TROUBLE IN TRANSYLVANIA

TROUBLE
IN
TRANSYLVANIA

A CASSANDRA REILLY MYSTERY

BARBARA WILSON

SEAL PRESS

Design and cover art by Clare Conrad

Library of Congress Cataloging-in-Publication Data

Wilson, Barbara
    Trouble in Transylvania : a Cassandra Reilly Mystery / by Barbara
Wilson.
        p.   cm.
    ISBN 1-878067-49-4
    1. Women translators—Romania—Transylvania—Fiction. I. Title.
PS3573.145678T76   1993
813.'54-dc20   93-25036
                                                                        CIP

First Seal Press paperback edition, August 1994
10 9 8 7 6 5 4 3 2 1

Distributed to the trade by Publishers Group West
Foreign distribution:
In Canada: Publishers Group West
In the U.K. and Europe: Air Lift Book Company, London

ACKNOWLEDGEMENTS

I would like to thank Katherine Hanson and Michael Schick for their friendship and for sparking my initial interest in Romania. Many thanks also to the electric Molly Martin and the peripatetic Ines Rieder for detailed, thoughtful readings and galvanizing advice. Faith Conlon was an insightful, supportive editor and Martin Cobb a helpful multilingual copyeditor. Thank you to all at Seal, especially to Clare Conrad for her cover design, and to June Thomas, Carol Seajay and Rose Katz, Friends of Cassandra.

In the population of Transylvania there are four distinct nationalities: Saxons in the South, and mixed with them the Wallachs, who are the descendants of the Dacians; Magyars in the West, and Székelys in the East and North. I am going among the latter, who claim to be descended from Attila and the Huns. This may be so, for when the Magyars conquered the country in the eleventh century they found the Huns settled in it. I read that every known superstition in the world is gathered into the horseshoe of the Carpathians, as if it were the centre of some imaginative whirlpool; if so my stay may be very interesting.

—*from Jonathan Harker's Journal*
(Dracula *by Bram Stoker*)

TROUBLE IN
TRANSYLVANIA

❧ CHAPTER ONE ❧

I WAS ON my way to China, by way of Vienna and Budapest, when I first met Gladys Bentwhistle, her granddaughter Bree, and most of the Snapp family. Not everyone knows this, but an open-ended roundtrip ticket from Hungary to China on the Trans-Mongolian Express is one of the least expensive ways to visit Beijing. The only drawback is that you must first go to Budapest and reserve your ticket via Moscow, and then apply for the Chinese, Mongolian and Russian visas at their embassies—all this before suffering nine days of bumping across steppe, taiga and desert. Still, it's cheap if you have the time, and this trip I had particular reasons for not minding a possible stay of several weeks in Budapest. My old friend Jacqueline Opal, whom I had seen in London only two or three months before, had dropped me a postcard at my Hampstead mailing address, a postcard of the Danube which announced, in breathless capitals, that she was now co-owner of a secretarial agency in Budapest. This was so

1

manifestly unlike Jack, a high-spirited Australian drifter who had held nothing more taxing than a series of temp jobs in London, and those only in order to finance a series of low-budget, maximum-risk world adventures, that I felt I had to see what she was up to.

It was an April evening, darkly green and rainy. I'd arrived in Vienna from London, via jet-foil and a high-speed train that had propelled me through dozens of European cities so quickly that I'd hardly had time to read the station signs, much less distinguish enduring national characteristics, and had gotten off for a few hours to stretch and catch up with myself.

It had never been sunny during any of my brief visits to Vienna; I'd never seen its icing sparkle, had never gotten the least hint of its waltzing and prancing, its operettas and operatics. Grandeur was there, you couldn't really avoid it, in the enormous Habsburg palaces and Imperial museums and theaters all around the Ringstrasse, but it always seemed magnificence of a particularly pointless kind. Vienna had once been the capital of an empire of fifty million, a large family estate (some said a prison) composed of a dozen nationalities, all struggling to assert their historical identities. After defeat in the First World War the Austro-Hungarian Empire collapsed, and Vienna was left, with all its pomp, head of nothing more than a rather small country called Austria.

But my Vienna wasn't the Imperial city of the Habsburgs, nor was it fin de siècle, decadent and glittery. Much of what I liked about the city came from the uncertain but lively period sometime after the First World War, after the elegance had begun to thin, but before the political chaos of the thirties. My Vienna was intellectual, melancholy

2

and neurotic, well-suited to damp days, to walking through small squares with trees coming into leaf, which is what I did that particular afternoon, after I had made one important stop.

In every city I find an anchor. Sometimes it's a café, sometimes a street, sometimes a painting in a museum. It's what I claim as mine, what I visit when I pass through, what makes me feel at home. In Amsterdam it's a pub on the corner of two canals, where the sun strikes a worn walnut tabletop in an elegiac way on late afternoons in autumn. In Mexico City it's Frida Kahlo's blue house. In Bangkok it's the Chao Phraya River with its network of brackish canals and spicy floating markets.

In Vienna, my anchor is very small. She's a reddish-brown statue less than five inches tall, though photographs make her look enormous and overwhelming, with her pendulous breasts and ample belly. She lives in a glass case in a room next to gigantic dinosaur skeletons in the Museum of Natural History. I'm not sure why I like her so much, or why I find her so powerful. The Venus of Willendorf is thirty thousand years old, the oldest thing, besides the dinosaur bones, that I have ever seen.

It satisfied something in me to visit her again, and afterwards I stayed in a good mood for a long time, drifting around the wet streets of the inner city. Eventually I rediscovered the Café Museum, with its marble-topped tables and sills of potted plants, its lace-draped windows against which the rain streamed down. I ordered soup with liver dumplings and began to read Elias Canetti's memoir of the twenties. From time to time I looked up and saw myself in a large mirror with a Jugendstil frame: a tall, restless woman, middle-aged, in a black beret and a leather bomber jacket, a scarf muffling her neck and chin, freckles that had never quite faded, hazel-green eyes and a nose that seemed to grow ever more prominent.

I began to relax, to feel my mind and my senses wake up. I was on the road, moving again, traveling light, ripe for adventure. And just in time. Since the past November, I'd been cooped up in London, translating from Spanish a series of research papers for an environmental group, Save the Amazon Basin. Publishers weren't taking many chances on the literary work that had previously been my bread and butter. The luxuriously overdone magic realism of Gloria de los Angeles continued to sell, of course, but other authors of mine—the recondite, manic-depressive Uruguayan Luisa Montiflores, for instance—were out of favor and out of print.

The winter dragged on; I grew gloomier. My love life was non-existent, and my friends were in sour moods, talking of emigrating, of suicide, of getting jobs in Brussels. The flu season came on and I felt wearier and older every day. I reminded myself often that I didn't live in London—it was only one of my bases, just as Oakland was another—nevertheless, I kept having terrible fantasies of ending up in some lonely little bed-sit in Wood Green, not having gotten out in time.

As March came whistling through and the days grew longer, I became restive and longed to be off somewhere. The travel section at Foyle's beckoned every time I got off the tube at Tottenham Court Road to walk to the SAB office in Soho. I found myself spending long half-hours staring at maps of Madagascar and atlases of Antarctica. I needed to go somewhere, anywhere, but preferably somewhere vast and strange and as far away from Charing Cross Road as possible.

The crisis came when SAB offered me a permanent part-time position. My dear friend Nicola, the prominent bassoonist, whose hospitality I had availed myself of pretty much continuously for the last twenty-five years, said sternly, "Well, now perhaps you'll settle down and make a contribution to the world."

Two days later, I was on the train to China, by way of Budapest.

At seven I went to the Wien-Süd train station and continued my journey into the heart of the old Austro-Hungarian Empire. I was the only one in my compartment of time-softened maroon corduroy seats and slightly dusty drapes. What luxury to sit alone and gaze out at the darkening, rain-soaked landscape, reading Canetti's account of Vienna in the twenties, when anguished, voluble, oversexed poets and painters sat around talking psychoanalysis and avant-garde art. If I had lived then, my companion certainly would have been a woman called Anna, her father an architect of the International School, her mother a concert pianist with tuberculosis. Anna herself designed one-of-a-kind books; she wore men's clothing and used a cigarette holder. We would have lived in a modern flat with nothing comfortable to sit on, analyzed ourselves relentlessly and drunk only champagne, in spite of being ardent socialists.

"Evening," a voice boomed. "Mind if we join you?"

I looked up from my book as the glass door to the compartment slid heavily open. An American woman in her seventies, wearing twill slacks, an appliquéd Western shirt, and a bolo tie in the shape of two raspberry-colored dice, hoisted a backpack onto the overhead rack. Her white hair was cut severely; she had a sharp, fine nose, reading glasses slung around her neck and, I thought, dentures.

"My pleasure," I said, steeling myself for company.

"This way, Bree," she called down the corridor.

She dragged another bag inside, so it almost blocked the door, and began to distribute a variety of possessions around the compartment. Soon, all I had for myself was my seat by the window.

She settled herself across from me and leaned forward with an outstretched hand. "Gladys Bentwhistle. Coyote's Pet-n-Wash. Tucson, Arizona."

I shook her hand. "Cassandra Reilly. Romance Translator. No Fixed Address."

"On your way to Budapest, hon? Me too. It'll be my ninth or tenth country this trip. I've been traveling alone for two months now, but my granddaughter just caught up with me. We're going to Romania, going to stay in a spa. I'll tell you, I'm going to be ready for a spa by then!"

"Gram, I *wish* you wouldn't rush off like that!" A young woman, not yet twenty, slipped into the compartment. She was wearing a full, flowered skirt over leggings, red Doc Marten boots, and a Queer Nation tee-shirt under a black leather jacket. Her hair was dyed black and fell tangled to her shoulders. She had a nose ring and pale freckles, the color of weak chocolate milk, scattered over her soft, pretty face. She was carrying a camcorder and a state-of-the-art backpack, suitable for climbing Mount Everest.

The train whistle sounded its haunting farewell and we slid smoothly off into the twilight. More latecomers were bumping and pushing and staggering their way through the corridor, but they kept passing our door.

"I learned this from a gal in Spain," said Gladys. "You don't lie. If someone opens the door and asks *frei* or *libre* or something, you say *ja* or *oui*, but if you spread enough stuff out, they won't bother to ask."

"I can see you're a seasoned traveler," I said.

"It's my first trip to Europe," Gladys said. "I always planned to come sooner, with my friend Evelyn, but we never got around to it. Evelyn was in bad health for a couple of years and last year she passed away." Gladys paused. "Well, you get old. I'm working on a way around it, but so far, no luck."

"Here are three places, Dad," said another American voice out in the corridor. "Hurry up, Emma, come on."

I put Elias Canetti away.

An adolescent girl, rangy and awkward in Levis and a sweatshirt with the mournful profile of Virginia Woolf screened upon it, barged through the door to our compartment and, ignoring Gladys's denim jacket on one seat, her *Herald Tribune* on another, and her string bag of fruit and crackers on a third, shoved a big suitcase inside and called again, "Hurry up, Emma. Dad, where are you?"

Gladys gathered up her items and immediately switched into a welcoming tone. "Going to Budapest, hon?"

"Yes." The girl stuck out her lower lip. She had a strong nose pushing its way out of childish features, and blue eyes half-hidden under thick bangs of darkening blond hair. Fourteen, I guessed, maybe fifteen.

"Hello, everybody!" A man with a tan, soft felt hat pushed back from a good-natured, perhaps overzealous face was shepherding a small girl of about four into the compartment and dragging a large suitcase behind him. Compact and muscular in a sports jacket that strained a bit at the shoulders, he looked like a Little League coach or something equally athletic and wholesome.

"I'm Archie Snapp," he said, shaking everyone's hand. "And this is little Emma. And you've met my other daughter Cathy."

"Hi," Cathy said expressionlessly. She opened her backpack and took out a thick paperback edition of *The*

Magic Mountain. Although the compartment had eight seats, suddenly it seemed much too small. Only Gladys and Archie seemed truly enthusiastic about our chance proximity; they obviously belonged to that gregarious American sub-group: people-people.

"Sit down, Emma," said Cathy from behind her book. "You're kicking me."

The little girl had on a pastel-pink cardigan, jeans and sneakers with white socks, and her black curly hair was tied by a pink ribbon. She had plump, downy cheeks and dark, uncommunicative eyes. The small case she was holding close to her chest was shaped like a violin.

"Hello, Emma," said Gladys. "Is this your first trip to Europe?"

There was no answer. Emma put her thumb in her mouth and her father quickly pulled it out again.

"Our Emma's not much of a talker," said Archie hastily. "But it's not her first trip to Europe by any means. You could say that..."

"Emma, I'm going to peel you an orange," Cathy interrupted, and proceeded to do so. The sharp, sweet tang of citrus bloomed around us.

"I'm Gladys," the dog-washer persevered. "Coyote's Pet-n-Wash in Tucson, that's my business, had it for thirty years, my assistant is running it while I'm gone. This is my granddaughter Bree. It's her first trip to Europe, too. She's a college student at Berkeley, majoring in Film Studies, whatever the heck that is. Mostly sounds like it's a lot of sitting around watching old movies that you could see on late night television anyway."

Bree tossed back her tangled black hair. "Hi," she said to the compartment, making sure not to make eye contact with Cathy. The five years that separated them was an enormous gulf of time and experience, and she needed to

8

make sure everyone knew that.

"And this is Cassandra Reilly," Gladys said. "I don't know where she's from."

"Kalamazoo, Michigan is where I started out."

"That's not too far from us," Archie said, warming to thoughts of the Midwest. "We live just outside Ann Arbor. My wife Lynn is in the physics department at the university, though right now she's in Munich at the Max Planck Institute, that's why we're over here for a few months. Back home, I'm the editor of a small newspaper."

That explained the felt hat then. I knew I'd seen Archie before—in a film from the thirties about a small-town reporter on an important assignment to save Western Civilization. All that was missing was the cigarette dangling from his lip as he leaned forward with his steno pad and said . . .

"It's a local kind of thing, *The Washtenaw Weekly Gleaner*. Mostly advertising, but I manage to fill it up with whatever strikes me. Interviews, opinion pieces, human interest kind of stuff. Fresh angles on the same-old same old."

Behind *The Magic Mountain* there was an audibly rude sigh.

We were traveling through the last suburbs of Vienna. The rain was falling faster. It was dark now, and our compartment seemed small and bright and close. I felt as if we were hurtling through the universe in a booth at a Howard Johnson's restaurant. In truth, it wasn't that unpleasant. Even a hardened expat like myself gets a longing for her countrymen and women from time to time. For the flat midwestern accents of some Snapps, for the western bluffness of a Gladys, even for the sulky rebellion of over-indulged children dragged to Europe to accompany their relatives.

A conductor bustled his way in and asked to see our tickets and passports. The blue ones came out along with my burgundy one. The conductor gave the blues a cursory glance but looked carefully at mine.

"Oh, very good. Ireland," he said, and he quoted from Yeats:

Romantic Ireland's dead and gone
It's with O'Leary in the grave.

He departed with a bow.

"I thought you came from Kalamazoo?" said Archie, sensing a story.

"I travel a lot and an Irish passport is often more useful than an American one. It's saved me a couple of times. In fact the only place I have trouble is Heathrow."

"But that's fascinating," said Archie. "Are you married to an Irishman?"

"I got it through my grandparents. The Irish government doesn't consider that a family has left home until a couple of generations have passed. My grandparents were born in County Cork, so I was eligible for citizenship."

"You said you were a translator," Gladys remembered. "From what to what?"

"Mostly I translate from Spanish to English, but I've also taken stabs at French-English, Italian-English, and even (this was not entirely successful, though friends in Lisbon assured me it was quite amusing), English-Portuguese."

"Do you speak Romanian?" Bree wanted to know.

"Some," I said. *"Poti să dai drumul la caldura?"*

"What's that mean?"

"Can you turn on the heat?" I added, "It doesn't always work."

Gladys rummaged in her bag and thrust several brochures into my hands. "Here's the spa we're going to. It's in the Carpathians, in the Transylvanian part of Romania. Evelyn and I were going together. She heard about this place from a friend in Tucson. The doctors do all kinds of things here, they have some treatments you can't get anywhere else. Ionvital, it's kind of an anti-aging drug, they say it works. And if not, the mud packs should at least help my rheumatism."

The brochures were printed on thin paper in colors that managed to be lurid and faded at the same time. They showed happy spa-goers in bellbottoms and sideburns strolling in front of large hotels, and women in bathing suits and shower caps receiving various forms of treatment, including "galvanic baths," "mud wrappings" and "medical gymnastics."

I read aloud:

On the shores of these famous heliothermal lakes rises a complexity of hotels and spa which is one of the very most popular in all Europe. Well-situated on a salt massif, Arcata is known since antiquity times for many healing possibilities in its mineral-rich waters and fresh, healthful air. Under the directorship of Dr. Ion Pustulescu, Discoverer of Ionvital, a drug known widely to slow or even stop the aging process, Arcata has become the premiere destination for people everywhere suffering from rheumatological, gynecological and geriatric complaints.

Archie was looking over my shoulder. "Those galvanic baths look like they can give you quite the kick!" His laugh boomed and I saw Cathy wince.

"What are you going to do there?" I asked Bree. She was really very pretty, in a pale, postmodern kind of way, and self-possessed in a way I could never have managed at her age.

"Keep my eye on Gram," she smiled. "Make sure the

11

vampires don't bite her."

"My daughter pays good money for Bree to take classes on horror movies, can you beat that?" said Gladys.

"*Nosferatu*'s a classic, Gram." She glanced sideways at me. "So's *The Hunger*."

Gladys said, "I always liked the one with Bela Lugosi best."

I looked at the small map that showed the location of the spa. "Then you're in luck. Arcata is very near some of the real Dracula's special places in Transylvania. He was born in Sighişoara."

"Sighişoara!" said Archie. "Oh, that sounds like a fun place to visit, doesn't it, Kit-Kat?"

Cathy put her book down and stood up, taking Emma by the hand. "Come on, Emma, let's go for a walk."

Still silent, Emma got up and followed Cathy out into the corridor. She took her violin case with her.

"Isn't Emma a doll?" Archie asked us after they'd left. "My wife and I adopted her almost three years ago from Romania." He snapped open his leather briefcase and pulled out a folder of xeroxed newspaper clippings.

"These are the columns I wrote about going there and adopting Emma," he said, passing them around.

The first one read:

OPENING OUR HEARTS

by Archie Snapp

Readers of this column know that the Snapps are not the average family in every way. How could we be when Dr. Lynn is a world-renowned scientist and your editor has taken responsibility for raising the kids and doing the housework? But in some ways we are the typical nuclear family. We have two kids, a boy and a girl, a dog and a "fixer-upper" farmhouse.

Our life seemed set in an unchanging routine. We might get another dog, or maybe some chickens (daughter Cathy wanted a boa constrictor), but we certainly didn't plan to have any more kids. Until the first news of the thousands of abandoned babies in Romanian orphanages began to seep out.

We couldn't stand by at the thought of those friendless, scared, lonely little children, hidden away in dark, cold institutions all over the country. Not while we had the resources to help. While Dr. Lynn arranged time off from the university and scouted the stores for baby clothes and supplies to take with us, I did my research.

After Romania's dictator Nicolae Ceauşescu (pronounced Chow-chess-cu) was deposed and killed in December 1989, the world's eyes turned to scenes of unparalleled child neglect. Ceauşescu had banned abortion and birth control since the mid-sixties, causing the birthrate to skyrocket. The mandatory number of children was four, then five. Families, already reeling from the dictator's decision to export nearly all the country's food, were forced to put their children into orphanages.

Even worse, due to a contaminated blood supply and unsterilized needles, combined with the Romanian "health" notion of injecting newborns with blood, many of these orphans had tested positive for AIDS.

It sounded like a nightmare situation. Still, our minister and friends urged us to go ahead with our plan. We received papers from the U.S. Immigration and Naturalization Service that would enable any child we adopted to enter the U.S. Someone gave us the name of a Romanian lawyer in Bucharest.

Somehow, in all this whirlwind of activity, we never lost sight of the fact that somewhere, in Romania, there was a little baby waiting for us.

Other headlines told the rest of the story: ORPHANS OF CHANCE; LOVE TO THE RESCUE; WAITING FOR A MIRACLE; EMMA COMES HOME.

We were still reading the clippings and I had gotten to:

"Well, it took a little longer than we thought—two months longer in fact—but here we are back home, safe and sound, the proud parents of little Emma..." when the door slid open and Cathy and little Emma came back in.

"Dad, do you really have to show those to everybody?"

"Oh, Kit-Kat, relax. People are interested."

"I hate Romania," Cathy announced, slamming into her seat and taking up Thomas Mann again. "I don't know why we have to go there."

"You shouldn't say that, if Emma's Romanian," Bree admonished her.

"She's not Romanian, she's American," said Cathy.

"Gladys, I was wondering if you'd have time for an interview?" Archie tried to change the subject. "In fact, I'd like to interview all of you. You all seem so interesting. Pets, film, an Irish translator. That's what I love about trains, you meet all kinds of fascinating folks."

"I'm flattered," Gladys said. "I've never been interviewed before. Well, there was that little piece about me in the paper when I pulled the pitbull off Eddie Lamb, but that was only two paragraphs."

"So why are you going back to Romania if it's so awful?" persisted Bree. "Are you looking for more kids?"

Cathy groaned, but Archie laughed, "If I could, I'd adopt a dozen. But you can't anymore. It wasn't easy then and now it's impossible. No, we're happy, we've got our Emma. That's enough."

"Well, compared to my kids when they were young, Emma is sure a quiet one," remarked Gladys. "I remember Teresa—that's Bree's mother—never shut up. And Bree was just the same. Jabber, jabber, jabber."

"Gram, that's not true!"

"Emma doesn't speak at all," said Archie. "Not yet,

anyway. Now, tell me all about your grooming salon, Gladys." He took out a pad of paper. "You say it's called Coyote's Pet and Wash?"

"That's Pet-n-Wash," Gladys corrected him and spelled it. "I named it after Coyote because according to the Southwest Indians, Coyote is a trickster and a clown. He loves to get into things and he loves a good joke, and so do I."

"But doesn't Coyote also bring evil into the world?" I asked. "He's a glutton, a lecher, a thief. That's what I remember about the Coyote stories."

"Oh, he's trouble all right. When he gets a mind to, he stirs up all kinds of trouble." Gladys took off her glasses and gave me a wink. "But to my mind, trouble is more interesting than lying around waiting to die, any day of the week. And you can quote me on that, Mr. Snapp."

❧ CHAPTER TWO ❧

I HAD CALLED ahead and Jack was waiting for me at the train station in Budapest. She and I had met in Colombia some twenty years before and had taken to each other immediately. She'd been traveling alone then, armed with a blazingly white smile and a good strong bowie knife. In fact, she'd gotten me out of a tough situation in an alley behind the seedy hotel where we were lodging. Tough situations seemed to be Jack's line; when she was in London she always seemed rather wan and forlorn. She drank a bit too much and lived in an impossibly chaotic flat with three other Australians in Stoke Newington.

Lately she had turned, somewhat dramatically, to women's spirituality. The last time I'd run into her, at Camden Locks on a Saturday, had been just after the winter solstice, when she was returning from a tour of sacred stones of the British Isles. Jack had been wearing a layering of ethnic and athletic clothes, reminiscent of certain tribeswomen in a transitional state of civilization. She talked quite a lot about passage graves and stone circles and, most suspiciously, about the tour leader, an American called Charis Freespirit.

Obviously things with Charis hadn't worked out spectacularly well, for here was Jack in Budapest, in a cotton dress from the forties and a short, boxy sweater. Her curly brown hair was carefully cut, and she was even wearing a bit of eye makeup and lipstick. Could the woman next to her have anything to do with this new fashion development?

"This is Eva Kálvin," Jack flashed her white smile. "My new business partner."

Barely five feet tall, Eva had a heart-shaped face with thickly-lashed brown eyes and heavy blond eyebrows. Her light hair was tucked under a hat and she wore a sharp red suit and high heels that contrasted with a physical impression of coiled muscularity.

"Cassandra, welcome to Budapest," she said in beautiful, charmingly accented English.

From the corner of my eye I could see Gladys, Bree and the Snapps searching around for me on the platform. I'd purposefully said my good-byes in the compartment and had been one of the first off the train precisely in order to avoid the confused, beseeching looks that arrivals in foreign cities inevitably provoke. Although I was sure that the Snapps, at least, had hotel reservations, I also knew that even experienced travelers can undergo utter disorientation in a strange train station at night.

"Are those people waving at you?" Jack asked. "Do you want to say good-bye?"

"I've already put them out of my mind," I said firmly. "I don't expect to see any of them ever again."

*   *   *

18

Eva had a car, a tiny Polski Fiat shaped like a snub-nosed revolver. As we walked toward it I asked Jack, "Any problem booking me into that little place in the Buda Hills?"

Although it was my idea to come to Budapest, Jack had said on the phone that she would make all the arrangements, and not to worry; she was dying to see me, and if I wanted to I could bring her a bottle of Glenlivet. That had been two weeks ago; I'd remembered the Glenlivet but had somehow forgotten that Jack had trouble with follow-through.

"It's shocking," Jack said impatiently, looking at the queue for taxis in front of the station. "You can't get a taxi, you can't get a meal, you can't get a room. There are *tourists* everywhere, even now at the end of April. It's really terrible. You know how I love Germans—one of my best friends is Edith, you know that I'd do anything for her since that time in Tierra del Fuego; she was so incredibly resourceful with that sheepskin—but I have to tell you, Cassandra, the Germans have *discovered* Budapest. They come here with their Deutschmarks, which are just like gold really, and they can buy anything, do anything. The cafés are full of Germans, the concerts are full of Germans, the streets are packed with them—Cassandra, the Germans have *moved into* Budapest. Real estate, industrial investment, shopping complexes, this country is going to be completely transformed within a few years and it will all be because of the Deutschmark . . ."

"Jack," I interrupted. "Can we back up a moment? To the innocent phrase 'you can't get a room?' Does that mean what I think it means?" I said, my voice rising. "Does that mean you only remembered that I was coming about an hour ago and you called around and it's Friday night and all the rooms are booked?"

Jack squeezed my arm sympathetically. "Well, *I* don't even have a place to stay," she said. "I'm sleeping on a futon in our office. The first futon in Hungary, I think."

"I'm *not* sleeping in your office," I said.

"Of course not," Eva said calmly. "You'll be staying with me."

"Oh. Well. That's all right then." I was mollified.

"Cassandra, would I ever let you down?" Jack said plaintively. "Okay, don't answer that, I know you're thinking of that time when I let the boat sail without you to the Galápagos. But believe me, now that you're in Budapest Eva and I will show you a wonderful time."

At first I believed the wonderful time might start that night. I had plenty of energy and was ready to hit the new nightlife of the city. But Jack said she was exhausted and didn't think she was up for much. Could we drop her at the office? We'd all meet tomorrow. She whispered in my ear as I got out of the back seat to get into the front, "We only have a business relationship."

"Meaning?"

"Good luck!"

I got back in the car, scrunching my long legs up to my chest, and we drove off into the József District. Eva said her flat wasn't far; it was just off Baross Street. Did I know Budapest well?

I told her I'd been here several times, but not recently, and never for long. But even as we chatted about how rapidly Hungary was changing under capitalism, I was imagining Eva's threadbare old flat on the fifth floor, full of antiques her family had saved from before the war, a flat smelling pungently of paprika and apples and chocolate. Flowering begonias on the windowsill and complete editions of nineteenth-century Hungarian poets in leather bindings, along with old green Penguin editions of Chandler and Hammett. Perhaps a claw-footed piano draped in embroidery and lace, with framed sepia photographs of stout Hungarian generals and little children with enormous bows in their hair. But I was confusing Eva with someone else, Elias Canetti's mother perhaps, for although the Polski Fiat carried us into the right sort of neighborhood, badly lit, shabby but suggesting better days, its driver stopped in front of a complex of apartment towers, six of them, twelve stories high, that could have come straight from the Bronx, though there was less graffiti.

Still, not everyone could live in the past, there wasn't enough of it left. Anyway, at my age what did I want with romance, if it meant having to walk up five flights of stairs and wash in a sink with cold water? Elevators and showers were much better, I reminded myself, and Eva would give me tea and we'd have a good conversation about Eastern Europe's transition to a market economy.

"This is my home. Welcome!" said Eva in front of a door on the fourth floor that looked like all the other doors.

I wondered why she didn't put the key in. Oh dear, I suddenly thought, is there a Mr. Kálvin inside? Eva as a married woman didn't seem quite as attractive somehow.

She pressed the buzzer and the door opened immediately, as if whoever was on the other side had been watching us through the peephole. An elderly woman with an expression of worry etched into her forehead stood there smoothing her apron and staring at me with great disapproval.

"Cassandra, my aunt, Mrs. Nagy," Eva murmured.

"Enchanted," I said, inwardly cursing Jack. "So kind of

21

you to let me stay, probably only a night or two, other accommodations fell through, but I'll find something else,
don't worry about a thing."

"Cassandra," said Eva. "She doesn't speak English. But
it's late, come in. I've put you in my bedroom."

The flat was tiny, consisting of a kitchen, a bath, and
two other rooms, one of which was Eva's. There was also
a winter garden, a glass-enclosed balcony, full of potted
plants and boxes of potatoes and cabbage.

Mrs. Nagy was like one of those fascinating flip books
where you can put together different heads with different
torsos and legs. Her lower half did not correspond with
her upper; looking only at her feet, for instance, in their
little-girl white ankle socks and single-strap shoes, you
would not deduce a face with the consistency of moldy
Spam. Like Eva, Mrs. Nagy was very short, but her figure
went straight from the shoulder of her tightly buttoned
cardigan to the hem of her wool skirt. She held her arms
stiffly by her sides, as if afraid to touch anything in her
own flat. Yet her eyes were as inquisitive as a ferret's. Her
white hair was bundled on her head in a way that suggested she was just about to take it out with the garbage.

Mrs. Nagy may not have spoken English, but she knew
how to get her point across. Eva might have foreign
women friends, but her aunt didn't have to like them.
Mrs. Nagy gave me a push on the shoulder and pointed in
a threatening manner in the direction of the bathroom. It
appeared she was telling me not to use the shower. Eva
said brightly, "She says, Our home is your home."

Mrs. Nagy frowned and waved at the kitchen door; she
snapped her fingers and said, "Papf, papf." I thought she
might be warning me not to use a gas stove that might
blow up. Eva smiled. "She says, Help yourself to anything
you want to eat."

22

Mrs. Nagy pantomimed either a flood or a vast conflagration.

"My aunt wishes you a good sleep."

"Tell her not to worry. I won't destroy anything. Once my head hits the pillow I'll be out like a light. I won't be any trouble at all."

I thanked both of them for their kindness in putting me up and went into Eva's bedroom and closed the door. It was a long narrow room, with a single hard bed covered in cushions, a small desk and bookshelves that held economics textbooks in English and German. Over the desk there was a cork bulletin board, fluttering with notes, cartoons and postcards from countries around the world. There were some framed color photographs of a little gymnast doing handsprings and bar work with the Olympic logo in the background, but as I moved closer to study them, there came a harsh tapping on glass, and I looked up to see that the window at one end of Eva's room faced the winter garden. Mrs. Nagy was standing there, with her solid body and deranged hair, watching me suspiciously.

I waved in a friendly manner as I stepped away from the photographs; then I sat down on the edge of the bed and mimed yawning and closing my eyes. When I looked back up she was gone.

It wasn't what you would call private accommodation.

I got into my nightshirt and went out to the bathroom to brush my teeth and wash my face. When I came back to Eva's room the light was off. I turned it back on, all 30 watts, and got into bed to read Elias Canetti. Without a knock the door opened. Mrs. Nagy was standing there with a pained expression on her face. I couldn't have left a mess in the bathroom, could I? She pointed to the weak bulb in the lamp overhead and slapped her palm a few times with the fingers of her other hand. Eva appeared behind her, wearing a thin red slip that came straight out of *Cat on a Hot Tin Roof.* She said, apologetically, "My aunt wants to tell you that she is a widow."

"I'm very sorry to hear that," I said.

"On a pension," Eva translated.

"Yes?"

Suddenly the overhead light snapped off.

I said, "I guess she's careful about her electricity bills, right?"

Eva sighed. "See you in the morning, Cassandra."

I consoled myself by remembering that on some of my travels there'd been no light to turn off at all, and eventually fell asleep.

The next morning Eva brought me a tiny porcelain cup of instant coffee in bed. She was dressed again in the red suit and high heels, and smelled of duty-free Chanel. As usual I'd doffed my nightshirt during the night and was enticingly nude under the sheets.

Eva appeared not to notice.

"I told Jack I'd be at the office at eight-thirty. Here's the address. Will you join us later in the afternoon? Perhaps we can go to bathe at the Gellért Hotel, yes?"

"Ummm," I said, remembering that Budapest was full of bathhouses dating from the Turkish occupation.

I drifted then into an erotic dream painted by a French orientalist at the turn of the century. Immured in the harem of the Grand Seraglio, we odalisques reclined around pools of water that reflected the rich magenta and indigo of silk carpets and latticed windows. Eunuchs stood, arms crossed, in the background, while Eva and I soaped each other with langorous movements, and ladled perfumed water over each other's shoulders and breasts.

Afterwards we rested on divans piled with cushions, drinking coffee, smoking opium and feeding each other melon and delicately scented sherbet, while fountains bubbled in the pools at our feet.

I lay dreaming until I saw the solid and threatening figure of Eva's duenna through the glass window at the end of the room. I yawned and waved. She glared at me and looked at her watch. I got the impression she thought I needed to be up and about. And fast.

When I came out of the block of flats I found myself in one of the old Pest districts, which at the turn of the century had been jammed with workers and peasants flooding in from the countryside. The golden-brown stucco facades of the nineteenth-century buildings were still riddled with bullet holes from the last war and from the Soviet occupation of 1956.

It was early still, and the fresh green scent of the acacias and linden trees still had a fighting chance against the industrial and car pollution that would later become almost lethal. Budapest was an easier city to like than Vienna; it had been the capital of the other half of the Dual Monarchy, but even then, during the Habsburg era, Budapest had been the wilder younger sister who wanted to play music all night (Bartók, not Brahms), and invited all the unsavory ethnic neighbors into the living room for a party.

These days the Hungarians were throwing off the last remaining traces of forty years as a Soviet satellite. They'd dumped the Soviet statues into the river, and now they were enthusiastically changing all the street names. Maps were practically useless; everywhere you saw street signs with the names crossed out in red: a big scarlet slash through TANACS, through MAJAKOVSZKIJ. And everywhere were new names too: Burger King, Siemens, Philips, Sony, Minolta.

Andrássy út had once been the most fashionable boulevard in the city; it spent seven years as Stalin's Street and (very briefly) in 1956 became Hungarian Youth Boulevard, until it settled down resignedly to being the Avenue of the People's Republic. I was glad it had gone back to Andrássy út, because I never really could get my tongue around Népköztársaság útja.

My first stop that morning was the MÁV office on Andrássy, where I stood in line for over an hour in order to request a seat on the Trans-Mongolian Express. It would be at least a week, perhaps two before Moscow telexed back a reply and I could actually buy my ticket, but at least I'd set everything in motion. It was salutory, too, to stand in a queue that seemed not to move for fifteen minutes at a time; a good reminder that I was no longer in the West and needed more patience than usual. It's interesting how you adapt to circumstances. If I were standing in a grocery line in New York with six people in front of me and a checker taking his sweet time, I'd be in a state of frenzied indignation like everyone else, muttering loudly, Do I have all day to wait here or what? They oughta fire this guy.

Here I drew into myself, almost physically; my head dropped into my chest, my shoulders slumped forward. I was at the point of passing into the state known as "queuezen" where you no longer wonder when your turn will come or what the possible reason could be for such a delay or why the people in front of you are taking so unconscionably long with their trivial and idiotic requests...

when I saw a familiar face come into the crowded office. It was unmistakably Bree, with her long black hair and nose ring, her torn tee-shirt and leather jacket. She looked around curiously. Was she searching for her grandma, the loo, or just a map of the city? Then she recognized me too, and came over.

"Hi," she said eagerly. "Cassandra, right?"

"That's right. And you're Bree."

"I was just walking down the street and saw you through the window." She gave me a sideways, flirtatious glance. "How fantastic to run into you!"

"It's the railway booking office," I said. "I'm arranging my ticket to China."

"That's so fantastic you're going there. I'd love to go to China. Why don't you take me along?"

"Oh, I don't think your grandmother would like that," I answered, more sternly than gallantly.

I wasn't sure why I was so uncomfortable. Perhaps it was that around Bree dairy metaphors kept springing to mind. She was like a bowl of freshly whipped cream, a firm vanilla pudding, a pitcher of cold white milk. In contrast, I felt like a strip of beef jerky, or maybe just a hunk of barbecued tofu that someone had forgotten to put back in the refrigerator.

I felt ancient at forty-six, and age made me awkward.

"Oh, Gram couldn't care less what I do. She's cool. It's my mother who made me come," Bree explained. "Teresa suddenly got worried about Gram on her own in Eastern Europe. She talked me into skipping spring quarter with this *bribe* of seeing Europe and making sure nothing happened to my poor old grandmother. So this is what happens: I get to Paris, where I could easily have stayed the rest of the summer it was so fabulous, and Gladys is just fine and doesn't even really want me around. I can barely

keep up with her and now we're going off to Romania."
Bree laughed in a manner that was meant to sound sophisticated, but was instead despairing. "To a *geriatric* spa!"

"Well, you've got your camcorder. *Nosferatu* and all that."

"Yeah," she sighed. "I'm sure it's atmospheric as hell. But it was hard to leave my girlfriend in Berkeley. Not that we're monogamous or anything."

Again the sideways look. I said nothing.

"I'll come straight to the point," she said, then she dropped her voice nervously. "Are you a dyke? I personally just identify as queer, it doesn't matter who I sleep with, I'm always queer."

In the world I'd grown up in and still moved in, especially when I traveled, bluntness was not a virtue and actions spoke more quietly than words.

"Call me old-fashioned," I murmured. "It still seems to matter to me who I sleep with. Some twisted Catholic thing, I would imagine."

The line had moved up somewhat during this exchange, but not fast enough. I wasn't too worried about people overhearing. Even if they understood English they probably didn't understand this kind.

"Well, Gram is waiting," Bree said, but as if she wanted me to stop her, and perhaps suggest a tryst in Mrs. Nagy's flat. When I didn't, she reluctantly began to move off. "She's got a whole day of sightseeing planned, Castle Hill, the works. I'll probably be a wreck by tonight, and then she's got us on the train tomorrow morning at seven. Well, Cassandra, hope you don't have to wait here too long. If you have any time later..."

"I'm sorry," I said quickly, and gave her an awkwardly maternal pat on the shoulder. "Enjoy your trip to Transyl-

28

vania, and keep an eye on your grandmother. Gladys
might surprise you."

Was it possible that I had been her age once, that I had
once looked to older women for experience? But they
could never have been as old as I felt now.

I took my time getting over to Jack and Eva's office. After
leaving MÁV I refreshed myself with an espresso at one of
the leafy outdoor cafés on Andrássy and then wandered
through the side streets to the Jewish Museum and Syna-
gogue. I had a nice kosher lunch at a small restaurant
nearby, and continued reading Elias Canetti.

One of the reasons I'm such a good traveler is that I'm
endlessly interested in doing nothing much in particular.
There were ten of us in my family, and babysitting and
chores every spare minute. I missed parts of my childhood, and travel is, I sometimes think, an attempt to find
the curiosity and joy that I sensed but seldom had time to
explore growing up. On the other hand, travel could be,
as my mother always tells the rest of my family, just an excuse to be a bum.

The office was off Rákóczi út. It was in a nineteenth-
century building with an elevator that didn't function. I
walked up four flights and knocked on the door with the
small sign:

O.K. Temporary Secretarial Services
English and Hungarian receptionists, stenographers,
and business secretaries
Our motto: O.K.!

Opal and Kálvin? Okay. . . .

"Cassandra!" said Jack from a cross-legged yoga posi-

29

tion on the floor. "We've been waiting hours for you! Eva has gone out; she said she'd meet us at Gerbeaud's at four."

The offices consisted of several small rooms. This one had a rug, a couple of chairs, some tables with typewriters, and a reception desk kitted out with a phone, a fax and a Macintosh computer. Through one doorway I could see a futon and another desk; another door, with KÁLVIN EVA on a brass plate, was closed. There seemed to be no one else around.

"I don't think I've ever seen you in an office, Miss Opal," I said, crouching down beside her.

"Oh, you know I've temped for years. Every Australian does." Jack stretched out one of her long legs and put her head on her thigh. "I had a whole set of different clothes; I was good at taking shorthand, good at taking shit. After all, I was well-paid and it was temporary."

"But then you met Kálvin Eva and everything changed."

"It's not what you think. Okay, so I'd never made it with a former Olympic athlete before. Okay, she's cute and has that charming Zsa Zsa Gabor accent. But, believe it or not, there were ideals involved, feminist politics."

"And was there beer involved as well? Where did you meet her anyway?"

"At the Fallen Angel."

"I'm not surprised."

Jack held her position. "She started talking to me about women's desperate economic situation in the emerging democracies of Central and Eastern Europe. How women were losing everything: maternity leave, free childcare, the right to an abortion. How women were being betrayed by the same men with whom they'd worked to make the revolution. How women were the first to be laid off and the

30

last to be hired. How it wasn't enough just to talk about this problem, something had to be done."

"What about a temporary secretarial agency in Budapest that would only employ women!"

"Exactly."

"A joint venture between an Australian who has excellent secretarial skills, and a former Olympic gymnast with connections. What about the financial incentives that many of the Eastern European countries are giving to foreign investors and jointly-owned businesses? It's a great idea. You can't miss!"

Jack straightened herself suspiciously. "Have you been talking to Eva? How do you know all this?"

"A *Financial Times* I found on the Central Line. And was Eva really in the Olympics?"

"Montreal, 1976. But Nadia Comaneçi won everything."

Jack went into a headstand, slowly. "She said I didn't have to put much money in, just my name on the papers would be sufficient. . . ."

Her cheeks were suffusing with pink. "It's just getting going, this business. It has potential. I mean, I'm getting older. Was I just going to keep taking the tube to the City and home again, saving up money to go back to Bali? This is my chance, Cassandra."

I was roaming the small office. "So who's criticizing?"

Jack's legs came down with a thump. "Just the part of me that wants to be in Bali," she said sadly.

⚜ CHAPTER THREE ⚜

JACK IS ONE of those creamy-complexioned, blue-eyed, buxom Anglo-Saxons who look as if they would be most comfortable at the church fête in the village of Lower Crumble on Dent, yet who you will consistently find popping up all over the world, from Ouagadougou to Rawalpindi. Her parents had emigrated from Suffolk to Perth straight after the war so that her father could take a job as a geologist. He had died in a rock slide and Jack's mother had brought the girl up in stifling Australian-British nostalgia, complete with tea cosies and toast racks. Jack had taken off at nineteen for London, after a course at secretarial school.

She hadn't told her mother that she was going by way of Borneo, or that she didn't plan to return to Perth after the obligatory world tour to marry and raise a family. In that she was like many Australians I'd known: a year abroad turned into a lifetime. But Jack, though Australian to the core, also carried with her softer English traits. She might be a goddess-worshipping, knife-carrying, beer-guzzling adventurer, but she also, always, had to have her tea.

Now we sat, in satiated luxury, outside Gerbeaud's on Vörösmarty tér, one of the main city squares and certainly the most elegant, with a pot of black tea and the remains of two strudels, poppyseed and morello cherry.

She finished telling me the sad story of Charis Freespirit, who had turned out to be married to someone in the men's movement back in California, and then we turned to more cheerful topics.

"I'd love to be going to China," Jack said, and embroidered a long story I'd heard once before about a flight from hell that had taken her from Beijing to Harbin in the dead of winter. And then I told one about trying to get to Rangoon overland from Bangkok in a jeep that broke down in a jungle full of insurgents, and then, since we were on the subject of travels in that part of the world, Jack mentioned how long it had been since she'd been to Japan and had I ever heard the story of Yukiko, the punk rock star from Kyōto (I had), and then we reminisced about a winter we'd spent together many years before in Indonesia.

"Where were you on your way to then? I'm trying to remember," she said. "I know that I was heading back to Australia to see my mum. Come to think of it, it's the last time I was back in Perth."

"But that was, that must have been at least fifteen years ago!"

"Have we really known each other that long? My mum died, you know. And anyway, when's the last time you were in the States?"

"I get to California every year or two. My friend Lucy still keeps a bed for me in her attic in Oakland. I think she has my collection of *Virago Travelers* too. I was looking for

The Gobi Desert recently, couldn't find it anywhere. That's the one where the three lady evangelists travel through China to spread the word of God with their portable harmonium."

"And what about your family?" Jack countered. "I bet you never see them."

"What's to see? More nieces and nephews? I might have to start sending them presents if I met them. And I think there might be thirty or forty by now. Maybe fifty. My mother set a bad example."

"And what *about* your mum?"

"I assume she's still praying for me. You never know, someday it may make the difference between hell and purgatory."

Eva Kálvin came from the direction of the pedestrian street, Váci utca; she clattered quickly over the square on high heels. Her blond hair was in a French twist, and she wore small pearl earrings.

"So tell me quick, Jack, what's the story with Eva?"

"All I know is that she's divorced and says she'll never get married again."

"You know what I'm talking about."

In England and in our native countries, both Jack and I knew better than to get intentionally entangled with straight women (there was always the occasional Charis Freespirit, who simply forgot to mention her husband until later) but we'd both found that in the rest of the world, where there were no rules or different rules about gender and sexuality, behavior and naming that behavior were often two separate things. Jack had had several amorous encounters with married women in North Africa ("I'm irresistibly drawn to veils"), and while I drew the line at married women after an extremely unfriendly interaction with the lovely Flora's husband, a Bolivian policeman, I rarely said no to any woman—particularly spinster school-teachers with a pedagogic bent—who wanted to flirt with me and teach me the names of body parts in her language.

"I never got anywhere," said Jack. "And of course now we're in business together. But maybe you'll have better luck. If you can get past Mrs. Nagy."

Eva kissed each of us enthusiastically several times and sat down just as a phone began to ring somewhere in the vicinity.

"Excuse me," she said and, opening her handbag, pulled out a cellular phone.

"The new Hungary," Jack remarked. "In a nutshell."

Eva's conversation was soon over and she turned back to us.

"You can't imagine how well our secretarial service is doing, Cassandra. Already we have five women working for us speaking six languages among them. There hasn't been anything like this in Budapest before; American and British businesses have told me that they're very impressed with our staff. We're helping many women. And, we're going to get rich!"

Hungary was moving more quickly than I'd guessed, if feminism and capitalism could already be combined in such an unabashedly exuberant manner. It had taken Western feminists almost two decades to get through the anti-hierarchical, anti-financial-success stage. Though I suppose you could say the Hungarians had already done the collectivity thing.

"And of course they all love Jacqueline. They wish she was always available. But I save her for the top clients."

"But Jack doesn't speak any languages!" I said.

My friend looked disdainfully at me. "Well, I've never studied them, like you have," she said. "I speak them—sympathetically."

"She's even picked up Hungarian, in only two months," said Eva.

"Hungarian's impossible," I said. "It's like Finnish. It doesn't look like anything else."

"The secret is not to look," said Jack. "Not to use your left brain."

I thought back to various travels with Jack; she always had been adept at getting herself from place to place and making herself understood. I also recalled an impressive intervention on her part in Java when I seemed to be on the verge of purchasing a very large live tortoise rather than a colorful sarong.

"I suppose it's possible," I allowed. "Hungarian is based on root words. It's an agglutinating language."

"My point exactly," said Jack.

"I've heard that you're a translator, Cassandra," said Eva. "What languages do you speak?"

"The Romance languages." I smiled at her.

Jack agreed. "Romance is her speciality."

"Spanish, French, Italian," I said. "A smattering of Icelandic, Arabic and Tagalog. Serviceable German, some Mandarin, and Russian."

"We all had to learn Russian at school," said Eva. "I can't bear to speak it now. German I don't mind—we look forward to working with more German clients. But I would never speak it for pleasure."

"In that case, I suggest we stick to English." I looked inquiringly at Jack. "Unless you'd rather go on with your Hungarian, my dear?"

The Polski Fiat took us across the Danube from Pest to Buda. The two cities weren't connected by bridges across the river until the last century. Buda was much older, a

medieval fortress on a hill that during the Turkish occupation had turned into a city of minarets and domes. Although that skyline was gone, the Hotel Gellért and its adjoining baths, nestled at the foot of Gellért Hill, echoed the
Turkish past. The buildings were constructed in the early
part of the century in an art nouveau Ottoman style that
reminded me of glorious silent science fiction films. Mad
scientists and space voyagers could have easily been at
home in the mosque-like, round-roofed towers of the
baths, which looked as if they would slide open at any moment to launch a homemade rocket to another planet.

The main entrance to the baths led to more Mozarabic
elegance: a vaulted ceiling with skylights, a tiled floor,
marble pilasters and patterned mosaic walls, potted palms
and white marble copies of Greco-Roman statues, all
women in uplifted poses. We bought our tickets to the
thermal baths and swimming pool and went into the
women's dressing room, where we were each given a cubicle, a white muslin wrap and a plastic cap.

The air here had a secret mineral smell, like dirt, like
metal. After disrobing, Jack, Eva and I met up in a mosaic
and marble room with two sunken thermal pools. The
arched ceiling had a skylight of amber glass, the tiled walls
were aqua blue. Naked, we dropped into the warm, buoyant water that came bubbling up from the interior of the
earth.

The Romans were the first to tap into the waters of
Gellért Hill, but it was the Turks with their langorous no-
tions of the *hammam* who brought the bath to its steamy
perfection. I could never be in an establishment like this
without thinking of Ingres's *The Turkish Bath,* which I had
first seen, printed in black on a clear-plastic shower curtain, at the apartment of my high-school Spanish teacher,
Dede Paulsen, the first woman I was ever in love with.

Such was my cultural background that I never realized the image was taken from a famous painting (when I saw it years later in the Louvre I had to stop myself from exclaiming, "Dede's shower curtain!"). But such are also the wonderful powers of the adolescent erotic imagination that from this bathroom artifact I constructed an entire fantasy of gorgeously plump nude women lounging around a tiled sunken bath in various attitudes of sloe-eyed indolence. Ignorant of Ingres's orientalizing male voyeurism I could happily conjure up a Turkish bath *cum* harem where naked women soaped and steamed in close proximity.

All bathhouses had a homoerotic element; for men it was overtly sexualized, for women subtly. In the Turkish harems the odalisques spent hours soaking and scrubbing, being massaged and pumiced. They hennaed the hair on their heads and removed every strand of it elsewhere with harsh depilatories. The enforced interiority of their lives, the sumptuous idleness bred sensuous addictions to opium, to rich food and to each other. The women in the harems were slaves and concubines; they fought for position, they intrigued, they poisoned, smothered and drowned each other.

Of course I had to admit, as I looked at the women in and out of the two thermal pools, I wasn't exactly surrounded by nubile Circassian slaves or indolent pampered sultanas. Except for the three of us, and none of us were in our youth, the average age here was about seventy. These were women whose lives you could see on their bodies, from their humped shoulders to their swollen ankles. Some were stiff and withered, almost fleshless, as they let themselves down ever so slowly into the healing waters. Others had the big collapsed bellies and elongated breasts of many pregnancies, or the elephantine legs of gout. Hard work and gravity had pressed them almost into the earth;

their spines were twisted, their arms were heavy and their legs barely moved. Yet once in the water they floated like lilies, the tentative, halting land movements became luxurious and sure, their cracked, shriveled skin plumped up like raisins and the sparse hair below their bellies streamed like underwater plants.

Submerged in this warm mineral sea of menopausal crones, I relaxed my own thin, freckled limbs, and thought of purification and renewal. Water washed the soul clean, it baptized, it was sacred and holy. But it was also profane; heated, water relaxed the muscles and opened the pores. It brought back memories of the womb, of being lightly held in a pool of fluid. Warm water was erotic; it loosened inhibition, encouraged nudity. Cloudy with steam or mist, yet transparent, it allowed the bather to half hide, half reveal; it allowed the voyeur to see yet pretend to be blind.

Jack found a spot under a small waterfall and, raising herself slightly, let a stream of water come down on her neck and shoulders. I saw for the first time that she had a scar on her lower abdomen and that it had healed jaggedly.

"Had my appendix out in Nepal last year," she said following my gaze. "I don't recommend it. I was laid up for weeks."

And there it was again, that faint rhythmic drumbeat of age that I had begun to hear in the clacking of the train on the Northern Line coming down to Tottenham Court Road, and that was still beating, however much I tried to distance myself. I saw my own loosening, wrinkling, scarred flesh on my friend's body, saw myself old and crippled and getting ready to die, not like my father whose heart attack killed him quickly, but like my Aunt Maeve, trapped in an old people's home with a wasting disease.

"Eva's got her eye on you," Jack whispered. "Go for it."

I felt the warm water slip like silk between my legs and flutter teasingly in and out of my hidden places, and suddenly I was alive again. The only thing that prevented me from totally giving into lust was the knowledge that I had a rather battered shower cap on my head.

On Eva the shower cap looked cute, as if she were in a bubblebath in a movie from the fifties. She floated peacefully, her breasts bobbing. Just before she'd stepped into the pool I'd seen how athletic her body was still: the hard tight calves and strong thigh muscles, the broad shoulders tapering to a narrow waist.

I wanted to talk about romance. Eva wanted to talk about business.

"If you wanted to work for us, Cassandra," she said, "I'm sure, with your languages and background as a translator, I could get you many jobs."

"Thanks," I said. "I don't have a head for business. It's a great weakness."

"Oh, I'm sure that is only modesty."

"I wish I could be modest," I said. "All too often I'm given to bragging about the things I do well."

"And those things are?"

"Reading train timetables, bargaining, writing postcards. Crossing borders. Transgressing boundaries. And of course translation."

"But your Spanish would come in so handy at O.K. I have a businessman from Madrid in town right now whose English is rather poor. . . . Of course!"

Eva lifted herself out of the pool and reached for the bag she'd brought into the thermal baths with her. She took out the cellular phone. Moisture ran down her nose from her piled-up blond hair as she dialed.

"Señor Martínez, do you have dinner plans?" she said smoothly, and then laughed, "No, no, but I have someone I'd like you to meet, one of our newest secretaries. . . . She speaks excellent Spanish. Ms. Reilly is her name. We're in the baths at the Gellért Hotel. Why don't you meet us at eight o'clock in the restaurant upstairs? Jack too. Yes, yes," Eva's laugh glittered. "My bodyguards."

Before I could protest, Eva silenced me with her finger on my lips. "You would be doing us an enormous favor. Señor Martínez is only here for a short time. Surely you could spare an hour or two a day from your busy schedule."

She knew, of course, that I had nothing more compelling going on than to wait for my visas and tickets to China.

"I would really quite enjoy getting to know you better too, Cassandra," Eva said. "I think you and Jacqueline are rather remarkable. I've never met any women like you before."

The buoyant breasts came maddeningly near and then bobbed off again. Some women would find this frustrating. As an ex-Catholic girl, however, I'm used to ambiguous desire and prolonged courtship.

If Eva had the interest, I had the time.

"Count me out," Jack said, when Eva told her that our evening date included her. "I'm not spending another evening chatting up men I don't like."

"But Jack," said Eva reasonably and firmly. "In a business like ours networking is frightfully important. We want to make a good impression on Señor Martínez so that he will keep doing business with us."

42

"All Señor Martínez wants is to get into your knickers," Jack said.

"That's why I need both of you with me," Eva said. "Do you think I *like* the idea of these men pawing me and making suggestive remarks just because I'm little and have blond hair? Well, I don't. But I'm not going to spend my life living with my aunt in a small flat. I'm going to make something of myself and I'm going to make a difference in Hungarian women's lives!"

The intensity of this ringing declaration was slightly muffled by Eva swallowing some water and sputtering. Jack pulled her up and pounded her on the back a few times.

"Dinner and that's it," she said firmly.

Eva beamed at her. "We're meeting him at eight upstairs in the restaurant," she said.

"I hope you like violins," said Jack cryptically to me before swimming off like the dormouse in *Alice in Wonderland*.

❧ CHAPTER FOUR ❧

THE GELLÉRT BATHS were connected to deep under ground hot springs. Leaving Eva to answer her cellular phone in the thermal pools, Jack and I got out to explore further. Everywhere the steady drip and gurgle of condensed and flowing water drew us onward through echoing corridors and arched rooms carved from the hillside. It was like the vast subterranean palace of a Minoan priestess, a labyrinth of moistness, where the female figures that passed us were terry-clothed votaries of sacred watery rites. We found a huge colonnaded pool surrounded by shiny green palms in clay pots and by white cast-iron benches, with a bronze lion spouting water at one end, and a glass and iron ceiling reminiscent of the hothouses at Kew Gardens. Here we swam back and forth in blue luxury for a long time, recalling pristine sand beaches in the South Pacific and the aqua waters of the Caribbean. Afterwards, we came to a series of sauna rooms, each hotter than the next, and sat in blazing African radiance, ignoring the women around us whose makeup ran with sweat, and inciting each other with stories of summers in Bengal, Alice Springs and Arizona.

It was almost a fault with me and Jack that one memory led to another, and another, and another, until geography was thrown out the window and seas ran into seas and mountain ranges gave way to deserts and deserts turned into jungles in a glorious and enervating abundance of travel stories. Jack was the first to give out. She said she thought her heart might be failing, and she returned to the changing rooms.

But I went on and pried open a heavy door with a foggy glass window. A hot white cloud gushed out to envelop me and pull me inside. I could see nothing at first, and then very slowly I realized there were tiers of slatted wooden shelves and, perched upon them, the shadowy shapes of women's bodies, all lined up in rows like saints in an early Renaissance church fresco, or (as Jack would probably have it) goddesses lounging in the swirling clouds of heaven. With cautious steps I made my way over to the wall and clambered up to a middle shelf to take my place in the steam bath's frieze of celestial beings. The heat wrapped me close as a lover and turned my lungs to twin thermoses full of hot tea. I felt my internal temperature gauge resignedly revving itself up, like a refrigerator after the door has been left open too long, and wondered if I, too, may have overdone it, but just as I was about to leave, I heard, from the tier above, the sibilant interrogative of my own name.

"Cassandra . . . ? Aren't you the lady from the train?"

I looked up and recognized through the mist the big-boned teenager Cathy Snapp.

"We're staying here for a few days," she said. "At the hotel."

There was a slight pause, during which the sound of my heart sinking must have been audible.

"If you'd rather just sit and be quiet, I understand," she said with aggrieved patience.

"Oh no," I said immediately. "Hi. How're you doing?"

"Terrible," she said, and stopped whispering. "My dad is driving me crazy," she said. "I can't believe he's taking us to Romania. He's completely out of control."

"He looks pretty normal to me."

"He's *not*. You don't know him. He's always on some kick, ever since I can remember. He has *causes*. He has *manias*. He's interested in *everything*. He was into recycling before anybody else. He subscribes to a magazine called *Garbage*. And we always had to compost everything with worms and he would buy furniture out of catalogs and put it together and we're, like, sleeping in these beds that always fall down, and have lamps around made of teakettles that suddenly blow up and start fires. And he's always writing about us in his stupid column, in between interviewing crackpots who've been fasting for peace for two months and people who run their cars on gas from chicken droppings. My brother Mark is always Mark the Mathematician and I'm always daughter Cathy the Voracious Reader or Scrabble Champion or some idiotic thing. Now I'm Cathy, Eldest Daughter. I used to be just Cathy, now I'm Eldest Daughter."

This was said with great bitterness.

"What about your mother?" I said.

"My mom is almost as bad. My mom is totally in another world. She's so out of it that she doesn't think anything my dad does is weird. Like, she comes home and all there is to eat is some seaweed casserole, and she just goes, Oh this is interesting. Or maybe she doesn't even notice, I can't tell. She has this weird sense of humor, like she's laughing at things that aren't even funny. She thinks my *dad* is funny, she *likes* him. Well, she doesn't have to spend time with him is all I have to say. The whole time we were growing up she was working and my dad took care of us, that's the problem! And it's not bad enough that Mark and me are total social misfits, but now we have Emma on our hands. I mean, children are supposed to start talking before they're a year old. Emma is four and she's never said one word!"

"She's not deaf, is she?"

"Deaf? She's a musical genius. She loves to have the radio on and she was playing the xylophone from the minute she saw it. Mom started her on the Suzuki method about three months ago and now it's Mozart day and night. It drives you nuts."

"How old was Emma when they adopted her?"

"She was nine months. That's another thing. My parents were gone for two months! They just left Mark and me at a neighbor's house, saying they were going to Romania for two weeks to get an orphan baby, and they don't come back for *two months*. I know they had a horrible time, even though they didn't want to talk about it much. My dad *never* talks like anything *bad* happens in the world. He just writes about how lucky they were to finally get Emma. Some luck! What's she going to do in school if she can't talk?"

"Send her to Catholic school," I suggested. "They'll like her."

The heat had gone to my head. When I was growing up I never would have thought to confide in an adult about family secrets the way Cathy was confiding in me. Secrets were for the priest in the confessional, and even then you knew enough not to confide your really big secrets to un-

seen, low-voiced men in dark churches. The best secrets—
like crushes—you reserved for your friends. The worst secrets—like not always having money for a movie or even
for lunch—you didn't tell anyone.

Cathy was raging on. "*Romania*. Why did they have to
get a kid from Transylvania? Most people don't even
know Transylvania is a real place. I have to watch stupid
kids drawing back their lips and making vampire eyes and
sucking noises."

"So is your dad taking you to visit Romania for any special reason?"

"He *says* it's because we're here in Europe and should
take advantage of the culture all around. My brother Mark
is at Harvard, but I had to come along and my dad is supposedly teaching me in Munich. I have to read all German
writers, that's why I'm reading Thomas Mann, I don't
even understand it in *English*. We've already been to Paris
and Amsterdam and Berlin, and now it's supposed to be
two weeks in Eastern Europe. He *says* he wants to write
some article about Hungary and Romania. But I think he's
got some plan to find some of Emma's relatives and see if
there's a reason Emma doesn't talk. It would be just like
him."

I realized I had been in the steam room too long and that
I was feeling faint. I began to get up, but Cathy suddenly
grabbed my arm.

"I know you probably think this is totally strange. . . . I
just wondered, would you mind—I mean, I'd really appreciate it—if you could give me your phone number here
in Budapest where I could reach you, just in case. . . ."

"In case what?" I prompted.

"I don't know." She looked upset and embarrassed to
be upset. "I'm sure I wouldn't really call you. The phones

probably don't even work in Romania. But, at least I'd have *one* contact in case something really awful happened."

I hunted in my plastic bag for Jack's business card. Over the years I'd given many anxious fellow travelers my phone number, secure in the knowledge that any attempt to make a call on a foreign telephone would inevitably prove more daunting than whatever crisis was at hand.

"You could leave a message for me there," I said. "But I only expect to be in Budapest a couple of weeks."

"Thank you," she said. "You're really nice, Cassandra. Are you really from Kalamazoo?"

"A long time ago," I said.

The menu at the Gellért restaurant was full of paprika and goulash and intriguing items like "Roast stag à la Forester's Daughter."

"Paprika, paprika! I'm not sure it's healthy to eat so much orange food," said Jack, settling for salad.

Not being vegetarian, I had a wider choice, and ordered duck in plum sauce and some roast potatoes.

Eva's red suit was elegant enough for the dining room, and her loosely pinned-up blond hair was more sexy than disheveled, but Jack and I looked distinctly damp and casual. I was wearing jeans with my (extremely) crushed linen shirt, and Jack's forties-style dress was looking every one of its decades.

While we waited for Señor Martínez to join us I told Jack and Eva about my encounter with Cathy Snapp in the steam room.

"The little girl is four and she doesn't speak at all? Something terrible must have happened to her," said Eva.

"How old was she when they got her? Nine months?"

asked Jack. "She must have been adopted right at the age when she would have started speaking. Maybe the change from Romanian to English was too confusing."

"If you believe Chomsky, that all languages are fundamentally alike, then it shouldn't matter that Emma was born into a Romanian-speaking family and only heard Romanian in her very formative months. She should have been able to switch into English without any problem. What I wonder is if no one talked to Emma at all. Another school of thought from Chomsky says you have to learn your language from an adult with whom you have a strong relationship."

"That sounds like you and your Spanish teacher, Cassandra," said Jack. "What was her name?"

"Dede," I sighed. "Miss Paulsen."

"How old were you?"

"Seventeen. She was twenty-five. She was from northern Michigan and had majored in Spanish and Education. She'd only been to Spain once, for a month. Her apartment was full of things like posters of bullfights and those leather wine bags. She left me with a very bad Spanish accent."

"I think your parents are very important," Eva interrupted. It seemed to make her nervous when Jack and I talked so familiarly about old lovers. "My father was a teacher and he always read to me and talked to me. I pronounce many words just as he did."

"My mother talked to me," said Jack. "Endlessly. But I managed to tune her out except for a few ladylike phrases that pop out from time to time in the most unexpected situations. I go for Chomsky. I know it's why I never worry about speaking a foreign language. To me they're all exactly the same."

"Chomsky," I told them, "theorizes that language is in-

51

nate; 'an organ of the mind,' he calls it. It's in our genes, we don't invent it. He says that children don't learn language, they bring it with them when they're born."

"If you bring language with you when you're born," asked Jack, "what language is it?"

"It's more of a template," I said.

"How do you know that the little girl wasn't born to Hungarian-speaking people?" Eva wanted to know. "She comes from Transylvania, which used to belong to Hungary."

"No wonder then," said Jack. "If she has a Hungarian language template on her brain, no wonder she's confused. Probably she's got a paprika deficiency, causing the root words to agglutinate in her poor little mind."

"The trouble is," I went on, "all theories about language are quite difficult to test. Almost no children grow up without language, so it's hard to have a pure research subject. To really test out Chomsky's theories, you'd have to let a child grow up on an isolated island and see if the child developed a language or not, and whether it was like the languages we know. But of course, morally, you can't do an experiment like that."

"Of course you can," countered Jack. "We call it speaking Strine. That's Australian English to you, Eva."

Señor Martínez was a rotund man of fifty, with a damp enthusiastic handshake and what the Japanese have taken to calling a "bar-code head"—in which long strands of what hair remains on a man's head are pasted in straight lines across a pale round expanse of skull. The face under the black and white design was eager and even lusty. As he told us, he was from Bilbao but he'd had an Andalucían mother and this had given him a great zest for life, a zest that became more apparent as the glasses of red "Bull's Blood" wine disappeared.

Señor Martínez fell into my Spanish as passionately as into a beloved's arms. Not that he'd previously been parsimonious (according to Jack) with his ungrammatical English, but his Spanish was a force of nature that now gushed out of his mouth like water from a blocked pipe.

In this case the metaphor was particularly appropriate. Señor Martínez was a salesman for a large Spanish bathroom fixture factory and he was here to sell well-designed toilets, bidets, sinks and tubs to the Hungarians. He happened to have his portfolio with him and was not at all shy about immediately showing me glossy color photographs. I felt almost as if we were looking at pornography, particularly the way his stubby, ringed hand lingered over the curved porcelain smoothness of the bidets.

"And you're the one who will be my translator?" he said to me in Spanish. "Then please tell Señora Eva that her eyes are as blue as the Mediterranean."

"Señor Martínez says he's dying to try some paprika chicken," I said. "But I suggested the stuffed carp."

Eva handed him her menu. "Please."

"I speak of love, not food." He pushed it away and fixed her with a tender look.

"I can't persuade him," I said. "It's gotta be the chicken."

The Gypsy musicians had appeared and, without preliminaries, launched into a wild *csárdás,* startling a party of elderly British tourists who had been quietly whingeing about the prices on the menu ("I thought you said Eastern Europe was a bargain, Colin."). There were four musicians, dressed in blousey white embroidered shirts and tight black trousers. It was impossible to tell what they were thinking, but on the surface they were as shiny as copper pennies. The lead violinist had spotted Eva as both Hungarian and gorgeous, and our soup had hardly been set in front of us before he and his violin were leaning over her shoulder. His bowing was so intense it was more like archery.

Eva toasted the violinist with her wine and asked for a special song, not another wild tune, but something haunting and strange.

"Tell Señor Martínez this is a real Gypsy tune, not for tourists."

I translated and Señor Martínez sighed eloquently, his hand at his heart, "The Spanish and the Hungarians are very much alike. We have the wildness and also the sadness, what we call *duende*. We have both been conquered peoples, we have the souls of Gypsies and the heads for business. That is why I think I can sell our beautiful bathroom fixtures here. I believe they will be understood. And now you have democracy. Hungary, I salute you!" He raised his glass. "Down with fascism!"

"What's he saying?" asked Eva.

"He says he wishes that paprika chicken would hurry up. He's starving!"

But Señor Martínez was a single-minded man when it came to the similarities between Hungary and Spain, and the possibility of a spectacular union, plumbing and otherwise, between them.

While the Gypsies made wild music over our shoulders, Señor Martínez outlined a theory of history. "Both Christian Spain and Christian Hungary fought against the infidel Arabs," he said. "We stopped the Mohammedans from overrunning Europe."

"But surely you must admit, Señor Martínez," I corrected him, "that the Moors in Spain created a brilliant civilization of poetry, philosophy, gardens. Not only did

54

they have the first lighted, paved streets in Europe, they had the first sewage system in the world. Plumbing, Señor, they had plumbing."

"The *Reconquista* was Spain's finest moment," he disagreed.

"What's he saying?" Eva demanded.

"He thinks the Turks have gotten a bad rap," I said. "He says, Really, what's so bad about a culture that drinks coffee and sits around in bathtubs all day?"

"The Turkish infidels?" said Eva, shocked.

"What does Eva say?" he asked.

"She says she wishes these Gypsy musicians would take a hike. They're starting to remind her of a Luftwaffe raid, except there are no bomb shelters."

Señor Martínez stared at me a moment and then spoke in laborious English, with a pleading glance at Eva, "I am think Señora Reilly is have fun with me."

"Oh no, Señor Martínez, you're wrong about that. Believe me, I'm not having much fun at all."

Eva whispered, "Cassandra, don't tease the poor man so much. He's paying for our meal."

"Cassandra, you *are* being just the slightest bit *rude,* dear." Jack smiled wickedly. "See? There's my mother speaking."

I opened my mouth for another jibe, but put in a bite of duck in plum sauce instead. I'd just caught, from the corner of my eye, the entrance of the Snapp family into the restaurant. Cathy saw me first and waved, and then Archie dragged them all over to say hello. I wondered why Emma was staring so hard. But then I realized she wasn't looking at me at all. Her attention was completely absorbed by the frenzied musician between me and Eva and, of course, by his violin.

"Don't let us disturb you," said Archie, as he crowded

his children almost on top of us.

"Not at all, not at all, sit down here with us," I said, with a heartiness that astounded Jack. "Let me introduce you all around. This is Eva Kálvin, and Jacqueline Opal, and I'm especially delighted for you to meet Señor Martínez from Spain. Señor Martínez is in the bathroom fixture business. I think he'd make a great interview for your newspaper. He grew up in the Franco period, so of course he sympathizes with the Hungarians getting their first taste of freedom, with all the excitement and pitfalls that go along with a market economy. . . . "

"Just the kind of information I've been wanting to get," said Archie happily. "*Cómo está usted,* Señor? I forgot to tell you in the train, Cassandra, that I speak a little Spanish myself."

"All the better," I said. "All the better."

❧ CHAPTER FIVE ❧

A WEEK HAD PASSED since my arrival in Budapest, and already I'd established my little routines, although they were not the routines I'd imagined for myself on the train from Vienna. No, I'd envisioned a leisurely spring experience in the heart of Central Europe: reading newspapers in cafés, strolling along the Corso above the Danube, queuing for tickets outside the Opera House. And if I'd also hoped for a wild, though brief, romance, who could blame me?

But instead, the days had slipped into a dispiriting sameness. Yes, I was awakened every morning with a kiss on the cheek and a cup of coffee from blond, red-suited Eva. But the sweet nothings she whispered to me were only invitations to join her in the office at nine o'clock sharp. And even if I'd had an inclination to lie in bed all morning, the sight of Mrs. Nagy, lurking in the winter garden with her crazed hair and tightly buttoned cardigan, was enough to get me on my feet.

Señor Martínez was still hanging around Budapest, attempting to sell his line of bathroom fixtures to hotels and office buildings. I accompanied him on several sales trips. He poured his heart out to me about Eva, and I told him that underneath her flirtatious exterior she was a hard-hearted businesswoman and a raging feminist, but this put him off somewhat less than I had hoped.

Of course, I could have moved out of Mrs. Nagy's flat and found myself a nice room in a hotel and lived just the way I wanted while waiting for my ticket to China to be confirmed. Call it curiosity, call it infatuation . . . or call it a simple case of inflation. Prices had jumped since I'd last been to Hungary. In spite of my constant travels, which hint at trust funds or other fabulous resources, I live on a slim budget provided by my work as a translator. The money to travel to China had come mainly from six months in the SAB office. I hated to admit it, but the forints from O.K. Temporary Secretarial Services were coming in handy.

Still, I was restless, and when I got my train reservations and found out I couldn't leave for another two weeks, I chafed. Jack was restless too. Every afternoon, if we could manage it, we met at four for tea and pastries somewhere, at either a small espresso bar near the O.K. office or at one of the deliciously expensive cafés, Ruszwurm's on Castle Hill or Gerbeaud's in Pest. There we'd briefly commiserate about our current, if temporary, fate as secretaries in Budapest, and then spend the rest of the time arguing about how serious Jack had really been about converting to Hinduism in Java, if it had really rained the entire month we were in Chile and whether I still owed Jack money for the train fare to Recife from São Paulo.

Late one afternoon, as we were on our second strudel at the espresso bar, the door opened and in came Eva, clutching her cellular phone in some agitation. Jack and I both started guiltily—such was the effect this hard-working Hungarian entrepreneur had on us. My first thought was that Señor Martínez had come to grief somewhere in Szeged, where he'd gone to introduce his fixtures and where I'd refused to accompany him. But that was incorrect.

"It's a murder," Eva said, pointing at the phone as if the terrible news were still flowing out of it.

It was some time before we could get all the details.

"But I don't *know* how this Bree—is she a cheese?—has got my phone number," repeated Eva irritably. "I only know I'm in a taxi after my meeting and the phone rings. It's a girl asking for Cassandra. She says she's calling from a place in Romania and something bad has happened to her grandmother. A murder."

"But you're sure she didn't say that Gladys had been killed?"

"No, I told you! She said that her grandmother has *done* the murder. No, I mean, the police think she has done the murder, but of course she hasn't."

"Of course not," I said warmly. It was completely impossible to imagine Gladys Bentwhistle with her raspberry dice bolo tie *killing* anyone, especially in Romania. "And *where* was she calling from, did you say?"

"The Arcata Spa Hotel, in the village of Arcata. It's in Transylvania, in the Carpathian Mountains."

"But how did she know how to reach me in Budapest?" I asked again.

"For the hundredth time, Cassandra, *I don't know!* But I do know she wants you to go there because you speak Romanian. She was very upset."

Jack had been eating our second strudels through most of this. Now she said calmly, "Well, of course you have to go, Cassandra. It's your duty to help them. And I'll have to go with you to make sure nothing happens to you, in case it's a dangerous situation. And Eva will have to drive us there because she knows where the hell the Carpathians are and because she speaks Hungarian."

Jack looked more lively than she had since I'd arrived. "I've never been to Romania. I suppose we'll have to take lots of supplies."

Eva was staring at her. "But we can't just drop the business, Jack. It's not... professional."

Jack glanced at her watch. "It's only five o'clock. How long would it take to drive there?"

Eva shook her head. "I don't know. Four or five hours to the border at Oradea and then perhaps another six, depending on the roads, to Arcata."

"There you have it. It's Friday night. Ten hours and we're at the scene of the crime. You and Cassandra help sort this thing out and we're in the car and headed back to Budapest. Maybe we'll even have time for some sightseeing in Transylvania."

I had been about to protest that I was on my way to China and didn't need a side trip to Romania, whatever the reason, but Jack caught me up in her desire to be away and quickly. Eva had not seen this side of her partner yet, but I certainly had. Any sort of jaunt always brightened Jack's face; she was pining away for a change of scene after two months in Budapest.

I had to admit too, I was curious—and worried—about Gladys. Romania wasn't technically a police state anymore, but I wasn't completely confident in their legal system. If Gladys was in any kind of trouble, she would definitely need help.

"But we have dinner arranged with Señor Martínez to-night!" said Eva.

That settled it.

Jack and I stood up at the same time. "If you're not going with us, we're renting a car and driving there ourselves," Jack announced. "And who knows if we'll ever come back?"

An hour later the three of us were stuffed into the Polski Fiat, me in the front with my legs jammed up to my chin and Jack in the back seat amidst a hastily purchased basketful of sausages, fruit, biscuits and wine.

Like most Hungarians Eva believed that Romania was the Devil's own country, filled with backward, starving serfs, ruled by vicious, Magyar-bashing communists. She reminded me of the Hungarian proverb: "Outside of Hungary there is no life, and if there is life, it is not the same."

"Of course, if we go to Transylvania, it is not like we are going to Romania," she consoled herself, as we headed out of the city and found our way to the highway that would take us across the Hungarian plain to the border.

"How's that again?" inquired Jack, trying to get settled so her elbow was not in my ear, nor her dress above her waist.

"Transylvania was part of Hungary for a thousand years," Eva said. "And then, after the First World War—which Hungary was *forced* to join, because it had been *forced* to be part of the Habsburg Empire—we lost two-thirds of our land. Some went to Yugoslavia and Czechoslovakia, but most of it went to Romania. Because the Romanians and the French," Eva held up two crossed fingers, "they were like *this*."

"The Treaty of Trianon," I nodded. "It carved up the Austro-Hungarian Empire in a way that satisfied no one. But then, how could they satisfy everyone? In this part of Europe, political borders have never coincided with the ethnic boundaries."

"But Cassandra, you must admit that there are two and a half million Hungarians trapped inside Romania, trapped for seventy years now."

"Seventy years and they're still arguing?" said Jack.

"How long have the Arabs and Jews been at it? What about the Hindus and Moslems, or the Catholics and Protestants in Ireland? I won't even mention ex-Yugoslavia. In the Balkans, seventy years is *nothing*," I said. "Part of the problem is that Transylvania doesn't actually border the current state of Hungary anymore. It's two hundred miles to the east. And there are several million Romanians living in Transylvania now—what would happen to them? I know that Ceauşescu encouraged them to move there—but there's some evidence to suggest that the Romanians have been in Transylvania for centuries. They believe that anyway, that they're descended from the Roman colonists of ancient Dacia..."

"The Romanians just are liars, if they told you that," interrupted Eva.

"You can read it in any history book," I said.

"Not in Hungarian history books!"

From the back seat we heard the rustle of cellophane and cardboard as Jack unwrapped the first box of biscuits. "I don't know," she said through a mouthful of chocolate biscuit, "I was never great at history, but I've never understood all this ethnic squabbling in Europe. Back and forth, and forth and back, across the same boring old territory. First one group is in power and oppresses the other, then the other group is in power and oppresses the first. But way before the Hungarians and the Romanians, way before the Romans and the Huns this was Old Europe, home of one of the Great Goddess civilizations. There are paleolithic and neolithic sites all through this area of the Balkans."

"I thought you weren't great at history," I said, impressed. I wasn't sure I knew the difference between paleo and neo.

"It's prehistory I'm interested in, not patriarchal bullshit like kings, wars and empires. Charis Freespirit told us all about the work of Riane Eisler and Marija Gimbutas this winter on our tour. Gimbutas is an archeologist and Eisler based some of her new theories about dominator and partnership societies on Gimbutas's research. The Great Goddess cultures weren't dominator societies, they were partnership communities. None of the ruins that have been excavated show fortresses or anything that would suggest they fought with each other. Most of the statues are fertility figures."

I thought of the little statue in Vienna. "So, did the Venus of Willendorf come from around here?"

"Yeah, but she's no Venus. That was just something that the male archeologists said, because they couldn't imagine a powerful figure without sexualizing her. But in the old agrarian Goddess societies, she was a fertility figure—back in the days when fertility belonged to women and wasn't controlled by men."

"Still, Cassandra," interrupted Eva. "You must admit that the Hungarians were treated very badly in Transylvania by Ceauşescu."

"The Hungarians have no great claims as defenders of human rights. You want to talk about what happened to the Jews who were shipped off to Auschwitz the last year of the war? You want to talk about how the Hungarians treat their own population of Gypsies?"

"The Romanians treat the Gypsies worse! All the Romanian Gypsies have run away to Germany and now Germany is selling them back to Romania."

"In a partnership society," said Jack, "we wouldn't know how to talk like this about other people. The words wouldn't even begin to make sense."

"In a partnership society, wouldn't we be sharing the biscuits?" I said, taking the package away from her before she could devour them all.

"You'll see when we get to Romania," said Eva, who was determined to get the last word in. "That's the real Stone Age there. And they don't have chocolate biscuits, either!"

It had been dark when we set out, but away from the city it was darker still. We were crossing the *puszta,* once a thick forest, then, after the trees were chopped down, a bog. Still later, by some peculiar twist of geography and climate, the *puszta* turned into grasslands like the American prairies or the Argentinian pampas. Years before I'd been to a great livestock fair in Debrecen. It had been like some version of America's Wild West, with cowboys and hundreds of head of steer.

We were in marchland, borderland, a buffer zone, where the frontiers had shifted dozens of times over the centuries and the maps had been drawn and redrawn. But where maps showed lines, the landscape rarely did. Sometimes there was a river or a mountain chain, sometimes there was nothing but a fence through a pasture, and sometimes there was nothing at all. Sometimes when you passed from one country to the next, there was a sharp and immediate change. Sometimes the barbed wire, armed sentries and floodlights spoke of enmity and tragedy. Sometimes there was only a softening, a gentle blurring, people speaking two languages, eating similiar foods, sharing relatives, customs and memories.

The real borders now were economic. Fortress Europe had pulled up the drawbridge on the former Soviet bloc countries, all begging to be part of the European Community. Hungary might manage it in the years to come; Romania would not. Traveling into Romania from the West was like leaving the wealthy drawing room upstairs for the downstairs servants' quarters. Hungary might be a butler, able to mix in both worlds; Romania was the scullery cook.

Near the border Eva stopped and filled the tank with petrol. She opened the hood and peered inside.

"Is something wrong?" I asked.

"I don't think so. . . . Sometimes I think I hear a kind of thumping noise. I'm probably just imagining it."

"Good," I said. Car maintenance was never my, nor Jack's, strong point.

The night was eerily lit here, greenish-white, and the roar of heavy trucks filled the air and then departed, leaving thick silence. The wind came cold and hard across the plain, but there were stars overhead, and the sky was clear.

"Did you know, there were great witch-hunts around here, two, three hundred years ago?" said Eva, as we inserted ourselves back into the tiny car.

"Witches!" said Jack, perking right up.

"Yes. The Calvinists were strong here, but the Hungarian state was Catholic. There were many struggles during the Counter-Reformation. Many trials, not against the village wise men, but against the midwives and the *boszorkány,* the women whose beliefs went back to pagan times."

"You see," said Jack. "I knew this was an area with a lot of energy. The witches were directly connected with the Great Goddess cultures."

"I don't know if you can really call them witches," I objected. "Most of them were peasant women accused of killing their neighbor's cow. They were caught up in a general hysteria of hatred directed towards women."

"Towards women's sexuality," said Jack. "Most of the crimes they were accused of had to do with sex. In the old Goddess religions women's sexuality was celebrated, but the Catholic church condemned all pleasure in sexuality, and said it came from the Devil."

"I hate to remind you," I said, "but when I took First Communion in the fifties, that was still the general gist of church teaching."

"They also accused the women of giving contraceptive aid and performing abortions," said Eva. "The authorities did not like that the midwives had knowledge of healing and herbs."

"I'm telling you," said Jack, "it's a sex thing. Men hate and fear women's sexuality. They use women for sex and then they blame them. The bedrock of male authority is the control of women's bodies."

"You don't need to convince me," I said. "I had my revelation thirty years ago when my sister Maureen got pregnant and had to get married."

The Stygian crossing took longer than we expected. There were visas to buy and Eva's car was inspected thoroughly—for contraband, unfortunately, not for engine trouble. Eva didn't make it any easier with her haughty attitude towards the Romanian guards, and it was not until after eleven that we were back on the road. I offered to

66

drive and Eva got into the back seat and said she'd try to sleep a little.

"Let's play a game," said Jack to me.

Jack and I, when we'd traveled together and had needed to pass long stretches of time in as lively a manner as possible, had had a number of games. Some of the geographical ones were easy—to recite all the countries in South America and their major cities—and some were more difficult: "If you were traveling from Gambia to Bolivia, which way would you go and how?" or "Say you had to get from Bergen, Norway, to Bombay. Which railways would you use and how long would it take you?" One of our favorite amusements, however, was to name a country and then ask, "If you were going to Brazil and could only take ten things with you, what would they be?"

Since there were no size or weight limits, we usually started out with quite fantastic objects, for instance an airplane or a gorgeous Portuguese-speaking guide or a portable schoolhouse. Once I'd said, "The British Museum library," and we'd had a quarrel about whether that included the books. But gradually we'd reduce the number of things we could take with us. "If you could only take five things," and "If you could only take two things."

By the time we were down to the essentials I usually opted for either a Swiss Army knife or a large supply of insect repellent, while Jack almost always chose ear plugs or a foam pad. "Because if I don't get my sleep, I really can't cope."

"Say you're going to Romania," said Jack. "What's on your ten list?"

"A good French bistro, a vegetable shop, a petrol station . . ." I ended up with: "and a garlic necklace of course."

"Just in case . . ."

67

We drove through Romania's Western Marches and passed through Cluj. Like all the Transylvanian cities it had three names. It was once Klausenburg, founded by Germans from Saxony seven hundred years ago. The Hungarian name was Koloszvár. I had not been much in this part of Romania, but I thought of Cluj as one of the most Habsburg of the northern Transylvanian cities, with butter-yellow baroque buildings, and a number of cafés. It was a university city, and very old. The great Hungarian king Mátyás Korvinus had been born here during the Renaissance.

At least that was what I remembered about the place. Jack, who was turning out to be an authority on such subjects, said that right near Cluj the oldest script in the world had been discovered. It had been created by one of those old Goddess cultures (why did such information not surprise me anymore?) and predated the cuneiform tablets of ancient Sumer by a couple of thousand years. Further, unlike the Sumerian script, which often dealt with economic and administrative functions (men were so linear), the Vinča script had a sacred purpose. At least Gimbutas thought so. Nobody could actually read it yet; the scratchings might only say something like "Pick up some more berries for dessert tonight."

After Cluj the highway got worse and so did my tiredness. Eva was curled up asleep in the back seat. We came to Tîrgu Mureş, and I turned off for what Jack, peering at the map with her flashlight (fortunately on her list of ten real things to bring to Romania), said was a shortcut to Arcata. It was about two in the morning, and no cars had passed us for a very long time.

"I don't know if you've noticed," Jack said after we had gone a few kilometers, "but that thumping noise seems to have got worse."

I'd heard it too, but had been trying to ignore it. "I suppose something's just a little loose," I said. "In the engine. You know these Eastern European cars. They sound awful, but they last forever." With that airy generalization I speeded up. The road was empty and the sign had said it was only another 25km to Arcata.

If I thought I could outrun the thumping, the car had other ideas. The noise grew louder and louder; the car bucked under us like a bronco. I slowed down to a crawl.

"I don't think we can continue like this," said Jack. "Shall I wake Eva?"

"I'll pull off the road," I said as, with a last shudder, the Polski Fiat lost its will to go on and stopped dead.

We were alone in the Transylvanian night, in an ancient forest of wolves, foxes, elk and wild boars. Because our entire journey had taken place in the dark, through sleeping villages and deserted cities, on roads where there were few or no cars, it felt as if we had come to the middle of this ancient land by a sinister magic.

And all those scary passages from the opening of *Dracula,* when Jonathan Harker's carriage is rattling through a gorge of "great frowning rocks" and the rising wind is barely drowning out the baying of the wolves, on the road to the Count's castle in the Borgo Pass, seemed to spring vividly to mind.

"Why does the idea of Mrs. Nagy and her flat have a certain appeal at the moment?" I wondered aloud.

Jack and I didn't have the nerve to wake Eva, who had managed to sleep through the entire self-destruction of her little vehicle. We got out and pushed the car to the side of the road and then quickly and breathlessly hopped back inside and locked all the doors.

"If you were going to Romania, what would you bring?"

"An auto mechanic," I said. "And some parts."

But eventually, even though we were surrounded by werewolves and vampires and the ghostly victims of bloodthirsty counts, we, like Eva, slept soundly.

"And don't start with any of your travel stories," I woke to hear Eva telling Jack. "I don't want to listen to you and Cassandra talking about how this is nothing compared to the time you were stranded in the Andes without food or water."

"But it's good to remember when times were worse."

"At least you've learned something from experience," brooded Eva. "We've got plenty of food."

I opened my eyes. "But this is beautiful," I said.

We were not in dark deep woods at all, but in a narrow valley between rounded, low-lying emerald hills, scattered with copses of newly leafed birch. The sky was light, but the sun hadn't yet come over the hills; a soft white mist clung here and there. I got out of the car and stretched. The air was pure and fresh. There were birds singing all around us.

"It's like Ireland," I said. "It's just as green."

"Any place you like reminds you of Ireland," said Jack. "I've noticed that."

She and Eva had the hood up and Eva was looking doubtfully at the jungle of blackened metal within. "When the thumping got so bad, why didn't you pull off at Tîrgu Mureş? Now we're in the middle of nowhere."

I was still walking around, breathing deeply. Transylvania means "the land beyond the forest" and it did feel as if we had emerged on the other side of the woods, the other side of night and fear. In about fifteen minutes my body would begin screaming for caffeine, so I might as

70

well enjoy this blessed state as long as I could.

"We'll have to walk," said Jack. "The question is, should we walk back to Tîrgu Mureş and find a garage, or on to Arcata? I think we're closer to Tîrgu Mureş, but I don't know how much closer."

Eva thought Tîrgu Mureş, too.

"What about Gladys?" I said. "She might be in a Romanian jail. We can't backtrack now."

Before a serious disagreement could develop however, a woman driving a horse and cart appeared over the hill behind us. She was going in the direction of Arcata, and she offered us a lift.

Two hours later, having been picked up by two carts and finally by a Dacia, the Romanian-made car, the three of us came to the small town of Arcata, in the foothills of the Carpathians. We had traveled through a valley of forests and small farms, of villages of blue- and green-painted houses very neatly kept. Some of the houses had elaborately carved wooden gates in front, wide as the length of the house. Words we couldn't read formed patterns with vines and flowers on the gates, sometimes freshly painted, sometimes splintered and worn. Most of the gates had long birdhouses like dormitories built along the top.

Large, ungainly stork nests balanced on roofs and on electrical poles by the side of the roads. Occasionally a long-beaked head poked out to look at us. We passed farmers in the fields ploughing furrows for planting; sometimes they worked the land with horses, more often by hand. The men wore fedoras and the women kerchiefs. Here and there were Gypsy families too, in brighter colors, hoeing poorer land.

Arcata was a real town, not a village. The Dacia

dropped us off on the main street and we started up a steep hill, along a road fringed with pine and fir, in the direction of a sign that said Arcata Spa Hotel. Up here the sun angled through the dark needles of the trees and dappled the gardens of houses that grew larger and more ornate the higher we climbed. There was a holiday feeling to the place, and the evergreen air was deliciously cool and intoxicating.

I sang to Eva, who was lagging:

Kathleen Mavourneen, the gray dawn is breaking
The horn of the hunter is heard on the hill
The lark from the light wing
The bright dew is shaking
Kathleen Mavourneen! What, slumbering still?

"I'm not slumbering," said Eva ill-temperedly.

"Don't get Cassandra started on her Irish songs," warned Jack. "Her enthusiasm and her ability to keep a tune are unrelated. Believe me, I heard every song Cassandra knows while we were traveling in South America. Motown is one thing, but watch out for 'Danny Boy' and 'The Green Hills of Antrim.' Your eardrums will never be the same."

"Anyone can keep a tune," I said. "But I remember all the words. Are you ready for the chorus?"

"No!"

I would have sung it anyway, but the sight of something ahead stopped me. In a bright blue training suit, a familiar figure came speed-walking, elbows out, knees high, down the hill right towards us.

It was Gladys. And she was not alone.

Three scruffy black dogs ran after her.

❧ CHAPTER SIX ❧

G LADYS, ARE YOU escaping?" I half-expected to see
armed militiamen racing after her.

"Well, hello there, Cassie." She stopped in front of us,
hardly winded. Her white hair was slicked back from her
forehead in a smooth wave, and her cheeks were a fresh
pink. The dogs, after a cursory greeting, slipped off to
some nearby bushes for a sniff and a squirt. They were
ugly, wild-looking beasts, large enough to be wolves, and
their fur was black and matted. "I guess you got Bree's
message, huh? The poor kid was real worried about me.
No, I guess I'm not going anywhere...not for a while
yet. I'm just taking my morning constitutional before I
start my treatments."

"But what about this murder then? Has it been solved?
Who were you supposed to have killed? Did they find the
real murderer?"

"Nope, they didn't. I reckon that still makes me the
main suspect. They might get around to locking me up

one of these days." The thought made her laugh. "Me—in a Romanian jail! What the heck would I do there? But Cassie, why don't you introduce me to your friends and then let's go back on up the hill and sit down somewhere so I can tell you about it. See these dogs? I collect them everywhere I go. I'd love to get them into a bath, but I don't think that would go over too good around here. I bet you could use some coffee, you all look pretty near worn out." She plucked a piece of straw from my hair. "You got here awful fast, but how? Where's your car?"

Jack said, "It died."

"We believe it can come to life again though," I added.

Eva put her hand to her forehead and groaned.

The town of Arcata was divided into two sections. The lower part, where we'd been dropped off, consisted of a few streets of official buildings and shops: an *alimentari* or grocery store with little in the windows, a beauty salon, a clothing store, two pubs. There did not appear to be a garage or petrol station anywhere. The houses in the lower section were set among small orchards and newly planted gardens; some had the carved wooden gates we'd noticed before and many had pretty scalloping and other scrollwork on the lintels and eaves. They were tidy but slightly worn-looking, and that gave them a soft magical charm. On the hillside where we met Gladys, the houses turned into villas that could hold a dozen guests; they were gingerbread marvels of dormers and cupolas and porches, all with the same shabby, lively, slightly fantastic air as the smaller houses. As we climbed higher, followed by the original three black dogs and then two more, we passed several ice cream kiosks, a cinema showing a Bruce Lee film, a restaurant or two and a miniature, dark-timbered

Orthodox church set among the firs.

Eventually we arrived at a square at the top of the hill, next to a small, perfect lake. On the square were benches and a fountain and to the side, with a view of the lake, an open-air restaurant. If it hadn't been for the three tallish utilitarian hotels on the other side of the square, the setting would have been quite idyllic.

"This isn't what I imagined," said Jack. "It's so... poetic."

We seated ourselves in the outdoor restaurant above the lake, which was sparkling lightly in the morning sun. Eva ordered us coffee and bread and butter, and then we all turned to Gladys.

"I don't even know where to start," she said. "I never had anything like this happen to me before, and I'm around bathwater and electrical gadgets like clippers and hair dryers all the time."

"You electrocuted someone?" said Jack. "I mean, someone was electrocuted?"

"Let me tell it from the beginning." Gladys gestured to the largest hotel of the three, the one shaped like a cigarette box. "You see that low white building at the back of the Arcata Spa Hotel? That's the treatment center—the clinic, the spa. It's a great place, and everyone who works there is tops too. I'd been going there about a week, feeling better and better. I hadn't even seen this Pustulescu fellow—you know, the one who invented Ionvital and is so famous— because he was usually on the road, traveling around the other clinics and spas in Romania and to conferences to present his research and so on. I'd been seeing the doctor who seemed to be in charge, Dr. Gabor, Dr. Zoltán Gabor. He'd set up a schedule for me, all kinds of massages and baths, including a shot of Ionvital every day."

A large plate of bread arrived, a light, tasty sour rye,

with margarine and thick plum butter. Jack and I dug into it hungrily. Eva pulled a candy bar out of her bag and ate that instead.

"So I go to my usual appointment with Dr. Gabor to get my shot of Ionvital, and who do I see, sitting in Gabor's office as if it belongs to him? Dr. Pustulescu. And girls, I don't *like* him. Not one bit. He's wearing a moldy green and brown suit, like a reptile, and white shoes. White shoes, I ask you. You don't even see men in Arizona wearing white shoes anymore. You can't tell how old he is, he's kind of like Ronald Reagan, the same dark hair, except Pustulescu's is a toupee, and the same evil old eyes. He's wicked Old Man Coyote, personified. I ask him where Dr. Gabor is, and he says, Oh, I've temporarily relieved him of his duties."

Gladys held her nose to imitate the doctor's sinister, nasal accent.

"So what am I supposed to say? I ask if Dr. Gabor has done anything wrong. Pustulescu says, Wrong, dear lady? Oh no, nothing *wrong*. Let us just say, he and I did not see eye to eye over the running of the clinic. Then he changes the subject—he's looking at my chart. He says [again the pinched nose], I notice you've been following the prescribed regime except for one thing: you haven't been taking the galvanic baths to help your circulation. That is not good, dear lady.

"I tell him that I just can't get beyond my conditioning to feel comfortable putting my arms and legs in water together with an electrical rod. I'm not even gonna try it, because I don't like the whole idea of it. I'm here to relax and it's not good for the nervous system to be all het up, and anyway Dr. Gabor said I shouldn't do anything I didn't want to."

Jack looked appalled. "Let me get this straight, Gladys. This is some kind of electrical shock treatment?"

"It's mild," said Eva. "I have heard of it, it's not serious."

"Well, Old Man Coyote just laughs [Gladys gave a hideous nasal whinnying laugh]. I can tell he's the kind of bozo who never acts like he's upset and who always gets his way. One of my brothers-in-law is like that and he's gone far. Mrs. Bentwhistle, Pustulescu says, I tell you what we'll do. The schedule is full today, but tomorrow you meet me downstairs at the bath at eight o'clock, before the first patient, and I will give you a demonstration. I will put my hands in the water first—to show you that there is no danger at all."

Jack and I looked at each other in consternation.

"Well, I think about skipping it," continued Gladys, "but after all he's the big cheese at the spa, he *invented* this stuff that's making me feel real good. So I think, Heck, what's the harm? So I meet him downstairs in the baths the next morning—yesterday. Nobody else was around, no nurses or bath attendants. I wasn't surprised because it was pretty early.

"I remember the whole thing like it was a dream—real clear, but with that strange slowed-down feeling. Pustulescu's wearing a white coat, not real clean, over his green slacks and a yellowish shirt. He rolls up his coat sleeves and then his shirt sleeves. His skin is old and wrinkled like a dried-up snake with liver spots all over. He's smiling at me, saying, You'll see, Mrs. Bentwhistle, it's really quite *galvanizing,* and then he sticks both his arms, up to the elbows, in the two basins of water. You see? he says. I'm fine. Now turn up the voltage dial as high as it will go. You will see that nothing happens.

77

"But the minute I turn the knob up, he gives this big old gasp and conks over on the floor. His heart stopped, just like that."

Jack and I were speechless and even Eva was taken aback.

"I've never heard of such a thing in Hungary," she said. "The equipment must be faulty here."

"What a way to go," said Jack.

"What happened then?" I asked.

"I screamed and then I must have fainted," said Gladys. "Because the next thing I know I'm on an examining table and my granddaughter's there, looking real worried, along with Dr. Gabor and a whole lot of other people. When I saw Dr. Gabor I thought maybe I'd imagined the whole thing, but I knew I hadn't. I don't think anybody really thought I could have killed Pustulescu, but I was still the only person around when it happened. I turned the knob up myself, for goodness sake. They got Nadia Pop, who's the tourist agent here, and then the cops showed up."

"What happened with the police?" I asked.

"They didn't know what the heck to do except try to look tough. They wanted to arrest me, but Gabor and Nadia wouldn't let them. There was a whole bunch of shouting. I don't think the cops had ever had a case like this on their hands before."

"Couldn't it have been an accident?" said Jack. "A short or something in the wiring?"

"That's what some people seemed to be telling the police," said Gladys. "But the cops weren't buying it. They took the voltage meter off to check it and they took Old Man Coyote away for an autopsy. They're leaving me alone for the time being, but who knows what's going to happen?"

She looked less frightened than bemused by the whole situation.

I asked, "Do you remember, Gladys, when you were originally talking to Dr. Pustulescu in Dr. Gabor's office, about the galvanic bath, was the door open?"

"No," she said. "Because he was giving me my shot. It's always closed then."

"Was anybody waiting outside?"

"Just the usual crowd. The Austrian gal Sophie and the Dutch couple, the Vanderbergs. We all get our shots around the same time. They were as ticked off as me about Dr. Gabor getting the boot."

"And what about Dr. Gabor?"

"He's back in place like nothing ever happened. Last night I saw him and he said, Don't forget your shot in the morning, Mrs. Bentwhistle."

Gladys looked at her watch. "That reminds me, I've only got half an hour before my appointment. Come on and I'll introduce you to Nadia Pop."

On the street level of the Arcata Spa Hotel, next to the lobby and facing the square, was a glass-fronted office. The western sun had faded the few posters in the windows, posters not of Arcata or of the villages of Transylvania and Bukovina, but of the hideous coastal resorts on the overdeveloped Black Sea. Inside the office was a long teak-veneer desk, with very little on it besides an old-fashioned heavy telephone and several pads of paper. A woman was sitting at the desk and staring at the phone; she started with surprise when the four of us came in.

Olivia Manning is always droning on in her *Balkan Trilogy* about "moon-faced Romanian beauties," but Nadia Pop was the first woman I'd ever met in Romania to fit that description. Hers was the plump, ivory-skinned, moustached beauty of the Bosphorus, full-cheeked and heavy-lidded . . . and unfortunately compromised with bright red lipstick, crumbling black mascara, and over-sized horn glasses sitting on a snub nose. She wore an orange polyester suit jacket over a pink and green flowered dress, and her hair was pulled back in an unbecoming bun. She was probably about thirty-five.

"Oh, Gladys," she said, in halting English. "Your friends coming, good they coming from Budapest to help." She addressed us, holding up her hands as if she were being robbed at gunpoint. "Most unhappy situation. Very."

Eva spoke to her in Hungarian, but Nadia shook her head apologetically. "I don't learn Magyar, so sorry. Romanian?"

They pushed me forward, but after a halting beginning, I started over in French. The time had come to confess that my Romanian was limited. Better to find a language we could both speak well. I was right; like most educated Romanians Nadia Pop had studied French.

"*C'est une tragédie, une vraie tragédie. C'est incroyable.*" Turning to Gladys, she repeated, "A tragedy, a big tragedy. We got big problem but do not to worry, it is okay. Well, not okay now, but soon." And then in rapid French she asked me if I'd heard the story, and repeated the highlights again. With gestures, so that everyone could follow the innocence of the dip into water and the unfortunate result. She omitted the death gasp, for which I was thankful.

"Gladys said the police haven't charged her with anything."

"No, not yet, but perhaps more police come from Bucharest." She shifted her mascaraed eyes in Gladys's direction, "I told her if that happens we will call the American

Embassy right away. I am here for the tourists." She patted her well-developed chest. "My job is to protect them from problems."

This self-appointed mission cheered her up. She suddenly regarded the three of us with glee, and spoke in English. "Now, to business down, like you Americans say. You need hotel, we have hotel, many nice rooms. How many nights for you? A sightseeing trip to the Bicaz Gorge? To Bukovina? To Dracula spots? Anywhere you want to go, I got car, I take you. You want treatment? You got medical problems? This is the best—Gladys tells you. You tell them, Gladys."

Eva addressed her severely. She spoke in English and at length. About her business, about this regrettable trip to Romania, about Romanian roads and the lack of garages. "If Transylvania was still part of Hungary," she ended, "none of this would have happened."

Nadia's round face had assumed a bland, inoffensive, helpful look. "You got problem with your car. I fix it. That is what I am here for. To help. Only to help. Politics, I don't care. I am Romanian, Arcata is Magyar, we live together brother and sister, no problem. And the people come here from all over the world, brother and sister, no problem. No Yugoslavia here, okay? No Bosnia, no, no! I drive you to your car, I got tools, we fix. We fix everything!"

Nadia stood up and beamed a smile that showed one or two missing teeth. "Come on now, you get some rooms, some rest, you feel better."

We followed her into the hotel.

The rooms were cheap so we each took our own, all in a row on the sixth floor at the top. There was a big glass window in each of them with a spectacular view of the lake and the rising Carpathians, along with a balcony, a full bath and a comfortable double bed. I lay down on the bed without bothering to undress and immediately fell asleep.

I woke up a few hours later when someone knocked on my door. "Come in," I said, without moving. I assumed it was Jack. Eva had gone off with Nadia to look at the Polski Fiat. Somehow Nadia didn't look like a car mechanic, but these days, in these countries, knowing how to fix anything is an important skill to have.

Bree slipped diffidently in, stopping when she saw me in bed. "Oh, I'm really sorry," she said, and that same, slightly hungry look I'd seen in the MÁV office crept into her eyes. "You're asleep."

"I'm awake now. Is it lunchtime? I could eat something."

"I just heard from Gram that you got here. She's been in the treatment center all morning. She just isn't concerned. She thinks being an American makes you safe."

"It often does," I said, yawning and stretching. "Don't knock it till you've tried getting help with some other passport. Like a Haitian or Vietnamese one maybe."

"Thanks for coming. I thought of you because you said you knew Romanian and you seem so *experienced*. Gram said she told you all about it. Isn't it incredible? I called my mother, Teresa, she thinks we should come home right away. I told her that Gram didn't want to. I'm so glad I was able to get hold of you and have you come. I told Teresa about you, she said you sounded great."

Now I was fully awake. Bree had been coming closer and closer and now she was sitting on the bed with me. Her small soft breasts poked out braless under three layers of sleeveless tops that ended above her navel. Necklaces and thin chains dripped from her milky-pale young neck, and sharp little white teeth showed behind her parted, moist lips.

I jumped up and straightened my shirt and jeans. "I'm glad to do what I can for your grandmother. But I don't understand how you were able to get hold of Eva's business number. Did I mention Eva to you?"

"I got the number from Cathy Snapp. She and Archie and Emma are staying in Arcata too."

"I thought they were going to Sighişoara or someplace?"

"No, first they went to Tîrgu Mureş, then they came here to the hotel. Emma is supposed to be from a little village nearby. Cathy has been getting on my nerves. She's a nice kid, but she seems so *young*."

Bree was sitting cross-legged on my bed now as if she owned the mattress. I decided I had to get her out of here.

"I'm starving," I repeated, moving towards the door. "Where's lunch, downstairs?"

"In the dining room." Reluctantly Bree got up and followed me out. "But I guarantee you, it's not exactly the best food you've ever tasted. Gram and I have been eating a lot of cheese sandwiches."

"I've been to Romania before, you know," I said, rather impatiently. "And besides, the bread's great."

I'd forgotten how tired one can get of bread.

Like the hotel itself, the dining room had been constructed during times of greater prosperity, when health-seekers and conference-goers from many countries, particularly the Soviet satellites, had flocked here in the hundreds. The room could have easily seated three hundred trade delegates or a convention of structural engineers. It was elegantly proportioned, with floor-to-ceiling windows along one side and rows and rows of tables draped in white linen with starched napkins. From the entrance, the restaurant was impressive: waiters of both sexes stood at attention here and there, dressed in dark suits and white shirts, with napkins draped over one arm. However, moving into the room, one saw that the glasses on the tables were chipped, and that the plates were worn and faintly filmed with dust.

There was only one other diner in the whole vast room.

"That's the Austrian woman," whispered Bree. "She's always here for every meal, right on time. Her name is Sophie Ackermann. We call her Frau Sophie."

Frau Sophie beamed encouragingly at us and we seated ourselves at the table next to her. We could have sat anywhere, but something about the enormous room was intimidating. Given a wilderness or desert, humans will always cluster on top of each other.

"*Guten Tag,* Frau Ackermann," said Bree.

"*Gruss Gott,*" Frau Sophie responded with great heartiness.

"Do you speak German?" Bree asked me.

"Some." I said to Frau Sophie in German, "I'm a friend of Gladys and Bree, here for a day or two. Do you have anything to recommend on the menu?"

She chortled as if I had made a very fine joke. "*Aber das Essen ist ganz grauslich!*" The food is wretched!

She was a stout woman, nicely dressed in a green printed rayon dress with a small pink handkerchief folded perkily in a pocket above her vast bosom. Her hair was iron-gray, short and full, and absolutely cared for. Her face was the reddish-pink of strawberry jam.

One of the male waiters came over and stood solicitously with his heels together and his napkin neat over his arm. "*Was möchten Sie?*" he asked.

84

"They only speak German here," Bree said. "But it doesn't matter anyway. It's a trick question."

"What's on the menu?" I asked.

"*Schweinkoteletten*. Porkchops," he replied quickly and politely. "And fried potatoes."

"All right," I said. "And what about a salad?"

He looked as if he'd do anything to please. "Cucumbers?"

I nodded, and Bree did too. "Swine—nix," she said.

He clicked his heels and bowed in a grave and friendly manner and sped off, keeping his upper body perfectly still.

Frau Sophie was shaking in silent laughter. "*Ganz grauslich,*" she said again merrily, downing a small glass of vodka and starting on her red wine.

"I forgot to mention, you can drink all you want here," said Bree. "I don't drink . . . wine, anyway."

"Aren't there any other guests?" I looked around. "How can they keep the hotel going?"

"Probably by charging people like Frau Sophie and Gram an arm and a leg," said Bree. "It's not such a bad place, except for the food. There's one really wild waitress here. I could really go for her. . . . " Bree gave me her sideways look.

"So as far as I understand, the police seem to think it's murder but they haven't really charged your grandmother with anything, is that right?"

"I think Gram was just in the wrong place at the wrong time."

"Do you think someone could have reset the voltage meter before Gladys got there and then tampered with it again while she was lying there in a faint?"

Bree shook her head. "I never figured out how that thing worked. It looks like some torture contraption from

85

a 1920s horror movie, *Dr. Pustulescu's Nightmare Bathing Machine.*"

"If the galvanic bath is so rickety, it's strange that the police would even think it was murder instead of an accident or a heart attack. It makes me wonder about Dr. Pustulescu's popularity here at the spa."

"From what Gram says, he wasn't very well liked. I can take you over to the clinic after lunch and introduce you to Dr. Gabor. He was Gram's doctor before Pustulescu came along."

Our food appeared, two salads consisting of cucumbers in watery vinegar, a cheese sandwich for Bree and my lunch, a plate piled high with thick, gleaming yellow French fries, with a greasy hot porkchop perched on top of the fries like a barge run aground on logs.

"I think what really freaked me out was when I saw the police," Bree said, spearing a droopy-looking cucumber slice from its weak vinaigrette. "They've got these extremely intense uniforms, and they don't smile. Nadia was translating back and forth. I could tell she was stopping them from doing anything drastic."

I looked at my porkchop and ate a fry or two. The oil had been many times reused. "I remember the Romanian police," I said. "I used to have two friends, sisters, in Bucharest. I met them on the Orient Express on my way to Turkey and afterwards I'd visit them from time to time. Once we were walking in the street and someone asked if I wanted to change money. I said no, the man got abusive, the next thing I knew we were surrounded by Securitate, the Romanian secret police. We weren't doing anything, but just the fact that I was a foreigner was enough. They'd tried to set me up. Of course Tatiana and Ana were harassed all the time, simply for being Jewish. They finally were able to get out after the revolution; they emigrated to Canada."

"I guess things were pretty bad under Ceauşescu," said Bree.

"Almost twenty-five years of state terrorism," I said. "Of course he wasn't so bad when he first became president in 1965. But by the mid-seventies he'd consolidated his power. The West liked him because he didn't toe the line with the Soviets, but Ceauşescu's brand of nationalistic communism was lethal to the Romanians. I remember when I came here in the eighties how there were huge paintings and photos of him everywhere. It was a totally repressive regime—censorship, imprisonment, constant surveillance. That's where the Securitate came in."

"But it's better now, isn't it, since 1989?"

"I think so...but I still wouldn't want your grandmother to end up in a Romanian jail on some manufactured charge."

Bree suddenly wasn't listening. "Who's that?" she asked as Jack threaded her way through the white tables to sit down with us.

"My friend Jack. This is Bree, Gladys's granddaughter," I introduced them. The forties-style cotton dresses that Jack had been wearing in Budapest to do her secretarial work had disappeared, and she had reverted to her typically eclectic style, which was to combine pieces of clothing from all over the world. At the moment she had on Bermuda shorts that showed off her legs, espadrilles and a short red silk kimono tied with a handwoven Guatemalan belt. Her smile turned rakish when she saw Bree.

I was irritated to notice that I felt slightly miffed when Bree smiled back. If I could virtuously abstain from cradle-snatching, then Jack could too.

"Did you get some sleep?" I asked.

"I went out for a walk," Jack said. "I can never sleep during the daytime."

"Oh, I'm the opposite," said Bree. "At home I'm up all night writing papers and then I can hardly stay awake during my classes. Sometimes when they show films, I go right to sleep."

"Bree is in Film Studies at Berkeley," I said. "Jack's not much of a film buff."

"Cassandra, that's not true!" said Jack, looking around vaguely for a menu and realizing there was none.

"Try the omelette," I suggested as our waiter took away my half-finished lunch.

"My problem," Jack said to Bree, moving closer to her, "is that I travel so much that I can't keep up with the output from Western countries. So when I get back from six months in India I can't understand what any of my friends are talking about; I'm hopelessly behind. But on the other hand, I've seen a lot of Indian films. Did you know that India is the biggest film-producing country in the world? Have you been to India, Bree?"

"No . . . but I'd like to go."

"You should definitely go while you're young. . . . How young are you?"

"Not that young," "Too young," Bree and I said at the same time.

At that moment Gladys appeared in the doorway, flushed with health and youth from her life-prolonging treatments, and wearing slacks and a Western shirt. As she got closer, I could see that her bolo tie was in the shape of a silver coyote with a twinkling obsidian eye.

"Hi, kids," she said. "Hi, Soph. What's on the menu? Just kidding. I'll take a cheese sandwich."

"I thought I might go over to the clinic and meet this

Dr. Gabor," I said, rising. Bree jumped up too. "I'll show you where it is."

"Then Jack, you'll have to keep me company," said Gladys.

Jack nodded, looking slightly disappointed.

Can I help it that I have a magnetic personality? Nevertheless I vowed to keep myself pure for Eva. At thirty-two Eva was probably less experienced than Bree at nineteen, but that only made Eva a more interesting challenge. I would have to figure out a way to discourage Bree.

❧ CHAPTER SEVEN ❧

THE SIGN ABOVE the door said TRATAMENT, and although everything about the peeling white stucco building was worn and shabby, the place bustled with an energy the restaurant lacked. People in various states of dress and undress—from the crinkly, paper-thin training suits that upwardly mobile Romanians seemed to favor, to ragged bathrobes, to ordinary wool skirts and suits, to the long, brightly patterned red and green skirts of the Gypsy women—sat on molded plastic chairs or walked up and down the stairs and through the corridors. Some wore bewildered expressions and clutched their schedules; others, the regulars, strolled calmly from one appointment to the next or chatted in groups about their ailments.

Not a great fan of hospitals, I found the atmosphere here more cheerful than sickly. Many of the passing nurses and attendants nodded at us.

"Have you been having treatments too?" I asked Bree.

"Me? No, they know me from Gram. Everyone's been

completely sympathetic."

Dr. Zoltán Gabor's office was on the first floor.

"Hallo, Bree," he said graciously in English and invited us in. "Is this the American friend you were telling me about? Dr. Gabor, at your service."

A youngish nurse with bleached blond hair, very short, and an anxious expression masked by a bright, professional smile, pushed forward two chairs. "This is my assistant, Margit," he said. She wore a perky cap and a uniform of that almost diaphanous white nylon that droops after the first washing.

She nodded vivaciously and then, flinging a stethoscope over her arm, zipped out the open door and closed it. "Always in a hurry," Dr. Gabor excused her.

He was a tall man with an imposing nose and blue-black hair, silver at the temples. Under his white lab coat he wore a striped suit with very wide lapels. It may have been in fashion in the seventies. His eyes were gray-blue and his eyebrows winged up at the corners, giving him an alert, slightly demonic appearance.

"And what can I do for you, Mrs.—Miss?—Really?" He leaned forward in the concentrated listening posture of the doctor, and suddenly I was aware that I had no particular standing here, no reason to be cross-examining him about the death of Dr. Pustulescu and Gladys's supposed part in it.

"Mrs.," I answered demurely. "I'm a widow actually." Beside me I heard a choking sound from Bree. "Perhaps we could speak alone a moment?"

"Yes, yes," he rose with great alacrity and showed the speechless Bree out.

"I too," he said. "I have also lost my wife. Very sad."

When he'd reseated himself behind the desk, I began again:

"We all get older, as you know. I was traveling in Europe to forget my tragedy, and met Gladys and her granddaughter on the train. Gladys told me about this spa and how much better she feels being here. I'm thinking of taking the treatment myself."

"But you're *young*," he said graciously, even as his hands reached for a pad of paper and a pen. "Surely you are only thirty-seven, thirty-eight?"

"Mid-forties," I sighed.

"Symptoms?"

"Nothing definite. Vague things. Stiffness in my joints in the morning, more aching than usual when it's cold or wet. . . ."

"Pain?"

"No . . . not really. . . ."

"Melancholy?" he suggested.

"Of course."

He got up and stuck his head out the door. "Margit," he called, and to me, "Please undress."

This was slightly more than I'd bargained for. I took off my shirt as slowly as possible, and talked more quickly. "I was so surprised to hear from Gladys about yesterday's events. What a pity. I'd heard so much about Dr. Pustulescu. I was eager to meet him."

"Yes, a pity," Dr. Gabor said, pulling out his stethoscope and listening to my heart.

"Had he been here long, at the spa, I mean? I know he invented Ionvital. Was he the director here?"

Margit had returned and with quick movements had the blood pressure cuff around my arm and was pumping it up. Her eyes looked everywhere but at my face. "Yes, but only in name. He had his own treatment center, in Bucharest, very famous. He just came here from time to time to check on us."

Why was Margit perspiring? Beads of sweat gathered on her forehead.

"Do you speak English?" I asked her.

"Oh, no. No, no," she stuttered, and took the cuff off.

"He was Romanian, wasn't he? Not Hungarian?"

"He was the only Romanian here," said Dr. Gabor, motioning me to sit down and starting to bend and tap various joints. "We are all Hungarian at the treatment center. Magyar."

"That must have caused some problems then?" I heard a distinct creaking coming from one of my knees as Dr. Gabor manipulated it.

"It's the beginnings of rheumatoid arthritis," he said.

"What!"

"It's normal as you age. You can dress now." He sat back down at his desk, and Margit dashed out the door again. "Are you taking medication? Do you have other health problems?"

"No, really, I'm fine. I mean—I'm interested in this Ionvital treatment."

"Yes, I can give you shots, or pills if you prefer. And you say you want to take the full course of treatment? Two weeks of baths and massage and mud, you will be a new woman. A recent widow?"

"Very recent." I was suddenly inspired. "André's parents were Hungarian émigrés, that's why I feel a great kinship with the Hungarians, wherever they may be: in America, in Hungary, in Transylvania, in the Czech and Slovak Republics, a great and wonderful people."

"Then you know, you know about Transylvania, our sad history," he said. His handsome, sympathetic face lit up. "We are a different race, we are not of the Orient, we belong to Mitteleuropa. That is where we turn for civiliza-

94

tion—to Vienna, to Prague, not to Bucharest or Sofia or Istanbul. You know the work of Václav Havel and Milan Kundera? Josef Škvorecký, Czeslaw Milosz?"

"Oh certainly . . ."

"Yes, of course you do. They are great men. And what they write is our culture too. Everything is translated into Hungarian, we know what is happening in Central Europe, the world. *That* is the civilization we belong to, we Transylvanian Magyars. The Romanians, they are ignorant of great literature and democratic ideals. Such authors are not translated into Romanian. The Romanians, the Serbs, the Slavs and the Greeks—they are all corrupt, all writing only lies. But the Germans, the Hungarians, the Czechs, they write the truth. The Romanians only write lies."

"Why do they lie?"

"It's the Orthodox church. From the beginning it was all symbols and icons, corruption and power and *spying*. Byzantine thinking. How else could a man like Ceauşescu come to power in Romania? The worst dictator in modern times after Stalin." He suddenly shook his fist at the wall. "Are you listening? You are *liars!*"

"Securitate?" I asked. "Still, after the revolution?"

"Hah, the revolution," he said. "We will have a revolution when the Magyars throw the Romanian communists out of Transylvania." He looked pleased with himself. "I have a dossier this tall, every day a black mark."

Margit had come back in with a thin piece of paper, the kind I'd seen other patients carrying around.

"So. Margit has put together your schedule. Every morning a warm saline bath, then you go to the mud packing and to the shower massage. You take the galvanic bath every other day, more often is not good."

It was on the tip of my tongue to shriek that I wouldn't touch the galvanic bath with a ten-foot (and certainly not a metal) pole, but I figured that I had to get to the scene of the crime somehow.

"It's too late now," he said, looking at his watch. "Treatment is over. But you can start tomorrow morning, eight-thirty. Now, you want to get the Ionvital shot every day?"

"Tell me again, what's in it?"

"Procaine, you know, like novocaine, for your teeth? It affects the metabolism positively. You're having your menopause? You've finished?"

"I've had a hot flash or two."

"Ionvital will help you with your glandular upheaval. Here," he added, seeing that I looked less than convinced. "I look for something in English for you to read. Margit," he called. "Every time I turn around that girl is gone. She is so restless." Margit came back in and Gabor said something in Hungarian that made her look even more vivaciously anxious. She rummaged around in a file cabinet and came up with a lurid orange pamphlet that said GERIATRIC CURES IN ROMANIA and another titled IONVITAL: THE ANSWER TO AGING?

"Read these," Gabor said, "and we discuss more tomorrow."

"Is everyone here getting shots?" I asked.

"You mean the foreigners? Oh yes, the foreigners are my speciality. The Vanderbergs, very regular patients. And Frau Ackermann, she comes here for ten years for the shots. They have a mild euphoric effect," he added thoughtfully.

"Do you take them?"

"Me!" He seemed surprised. "Oh, no. Not yet. Dr. Pustulescu, he took them. He was eighty-nine."

There was a knock on the door. It was Bree. "Are you all right in there?"

Clutching my pamphlets and the schedule of treatments, I stood up and shook Dr. Gabor's hand. Margit had vanished again.

"Rheumatoid arthritis," I told Bree, in my best elderly widow voice.

Around five o'clock Nadia and Eva rolled up in Nadia's Dacia. Jack and I were sitting on a bench in front of the Arcata Spa Hotel, enjoying the sparkling pine-scented air and the late afternoon sun on the lake. We had already made several acquaintances: a woman who had a cousin in Miami, her daughter, who taught English at an elementary school, and a small boy with whom we shared a bar of Hungarian chocolate. I hadn't seen anything of Bree since my recent widowhood, but Gladys was to be intermittently glimpsed around the perimeter of the lake with her dogs. There were now seven, each blacker and larger than the next.

The Dacia halted with a shudder and Eva and Nadia got out, both carrying greasy chunks of metal. Nadia was covered in oil and had a happy, satisfied smile on her round face while Eva, usually so neat, looked as if Nadia had driven over her a couple of times. She had streaks of grease across one cheek and in her blond hair.

"Did you fix it?" Jack asked.

In English Nadia crowed, "It's simple problem, easy solved." She held up a blackened little metal tube. "I get sister husband to find this one for us."

Eva said, "My car is ruined, it's completely ruined. She doesn't know what she's doing. She just unscrewed and took apart everything. She was going to leave these parts on the side of the road. I don't know what they are, but I know they were in the engine. They must be there for a reason."

"No, no, Eva," Nadia said, unruffled. "It is *this,* this part that is problem. It is *nothing!* I fix plenty cars. You got to in Romania. Now I go in my office, call sister husband, he finds new one." She remembered our other problem. "Gladys okay? No more police come today?"

"I've been to see Dr. Gabor," I said. "He thought it would be a good idea for me to take some treatments. I start tomorrow. He's quite the Magyar patriot, isn't he?"

"You take the treatments, good!" said Nadia. "You stay here. *C'est bon,* very good. Then we take some sightseeing trips in the afternoons. To Bicaz Gorge. Sighişoara to see birthplace Dracula. Only ten dollars, hard currency, per day."

She vanished with the metal tube into her office, in high good humor.

Eva decided to leave too. She went off muttering, "How are we going to get back to Budapest? I can't just leave my car in Transylvania. The Romanians will vandalize it."

I'd been wondering when we would see the Snapps. The next thing I knew Archie was taking a photo of me and Jack.

"Surprise!"

"Surprise," Jack said, with a cautious glance at me, as if to say, He *looks* familiar but. . . .

"Jack, you remember Archie, from the Gellért."

"Oh, yeah," she said. "During the attack of the Gypsy violinists."

"Jack, that's right! The Australian!" Archie said enthusi-

astically, sitting down beside us with his Nikon, tape recorder and steno pad. "Great to see you again, Jack. I'm
the editor of *The Washtenaw Weekly Gleaner,* back in Michigan. I'd love to interview you about Oz—isn't that what
you folks call it? And Cassandra—I never got a chance to
tape you on the train. . . "

"I hope that's not why you got me to Arcata," I said.

Archie looked briefly troubled. "No, it's this Pustulescu
mess. Of course it was some kind of accident; he was
probably a heart attack waiting to happen, but what bad
luck for Gladys to pull the trigger, so to speak, him being
the Drug Czar of the spa and all. He's the inventor of this
longevity stuff called Ionvital, you know. Gladys swears
by her shots, but I'll reserve judgment. It's the way you
live that keeps you young—like you Cassandra, always on
the move, that's the ticket. But I'll tell you one thing, I'm
sure not tempted to try the galvanic bath *now.* And we're
going to stick by Gladys, make sure nothing happens. I've
got a few connections in Bucharest, got to know the con-
sul there and of course our lawyer Eugen, they can help set
things straight. If worst comes to worst, I'll get in touch
with a wire service, make sure the news gets out."

Archie Snapp reminded me of someone's kid brother, of
the boy at school who wasn't as smart or as talented as his
older siblings, and so made up for it by being overly eager
and agreeable. His brown-gold eyes were like polished ag-
ates under his thinning but still shiny shock of brown hair.
You looked at him and thought: Norman Rockwell, 1932.
Today, in the warm afternoon, he wasn't wearing his soft
felt hat, but he had on a handknit sweater-vest over a
white long-sleeved shirt with cufflinks. I hadn't seen cufflinks since my Irish grandfather died in 1956.

Cathy Snapp had seen us and came quickly over, pulling
Emma by the hand. Her dark blond hair hid most of her

face, which had developed a bad case of acne, probably due to all the French fries at the restaurant. Her sweatshirt pictured a haggard Dostoyevsky. Emma wore jeans and a sweatshirt too—I hadn't known that Mozart sweatshirts came that small. As usual Emma was silent, and carrying her violin case close to her heart. She didn't appear to recognize me, but with Emma it was hard to tell.

"I've been looking for Bree," said Cathy. "We were supposed to play cards."

"She's around," said Jack. I looked at her suspiciously.

"It's a good thing I gave her your phone number, isn't it, Cassandra?" Cathy asked. "With everything going on."

"I hope I can help. I don't think Gladys is in big trouble."

"But did Dad tell you about the other stuff, about Zsoska? That's how we wound up to Arcata in the first place."

"Zsoska?"

"Kit-Kat, Emma is looking tired to me," Archie broke in. "And so do you." He turned to me and Jack. "We went for an excursion on the bus today to a wonderful little village where they make pottery and sell it. I love folk art and crafts! Anyway, Kit-Kat, I think you'd both better lie down for a little nap before dinner."

"A nap! But Dad . . ."

"You can read to Emma. Don't let her practice."

"Dad!" But she was still of an age and nature to be obedient, though resentful, and she turned in a huff, pulling Emma after her.

As soon as the girls had left us, Archie said to me, "You know, Cassandra, what say we do our interview right here and right now? I know my readers would love to hear about your life. The life of someone who's never settled down. From Kalamazoo to Timbuktu. And you're not a spring chicken anymore, how do you do it?"

He turned his tape recorder on and looked at me, boyishly expectant.

Jack howled with laughter.

"Wait a minute," I said. "Who is Zsoska, and what does she have to do with Gladys and Pustulescu?"

"Zsoska doesn't have anything to do with Gladys," Archie said. "She works here in Arcata."

"So?"

Archie paused. The merest hint of worry darkened his agate eyes. "She's also Emma's birth mother."

"Here? In Arcata?"

"She just works here. She lives in a small village called Lupea. We're hoping to visit it on one of our bus trips."

"But how did you track this Zsoska down?"

"Well, first we went to Tîrgu Mureş. That's the city where Lynn and I adopted Emma in the first place. We didn't get her from an orphanage, but from a hospital. They still had all the records. Apparently the mother had moved back to her parents' home in Lupea."

Archie looked at his tape recorder. Like most journalists he was more comfortable asking questions than answering them. "We're going to introduce ourselves pretty soon. We'll figure something out . . . make everybody happy. . . . Emma will start talking, you'll see, it'll be fine. . . . But what I'm really interested in, Cassandra—or can I call you Cass?—is whether or not you make a living as a translator. Is it lucrative? And if you translate from Spanish to English, why are you in Eastern Europe, on your way to China? Is travel just a way of life for you? Are you running away from something? Or are you just interested in geography and culture? Do you still feel American?"

"She's traveling to forget," Jack said with a solemn look. "She's a widow."

101

Damn that Bree! Why had she told Jack what I'd said to Dr. Gabor? Now I'd never live it down.

"Oh, I'm so sorry," said Archie, and there was a sincerity in his face that made me even more embarrassed.

"Well, he wasn't a very nice man," I said, with a vicious look at Jack. "We often thought of divorcing before his... fatal accident. Now about this Zsoska...." I was imagining a baby-faced girl who'd made a mistake a few years ago, one of the bath attendants perhaps, a slight, dark girl with big eyes and bangs. "You'll have to be careful how you tell her, don't you think? It might be a terrible shock."

"Perhaps you could help us, Cass," he said. "Or you," he included Jack.

"Do you need a translator?" I asked. "Eva could help. Or Nadia. What language does she speak?"

"It's not just the language problem," Archie said nervously. "Truth to tell, we hadn't quite thought through some of this. I'm afraid the Kit-Kat is a little upset..."

"Get to the point, man," said Jack. "Where does she work here? Do you have a plan to try to talk with her?"

"Well, I thought, at one of the meals, one of the dinners, I might.... She's usually there at dinner. She's one of the waitresses."

"Well," I said, looking at my watch. "I guess we'll all have the chance to meet her soon."

Dinner was better attended than lunch, but only slightly. Frau Sophie occupied her usual place and had been joined at the next table by the elderly Dutch couple, the Vanderbergs, who immediately ordered and drank several small glasses of gin. The Snapps had a table to themselves next to Gladys and Bree. Eva, Jack and I made up the fifth table in the huge dining hall. We were all close enough to talk.

The slender male waiter was there again, scrupulously attending to the needs of the Vanderbergs and Frau Sophie. He carried the usual napkin over one arm and moved swiftly on the balls of his feet. I hoped they tipped him well.

"*Gruss Gott!*" Frau Sophie called over to us and pointed at her dish. "*Grauslich!*"

"She always says that," said Bree. "Do you really think she likes it?"

"It means disgusting or horrible in German," Cathy explained.

"Well, excuse me," said Bree and turned away pointedly.

Bree was tarted up tonight in a leather vest over a torn Marlene Dietrich tee-shirt, and multiple chains and bracelets, while Cathy had exchanged Dostoyevsky for Willa Cather, albeit Willa with a small, experimental rip over her left brow. I suspected that Bree, having had no one her age to talk to, had turned to Cathy and now regretted it, especially since older and more interesting women had appeared. But I felt sorry for Cathy, suffering from adolescent skin eruptions, and now obviously hurt and unsure whether to act miffed or indifferent, or to redouble her efforts to please.

"I just meant. . . ." said Cathy.

"Different cultures, different foods," said Gladys. "They are a little heavy on the meat side of things though. You wouldn't think, for such a poor country, they'd have so much pork. They could grow a nice crop of soybeans here. Tofu would be much more nutritious."

Suddenly the swinging doors to the kitchen burst open and a big tigress of a woman stormed forth, plates in hand. In her early twenties, she was tall and strapping, with wide shoulders and aggressive hips. She had a mane of black hair frosted so that it looked striped with gold. With her high cheekbones, aquiline nose and contemptuous full lips, she wouldn't have been out of place in a French restaurant in Manhattan, where her impoliteness would have been admired as hauteur. She clanked the plates down in front of the Snapps. Cathy glared at her, and Emma stared wordlessly at the omelette and fries on the table. "Thank you, Zsoska," murmured Archie. *"Köszönöm."*

She came over to our table and Eva spoke to her in Hungarian, perhaps asking for a menu. Zsoska shrugged and pointed at the other diners. All of them, except Emma and Bree, were eating porkchops. Bree was eating bread and cheese and Emma had her omelette.

Eva ordered a porkchop; Jack and I went for the omelette.

"Zsoska," I could hear Archie call in a friendly voice. "Could you come over here a minute . . . ?"

Zsoska ignored him and went banging back into the kitchen. She was as ferociously regal as a Tartar princess, and if she acted like this when she thought the Snapps were hotel guests, what was she going to be like when she found out they had adopted her daughter?

❧ CHAPTER EIGHT ❧

I WOKE EARLY the next morning from a deep sleep. The sun shimmered across the hills and valleys below, a long, unbroken stretch of light and dark green. I went downstairs to the bar, brought up a cup of coffee and settled down to read the material that Dr. Gabor had given me on the discovery and use of Ionvital.

The first pamphlet, IONVITAL: THE ANSWER TO AGING?, told me that the discovery of this miracle drug had been made in the early fifties, when Dr. Ion Pustulescu realized that a common anesthetic used in dentistry, that is to say novocaine, or in the world pharmacopoeia "procaine," had other uses. Injected intramuscularly, the procaine solution, now known as Ionvital, had a "vitaminic-type effect" (this term was not defined) on the organism. Acting on the central nervous system and, as a result, on the activity of the entire body, the drug was capable of great regenerative powers. Diseases and processes connected with aging were all positively affected. These included degenerative rheumatism, arteriosclerosis, angina pectoris, arthritis, gastric ulcers, neuralgia and Parkinson's disease. Improvement was also achieved with Alzheimer's disease, senile dementia and multiple sclerosis.

Many years of administering Ionvital had shown that patients who took regular treatments suffered less from depression, improved their memories, and increased their physical and intellectual capacities. Hearing was improved, as well as the sense of smell. The skin's elasticity and general appearance improved, the hair began to grow again, and brittleness in the bones was reduced while muscular strength increased. Wounds, burns and fractures healed more rapidly.

In the late fifties Dr. Pustulescu established a clinic outside of Bucharest, but eventually the treatment spread to other hotels and spas around the country. In spite of the great success of Ionvital in Romania, the treatment was subject to mixed reviews in the worldwide scientific community. Although Dr. Pustulescu traveled to conferences to present his findings, some journals were not impressed. In stuffy old England, for instance, it was impossible to make headway against the entrenched medical hierarchy represented by the *British Medical Journal*. But the *Daily Mail* published a series of illustrated reports on the medical successes of Dr. Pustulescu's clinic. An unnamed Nobel Prize winner, when asked about the drug's regenerative effects, was quoted as saying, "Anything's possible." And the secretary of a major German pharmaceutical company who visited the clinic several times exclaimed *"Donnerwetter!"* or "Thunderation!"

The rest of the brochure consisted of testimonials and excerpts from patients' letters. A typical one read:

Dear Dr. Pustulescu,

Last October I celebrated my ninety-fourth birthday. I am in perfect health after sixteen nonstop years of treatment with Ionvital. My eyesight is still good, my hair is still abundant and black, and I walk perfectly straight. I do kung-fu every morning and have written a novel a year since beginning treatment. In my youth I was sickly and unable to hold down a job for long. Ionvital has restored to me my faith in humanity. Thank you for your years of unselfish work dedicated to helping the debilitated, the senile and the victims of old age. The world is very lucky to have you.

The pamphlet ended with these stirring words:

There used to be an old Romanian saying: "Old age is a fatal process and nothing can be done about it."

Today, no one can say that. Ionvital has made the difference.

The second brochure, GERIATRIC CURES IN ROMANIA, also printed by rotogravure on thin slippery stock, gave a few more pseudo-scientific reasons for the curative powers of Ionvital: "Ionvital balances the neurovegetative discordance as well as glandular troubles provoked by old age; it is especially recommended in generalized distortions (the general phenomena of aging)."

There were photos of various clinics in Romania, mostly in and around Bucharest, where you could undertake the cure. I could hardly recognize the photo of the Arcata Spa Hotel, which must have been taken shortly after the place was constructed, twenty years before. The brochure rhapsodized about the setting and climate here in Arcata:

The natural surroundings in which the clinic is set as well as its comfort create a general atmosphere of relaxation, high mood and relief. Thanks to the stability of the weather, the action of the natural factors on the body is slightly exciting, favouring a rapid adjustment.

There was also a color photograph of Dr. Pustulescu in this brochure, and I scrutinized it closely. He was in a white lab coat, sitting behind an impressive desk. Although his lower face was sagging, his hair was still dark and his posture was alert and erect. It was impossible to guess his age in the photo or to know when it was taken. He could have been sixty or eighty or even, if he'd been taking his own medicine long enough, over a hundred.

It was eight-thirty and time for my first treatment. I still hadn't decided whether to go for the Ionvital injections or not. Was it better to become a "victim of old age," a passenger on a steadily moving train to the final destination? Or to turn into a living mummy with black hair and eyes that had seen too much? To see your entire generation wither and die around you while you became an ossified curiosity, kept alive by Ionvital shots? It sounded more lonely than anything. On the other hand, an extra twenty or thirty years were tempting, if only because the alternative was so final, and sometimes felt so close.

My fiftieth birthday was coming up in a few years. My father had died when he was fifty. I hadn't been to half the places I'd wanted to visit, done half the things I'd imagined I would when I stared out my bedroom window as a rebellious teenager and vowed I'd get away, I'd *do* something with my life. What had I, after all, accomplished? My head was an encyclopedia of train and ferry schedules to places all over the globe; my name appeared on the copyright pages of the books I translated and occasionally on the title page or back cover. Compañeras I had plenty of, and lovers more than my share. But I had no real home, no country in spite of two passports, no pension, no savings, no security. I did have about a hundred and fifty close relatives, but they were all Catholic and they were sure I was going to hell.

Maybe I'd feel better if I had a bath.

My first treatment, the saline bath, was the one I enjoyed most, in part because it required nothing of me. The water came from the lake, and had been warmed to a toasty forty degrees centigrade. It had a slippery, salty feel; I felt my muscles relax, my joints unstiffen, my bones float restfully inside the whole elongated package of my body. Ilona, the Mistress of the Waters, had the sympathetic face of a Crimean nurse ministering to a young British soldier who had lost a leg on the battlefield. Plump and sweet, she spoke a bit of English and a bit of German in a lovely musical voice.

"Are you ill or only to rest?" she asked me.

"Just a little tired," I said. "I'm thinking about taking the Ionvital shots. . . . I was just reading about them . . . about Dr. Pustulescu . . . isn't it a tragedy that he died? I would have liked to meet him."

"No, you would not like," she said decisively.

"But he was such a fine man, he did so much for humanity with his discovery."

"No! He bad man, chase the girls." She put on a lecherous expression that reminded me of Harpo Marx getting ready to speed after some unwary female.

"Chasing women at his age! How old was he, anyway?"

"Almost ninety! That too old for love! *And* if you say no, you lose job."

"So some women actually said yes?"

"I never say yes. I am married. But other girls here, they

got no choice. These baths the only work in Arcata except the dairy factory. . . . Excuse. . . . " She went off down the corridor to answer a call from someone in another bath.

I luxuriated uneasily. If Pustulescu had a reputation as a lecher and if almost all the workers at the spa were women, any or all of them could have planned the crime. It was a neat revenge fantasy: instead of an orgasm give him a jolt he'd never forget (or remember). A joint effort among his victims might explain why there was nobody but Gladys and Pustulescu in the galvanic bath room. But it didn't explain how anyone knew he was going to be there that morning unless he'd told someone besides Gladys. And what *about* poor Gladys, on the verge of being charged with his death? Would the real culprit(s) come forward? Not likely.

Ilona came back and helped me out of the bath and gave me a thin sheet to dry myself with. "You don't stay too long in bath. You faint," she said. "Now you go to mud, yes?"

To mud, yes. The brochure had said the mud came from nearby, that it was "saprogenic" which, though I had no dictionary with me, I vaguely recalled as having something to do with putrefaction. "The mud is prehistoric," Dr. Gabor had told me. "Like the Dead Sea. It has minerals. It is like estrogen. *Not* estrogen. But hormones. Good for women with problems in fertility."

I descended to the underworld of the clinic, to the basement where, in subterranean shadowlight, the mud wrapping took place.

This treatment was done on the assembly line: all the nine-thirty appointments—about a dozen women—entered at one time, and were each given a threadbare muslin sheet and a pair of plastic slippers. Two to a small cubicle, we undressed and lay down on our stomachs on tables

110

draped in more soft, yellowed sheets. None of the attendants here spoke anything but Hungarian, which presented a problem in terms of cross-examination. Not that there was much time to chat. I hadn't been on my table more than a few minutes when two women in heavy rubber aprons and thick rubber gloves came into the cubicle, wheeling a cart with big buckets of steaming black mud on it. Very rapidly they piled heaps of the mud on my back and legs and smeared it all over me. It smelled intensely like fertilizer, and I had to bite my lip so as not to cry out at the heat. Then they helped me turn over, and just as quickly slopped and smeared the mud up and down the front of my body. With practiced movements they wrapped me up tightly in half a dozen sheets. The whole operation couldn't have taken more than three minutes, and then they started on the woman next to me.

My temperature immediately began to rise. The mud was heavy and hot on my body, oily as blackened butter, gooey as molasses. Bound this securely, I couldn't move an inch; I could only feel the mud oozing between my flesh and the sheets. My nose began to itch. An attendant came by and put a cool cloth on my forehead and stroked my cheek and said something kind in Hungarian. I felt like a swaddled baby in the nursery, helpless and vulnerable. I felt like a child with a fever in the school nurse's office. I felt as if the world stood still. All the women had been slapped with mud and wrapped in sheets; we lay like a row of chrysalises. The silence was almost total. There was only the drip, drip, drip of water, and the glutinous squish of hot mud between my thighs.

When Camille Paglia accused women of being unable to contribute to civilization because of being hormonally mired in the chthonian swamp, was this what she was talking about? I certainly didn't feel cool and crystalline,

111

much less in full possession of my Apollonian faculties down here in the primordial realms of the procreative female. Deep in the twilight womb of the earth, inside my sloppy little cocoon of slimy hormones, I had become a vegetable goddess, an inchoate force of regeneration or destruction, bubbling and boiling, seething with hot volcanic energy and ready to erupt if they didn't . . .

Just in time, the same team came back to unwrap me with friendly efficiency. The air was cool and then cold against my skin as they scraped off the excess mud and pushed me off the table in the direction of the primitive showers with their slatted wooden platforms. The black mud was startling against my pale skin, and at first clung in lumps and clots; its fine, silt-like quality kept creating a kind of wash of black, even after I'd been scrubbing for a while. The silt rained over me like an etch-a-sketch gone wild.

Meanwhile the other women had emerged from their cocoons and were wandering dazedly over to the showers. They did not look like great scientists and artists of genius. In the dim light of this richly pungent netherworld they looked like tadpoles taking their first steps out of the primal soup.

After I finally got the mud off, I dressed again and staggered out into the hallway. It was only ten-thirty and I was worn out. But there was more to come.

I walked upstairs and into a changing area, where I disrobed for the third time since putting on my clothes this morning and was given a thin cotton robe and another pair of plastic slippers. This was something called a shower massage. I had no idea what to expect.

I was told to wait on a bench in a corridor. It was steamy in this section, and the water was not so much running as sloshing, lapping, spraying and gushing. There was a rhythmic undertone of hands slapping flesh, punctuated occasionally by a groan or two. This area was not divided by gender, as the salt baths and mud-wrapping swamp had been, and I was suddenly acutely conscious of being surrounded by elderly semi-undressed men, most with sheets wrapped around their lower parts, leaving sunken chests and bloated bellies bare.

To tell the truth, Camille, they didn't look like great scientists or artists of genius either.

Someone staggered past me and I realized it was my turn to enter the massage room. A man in a skimpy bathing suit, over which his belly protruded, smooth and round as a brownish-white dinosaur egg, came out into the corridor and called some version of my name. He was wearing smoke-gray goggles that gave him the look of a undersea diver, and as I followed him into the room I realized he was blind or nearly so. In German he ordered me up onto the sopping-wet massage table. The entire room was dripping; water ran down the walls and the windows.

I lay on my stomach as directed and he pulled a battery of shower nozzles directly over my head, spine and legs. As the warm water sprayed over me it created a kind of tingling numbness and at the same time a peculiar physical awareness, a strange sensory disorganization that increased violently when the blind masseur began to vigorously knead my flesh. There seemed to be no pattern to his massage. He didn't start by gently pressing my shoulders (asking if the pressure was okay for me, or, as did American bodyworkers, murmuring, If your muscles could speak, what would they be saying right now?) and then working his way down my spine and so forth, giving me time to adjust. This was more like being attacked by a school of sharks. I opened my mouth to shriek and water clogged my nose and throat.

"*Ist gut?*" he said, assaulting my thigh muscles with powerful fingers; my legs promptly clenched up as I braced myself against the table.

"*Nein! Halt!*" I glugged, as water poured down my throat. I wasn't only being mauled by sharks, I was drowning as well. "Not so damned hard! *Donnerwetter!*"

After a few more minutes, I begged him to stop and crawled off the table, half-drowned, trying to collect my senses and my wits and stuff them all back into the vulnerable bundle that was my body. I didn't know why Dr. Pustulescu's murderer had bothered with the galvanic baths. This shower massage was a near-death experience. I felt as if I were competing in a triathalon by this time; nevertheless I dried myself off as best I could with the thin sheet, dressed again and made my way over to the galvanic baths.

Fortunately, here I didn't have to get completely undressed again; I only had to take off my jeans, socks and boots and to roll up my sleeves. I was made to sit in a small plastic stenographer-type chair, surrounded by four small ceramic tubs of water: two at waist-level for the forearms and hands, and two on the floor for feet and legs up to mid-calf.

The attendant, a young woman with a morose expression, was fooling around with a machine to the side. It was a rectangular case the size of a shoebox, with a few dials and a half-circle of numbers. From where I sat I couldn't see how high the numbers went up.

I asked in Romanian if this was the voltage meter that had been here when Dr. Pustulescu was fried, but perhaps I didn't phrase it quite correctly, for although she said yes ("*Da, da.*"), her smile seemed more diabolical than mournful.

She signaled to me that I should now put my limbs in

the tubs. This I found hard to do. As an older child in a family of eight children I had been instructed over and over not to let any electricity ever come in contact with water and with me or my siblings. I could see that each of the tubs had a narrow strip of metal to the side and presumably the electric current came from that. I had visions of monster movies in which my eyes would bug out from my head and my hair would stand on end, straight for once, and for all time.

I had visions of Dr. Pustulescu.

However, I had to know how the contraption worked and so, closing my eyes and muttering a quick "Mary, Merciful Mother, protect me," I put my arms and legs in the water and the attendant switched on the current. I felt a slight tingling, as if thin needles were pricking at my skin. I could see her looking at the meter and I quickly said, "I think that's enough voltage." She indicated that I was hardly getting any and that if she had her way she'd definitely turn up the juice.

Intellectually I knew that even if she turned it up all the way I probably wouldn't be electrocuted. If Dr. Pustulescu had been murdered, it was because someone had fixed it so he would. I wished I knew more about electricity. How much current was too much? How could you tamper with the meter to increase the voltage? Who would have had the opportunity; who would have had a motive?

From the sound of it, almost everyone who knew Pustulescu had hated him.

When I knocked on Dr. Gabor's office door, there was a pause and then Margit rushed out, laughing nervously when she saw me. Dr. Gabor was seated behind his desk, reading what looked like a Hungarian political review.

115

"Oh, Mrs. Really," he said, "I have been expecting you. I have something for you." He gestured to a pile of small cardboard boxes on his desk. "Sit down. How are you?"

"I'm completely exhausted," I said, collapsing on the chair. "I haven't done as much in a morning since I left the Marine Corps."

"The cure is very taxing." Dr. Gabor nodded. "You must be careful to take long naps and not to overexert yourself with walking or dancing."

"Dancing?"

"There is a discotheque in Arcata, by the cinema," he said. "I am too old myself."

"I am too," I said. "What are these things?"

"Beauty treatments!" he said, opening one of the boxes and pulling out a sea-green plastic jar. On its lid, in gold script, it said: *Prof. Ion Pustulescu.*

"Did I ask for these?"

"You asked about Ionvital. Well, you should know it comes not only in shots and pills, but also facially. It will rejuvenate your wrinkles and feed your dry skin."

I tried reading the Romanian on the box. It was *cremă nutritivă* with *lanolină* and *vaselină*. That seemed safe enough.

"Okay," I said. "I'll try them. Hard currency?"

"Yes," he said carelessly. "Whatever you want. Five dollars, ten marks, even forints I take. I am trying to buy a good car. An Opel Kadett."

"Listen," I said. "I tried the galvanic bath. But I don't really understand how it works."

"It is meant to stimulate the nerves. It will help your circulation."

"But it makes my nerves nervous. I keep thinking about Dr. Pustulescu. I can't relax."

116

"Oh, it's perfectly safe," he said. "Except in that one case."

"Do you think Dr. Pustulescu's death was an accident then?"

Dr. Gabor's iron-blue eyes shifted to the wall. "You are worried about Mrs. Bentwhistle, that I understand. But there is no need to worry. They have put the voltage meter back. Nothing was wrong with it. The doctor was old. He simply had a heart attack. When they finish the autopsy, it will be clear. They will not put Mrs. Bentwhistle in jail unless they wish to make international fools of themselves."

He held up his journal. "Do you know what I am reading? It is report on the situation of we Magyars here in Transylvania. So shocking, you would not believe me, what happened during Ceauşescu times. Now it is better, but not so much, not when we are still controlled from Bucharest."

I could see that the way to Gabor's confidence was through his ethnicity. "How many Hungarian-speaking people live in Transylvania anyway?"

"Two million, three million. Once it was all Magyar, but then Ceauşescu had plans. First to move Romanians here to Transylvania, then to send students, professionals away from here. When I studied at Tîrgu Mureş at the medical school, everybody was sent away. I was sent away first, then I came back. So the population of Magyars in Transylvania got less and less. In 1988 Ceauşescu had a plan to destroy 8,000 villages, mostly in Transylvania. This way he would have more land, more control of people. They would have to leave villages, go live in big apartment blocks. He started to do this, then he was killed."

Dr. Gabor shook his handsome head. "You know the

117

saying about Ceauşescu? People said, 'We are a dream in the mind of a madman.' And that is true. Now we are waking up, but to what? A past that is a nightmare. They say there were ten million microphones. This, in a country of twenty-three million! When everyone was an informer, the whole country must be corrupt. And yes, Magyars informed too. But not like the Romanians. Why should we inform on each other when the Romanians will do all the informing?"

"It sounds to me that there was a reason to kill Dr. Pustulescu during the Ceauşescu years, but not now. He must have had far less power after the revolution."

"When the same people are in charge, how could the doctor have less power?" said Dr. Gabor. "Oh yes, he was a friend to Ceauşescu and for several months during the winter of the revolution he found it convenient to travel abroad. But after the elections, after Ilescu was elected, he knew it was safe to come back. That he could live the same life as before. Even now he had the same power over us. Do this, do that, come here, go there. But these days, sometimes, we said no. We said no!" He slammed his journal down forcefully on the desk. "He didn't like that, but without sending us to prison like in the old days, what could he do?"

"Then there was no reason for anyone here at the clinic or hotel to kill him?"

"You keep saying kill, but why? A simple heart attack."

"He may have been old, but he was healthy, wasn't he? He invented Ionvital! I read those pamphlets—he could have lived to be over a hundred."

"You must not believe everything you read."

"Well, answer me this. Why did it happen to be Gladys who had to switch the meter on? Was it because someone knew the Romanian courts would never convict a foreigner?"

"Questions, questions," Dr. Gabor said. "So many questions. Do you have any more questions for me?"

"Yes! Why does Margit always leave the room when I come in?"

"Margit?" Dr. Gabor hesitated. "There is nothing wrong with Margit. She's a happy girl, she's always smiling, and laughing. Very restless though, many times I have to tell her relax, relax."

He looked at his watch and pushed the little jars of *cremă nutritivă* towards me. "You try these, yes? Maybe later have injections?"

"You don't think it's bad for the hotel and spa's reputation that the inventor of Ionvital just met his death here?"

Dr. Gabor smiled. "No because, how do you say it in your country? *We have all got to go sometimes.*"

❧ CHAPTER NINE ❧

I F VERBS ARE the engines of language, then German is a series of freeway accidents. All the nouns and adjectives travel sedately in front while at the end of every sentence there's a traffic pile-up of verbs to sort out. I usually keep my German language skills firmly locked away in the emergency room of my brain, lest the syntax disrupt the smoother highways of French and Spanish, but sometimes I have to bring them out.

"Frau Ackermann, *Guten Tag,*" I said.

She was sitting in the main square, knitting what seemed to be a sweater.

"Who's that for?" I asked.

"Dr. Gabor," she said. "I knit him one every time I'm here."

"And how many times did you say you'd been here?"

"Ten. But it used to be much different."

"In what way?"

"The restaurant was full of people, many Germans and

Austrians came here, along with Romanians and Hungarians and even Russians. There were flowers on all the tables and a band in the evening for dancing. The government made sure there was food; there was sometimes lovely food—mushroom soup and roast pork and mutton with cream sauce, fresh rolls and cheese for breakfast, fruit and delicious pastries and cakes. Now, it's changed. The food is dreadful, I bring my own." She put down her knitting and pulled out of her leather handbag a small tube of liverwurst and some crackers.

"Would you like some?"

"Not right now, thanks...I wanted to ask you about Ionvital."

"Look at me!" Frau Sophie thumped her hefty chest. The starched little sail of her pressed handkerchief rode the wave of her bosom. "How old do you think I look?"

She looked about seventy. "Well," I prevaricated. "You look very young."

"I'm seventy!"

"No!"

"It's because of Ionvital that I still work. I'm a secretary back home in Graz. I have a zest for life that none of my friends do." Frau Sophie spread some liverwurst on a cracker and munched on it. "I come here every year for three weeks and that gives me enough stamina for the rest of the year."

"What does it feel like, this treatment?"

"It fills me with joy, and with energy. I feel the life coming back to my stiff shoulders and my knees. I feel like walking and singing. I feel hungry—but there's nothing to eat." She finished off her liverwurst with a sigh. "I must bring my own snacks. In a cooler."

"And you get the Ionvital as a shot, yes?"

"Every morning, a shot."

"Do you know anyone who might have killed Dr. Pustulescu?"

"He created a magnificent drug, but he himself was not a good person."

"I heard he chased girls."

"That I don't know. But I know he was greedy. For Dr. Gabor this work is a labor of love, a gift to humanity. For Dr. Pustulescu it was only money. He smiled at me because he thought I was a rich Austrian, but he treated the Hungarians badly. You should have heard how he talked to the nurses sometimes."

"Yes? What did he say?"

"I don't know Romanian. But his tone was always harsh and threatening. A few days ago, when Dr. Pustulescu arrived, he took over, pushed Dr. Gabor out of his office and took over his patients. Can you imagine?"

I would have liked to have pursued this line of questioning with Frau Sophie, but at that precise instant I recognized Eva's Polski Fiat coming slowly up the hill towards us on the square. I was relieved—then worried. Eva would want to get back to Budapest immediately. But there was, in fact, no danger that we'd have to be leaving soon, for I soon noticed that while Eva sat in the driver's seat, the power was provided by the shoulders of Nadia Pop and a burly man with a moustache.

The car came to a halt outside Nadia's office on the square. Leaving Frau Sophie to her knitting, I went off and asked what was going on.

"We start car, then it stop again," Nadia said, puffing hard. She had taken off her orange polyester suit jacket, but was still wearing the same pink and green flowered dress. It was hard to imagine that she'd helped push the car very far in those tottery heels. Sweat ran down her round face, and her bun draggled.

"They've destroyed my car!" said Eva, who looked almost as disheveled. "Romanians are idiots!"

"It going fine, until recently," said Nadia. "Polski Fiat, not good cars."

The brother-in-law didn't bother to add his remarks. He opened the hood and began rummaging around.

"Nicolae will find the problem!" Nadia said. "No worry about that."

At dinner that night there were fewer of us. Eva and Jack had gone off to eat biscuits and fruit from Budapest and to discuss what should be done about O.K. Temporary Secretarial Services during their absence. Eva refused to leave her car in Arcata, even temporarily, so convinced was she that Nadia's brother-in-law was planning to steal it or sell it for parts once she was gone. However, staying on indefinitely created problems. Eva wanted Jack to return to Budapest to at least answer the phone at the office and tell everyone what was happening.

Their absence left me and the Snapps and Gladys and Bree together at one large table. While Frau Sophie and the Vanderbergs were gracefully served their dinner by the male waiter, the six of us were in Zsoska's section and thus subject to her imperious ways.

Archie had brought with him *The Rough Guide to Eastern Europe,* as well as a Berlitz Hungarian phrase book that he'd picked up in Budapest.

"Last time we were in Romania," he said, "I didn't quite understand that there were all these Hungarians here, or that there was some kind of problem between the Hungarians and the Romanians. I'm going to read you my bare-bones version. I want to juice it up but first I wanted to try to get the facts straight."

Archie opened his notebook, as Cathy writhed. I had a feeling this might be a nightly feature at their dinner table.

TWO CULTURES IN CONFLICT

If you asked the average person on the street about the former country of Yugoslavia, most people would say it was a crying shame. And then they'd probably say they didn't understand what it was all about anyway. Living in America, a multicultural society made up of immigrants from all over the world, it's sometimes hard for us to understand what all the brouhaha in the Balkans is about.

Why can't people just get along?

None of the immigrant countries, like Canada, Australia or the U.S., is just one ethnicity. Our feeling of being a nation comes from—or should come from—shared values, not our ethnic or religious background. Our nation's creed is based on respect and tolerance for difference.

But Bosnia is only one of many areas in Eastern Europe that is experiencing ethnic strife. I am in the Transylvanian part of Romania with my two daughters, Eldest Daughter Cathy and young Emma, who was born here. After only a short time here, I can tell you that though the discord between the Romanians and Hungarians is nothing to the hatred that the Serbs, Croats and Muslims have for each other, it's still worth worrying about.

"Well," said Bree. "I don't know. I understand your need to reach the average reader, but I think it's misleading to paint America as such a tolerant, multicultural society. And it's *not* just an immigrant country. The Native Americans were there first and they were practically wiped out, and African Americans didn't exactly immigrate of their own free will."

"Oh, you're just so smart, aren't you?" Cathy sneered. "I'm *so* impressed." And then she turned to her father.

"Well, she's right, you know. Think about what the pioneers did to the Indians!"

"Kit-Kat, Bree has a good point there. I'm going to think about that, and work it in somehow. Thanks for being constructive, Bree."

"Dad, this is totally boring," said Cathy. She glanced at Bree to see if she agreed. Although the two didn't seem to be getting on at all, I could see that Cathy was still hoping to be friends. She had come to dinner with leggings under her jeans skirt and two different earrings—and the rip through Willa Cather's forehead was getting bigger. "I mean, who at home is going to be interested in why Romanians and Hungarians don't get along?"

"Why not just reduce it to ethnic stereotypes?" I suggested. "The Hungarians believe that the Romanians are corrupt, lying and lazy. The Romanians believe that the Hungarians are arrogant, power-mad and bloodthirsty. The Romanian myth about themselves is that they're a Mediterranean people who unfortunately ended up on the Black Sea, left behind by the Romans. They believe that their Latinate language and culture connects them more to France and Italy than Mitteleuropa. They think the Hungarians are the descendants of savage tribes who swept through the Carpathians to rape, murder and pillage. The Hungarian myth about themselves, on the other hand, is that they are a hard-working, proud, independent people, who bravely battled the Turks for centuries, and who created the Magyar culture that exists here, with all its important ties to Central Europe."

"Seems to me," said Gladys, "that people live in these countries like beans in a pressure cooker. Navy beans, kidney beans, lima beans, black beans. They could make a real nice chili but instead, they want to keep their shape, no matter how hot it gets."

126

"And don't forget to put in your article something about the the other minority cultures that are here or were here once." I instructed Archie. "Most of the Jews were deported to the camps during the war and the rest have emigrated to Israel. Ceauşescu let them go, at a price from the Israeli government. The Saxon Germans, who did as much to create Transylvanian culture as the Hungarians, are leaving their traditional cities for Germany in droves. And what about the Gypsies? There are more Gypsies in Romania than there are Hungarians, but nobody cares about them. Since the revolution they've become the scapegoats of the new order. You ask either a Hungarian or a Romanian about the Gypsies and they'll spit on the ground."

"The Gypsies are mighty picturesque," said Gladys, "but you're right. I've noticed that people here don't exactly cotton to them."

"It's interesting you should mention the Saxons," said Archie. "It's Transylvania where the children that the Pied Piper spirited away are supposed to have come out again. That's the legend of how the Saxons came to live in Transylvania. Kit-Kat, do you remember Robert Browning's 'The Pied Piper of Hamelin'?"

In Transylvania there's a tribe
Of alien people who ascribe
The outlandish ways and dress
On which their neighbours lay such stress,
To their fathers and mothers having risen
Out of some subterranean prison
Into which they had been trepanned
Long time ago, in a mighty band,
Out of Hamelin town in Brunswick land
But how or why they don't understand.

"Dad, please!" Cathy was ready to sink under the table. I noticed, though, that Emma, who had been sitting on her child's seat in her usual stolid, blank-faced way, was swaying, almost imperceptibly, to the rhythm of the words. Perhaps Emma's mother tongue was not words at all, but music.

Archie noticed too, and his face brightened. "Emma loves poetry," he said. "We do a lot of reading aloud at home, don't we, Emma-Demma?" Zsoska chose that moment to appear at our table. Pen and pad in hand she stood sullenly, waiting for us to all order the same thing. Although she could only have been a few years older than Bree, she projected the toughened fierceness of someone twice her age. She was beautiful, but in a frightening way.

Archie hastily whipped out *Hungarian for Travellers.* "Zsoska," he began. *"Hogy van?"*

"Swine? Fry potatoes? Salat?" Zsoska asked impatiently. Her English was bad, but to the point.

Archie tried again. "Hawd-y von?" ("It's how are you?" he told the rest of us.)

"Köszönöm, jól," Zsoska snapped.

"Wait a minute, wait a minute." Archie peered down at the phrase book. "Kursurnum yawl. . . . Okay, she's saying, 'Fine, thanks.'"

Zsoska turned to Gladys. "Swine?"

"No, hon, my stomach is acting up a tad. I think I'll just have an omelette."

"Me too," said Bree.

"Let's see, let's see. . . . *Honnan jött?*" said Archie. "Hawn-non jurt?"

Zsoska burst into a torrent of Hungarian, which none of us could understand, but which gave the distinct impression that she'd had about enough of this intercultural exchange.

"I just asked her where she came from," said Archie plaintively. "The more I look at Zsoska, the more I believe she might be from one of the ancient Székely tribes. The guidebook says that most of the Hungarian people in this part of the Carpathians are Székelys. They were a group of Tartar nomads who came here in the twelfth century and defended the border for the Kingdom of Hungary."

Cathy said, "I think Emma and I will have an omelette too."

"No, wait," said Archie, determined to make contact with Zsoska somehow, "*Tojást*... Tawyaasht. That's eggs in Hungarian. The little girl would like an omelette. Her name is Emma. Emma, this is Zsoska."

"You too, omelette?" Zsoska jerked her yellow and black mane in my direction.

"Yeah, okay."

I asked Archie if I could see his phrase book. The Berlitz people really tried to cover all contingencies, by supplying phrases for road accidents and health problems. To read the little book straight through was to become nervously aware that life on the road was nothing but a series of aggravations and catastrophes. Although my own travels had taken place on a different scale—I had rarely had occasion to ask, "Where's the nearest golf course?" for instance—the core needs in the book were familiar: I need a place to sleep; I need food; I need help; I need to go somewhere; I'm lost.

I flipped through the book to "Eating" and heard my stomach growl. Eggs stuffed with caviar, dumplings, apple soup, pike in cream and paprika sauce, sweet pancakes with nut-cream, flambéed.

The "Relaxing" section was also pretty useless, with its suggestions about movies and theatres, boxing matches and tennis. And, no, "Shopping" wasn't quite appropriate

129

for Arcata either. That afternoon Jack and I had investigated the one store and two kiosks down the hill from the square. They had very few things, out of the many consumer words listed here, for sale. Aside from a few basics, like bread and more bread, there were only plum brandy and canned whole plums and plum jam.

Flip, flip. Here was a phrase, under "Hotel," that might come in useful.

Mennyi a feszültség? Maenyee o faesewlshayg. What a tough language! I tried to memorize it before handing the dictionary back to Archie.

It meant "What's the voltage?"

"Now I've got a question for you, Archie," said Gladys. "Why do you see the country's name written sometimes as Rumania and sometimes as Romania?"

"I think Romania is the correct version now," said Archie. "What do you say, Cassandra?"

"The Romanians like *Romania* because it connects the current state with the Roman Empire and makes them feel good. The Hungarians always want to call it *Rumania*. Of course, some feminists prefer the more modern spelling of *Romynia,* so as not to privilege the men any longer, the people naturally being called *Romminians*. Finally," I added, watching Zsoska slam forward through the swinging doors, with her arms full of plates and a hostile look on her face, "some think the citizens are more properly called *Romaniacs.*"

A porkchop slid off one of the sharply angled plates Zsoska was carrying. She retrieved it and slapped it back on a pile of French fries, then handed the whole thing to Archie.

"Swine!"

He pretended not to notice.

"Zsoska," he said, thumbing quickly through the phrase book. "Zsoska..."

But before he could find the right words, she was gone again.

❧ CHAPTER TEN ❧

AFTER DINNER our party repaired to the square by the lake. Gladys's dogs were patiently waiting for her and crowded around as she fed them French fries and some pork bones. Bree had disappeared, saying she was going to look for Jack and Eva, and Emma and Cathy wandered away too. Archie sat down by me on one of the benches by the lake.

It was still light and the evening was, on the cusp of April and May, scented in layers. The fresh, piercing scents of the evergreens were like sopranos that soared over the altos and tenors of the spicy plum and apple blossoms in an a cappella group. The cuckoos sang their falling two notes with sweet regularity.

Archie had on his soft felt hat and a tweed jacket with suede elbow patches.

"I'm not getting anywhere with Zsoska," he said. "Do you think you might be able to help?"

"With that phrase book? Probably not."

"She speaks a little English. And she speaks Romanian, too, so you could talk to her."

"What about?"

"You know." Archie looked furtive.

"Archie, do you honestly think this is the best idea? The poor woman gave up her child three years ago. Isn't it going to be kind of a shock when you tell her Emma is hers?"

"It might be good for both of them. Listen, I thought how you could do it. Ask Zsoska if she would take you sightseeing tomorrow. She might be glad of the extra money. I'm not saying you have to tell her about Emma, though if it comes up, it comes up. But maybe you could find out something about her past and her circumstances now. It would be a start anyway."

"Archie, I can't. I'm here to help Gladys. I can't get embroiled in something else."

"It's just that I feel so frustrated," he burst out. "Cathy and Mark were such great kids. You wouldn't think so to see Cathy now, but she and I had a ball when she was growing up. We drew pictures, wrote stories, made our own post office. Mark had a mathematical bent like his mom, and pretty soon he outstripped me, but Cathy was always special to me. We made cities and harbors with Legos; we did science experiments, we looked at the stars through telescopes, and at the insect world through microscopes. I didn't mind staying home with the kids while Lynn worked. I loved it!

"But Emma's never been a kid. She doesn't play like Cathy and Mark did. She just sits staring at things, with that vague look on her face. Games don't interest her, toys don't interest her. She doesn't seem to know what they're for, however much you show and explain them to her."

"How soon did you notice that something was wrong with Emma?"

"Don't say wrong," said Archie. "Say different."

"Okay, when did you know she was different?"

"Lynn says she knew at the hospital, because Emma didn't cry or move very much. She thought once we got Emma home to Michigan everything would be all right. She was willing to take a chance. It took me longer to see Emma's problems, maybe because I didn't want to see them. You'd talk and she'd seem to look at your face and hear you, but she didn't respond.

"The pediatrician said she didn't seem to be deaf, but that she could be mildly retarded. That was a blow. But we were still optimistic. As the second year passed Emma learned to walk and to eat by herself. She could understand directions. She didn't seem developmentally disabled except for her speech. We couldn't get her to stop sucking her thumb and rocking in her bed at night, but during the day she seemed happy enough in her own little world. Sometimes when I read to her she would start rocking back and forth or beating her hand on the floor.

"And then Cathy noticed how Emma seemed to pay attention to music on the radio and enjoy it. We got her a xylophone and then one of those little Casio keyboards with a recorded tape that you can play along with. It amazed all of us, how Emma picked it up.

"It was Lynn who thought of giving her violin lessons. We started her in Ann Arbor and now she has a teacher in Munich. It's phenomenal how she's taken to it. I can't understand it—how Emma can hear music and imitate it just fine, but how she can't somehow get the idea that speech is the same thing. One child psychologist told us that what seems to be either missing or delayed is the sense of language as communication."

"You said that Cathy and Mark loved to learn," I said. "But it sounds to me that Emma has them both beat. For a four-year-old to play Mozart is quite astonishing, don't you think?"

Archie didn't say anything for a minute, then, in a lower tone of voice, he said, "I know I'm no genius. I've always felt it was my role in life to help people who were smarter than I was. Lynn is the brain of the family and Mark and Cathy take after her. Don't get me wrong, I'm proud of all of them. I gave the kids the childhood I never had. But sometimes, I guess I hoped that Emma would be more . . . average." He paused, and became the journalist again. "Tell me about *your* family, Cass."

To my surprise, I found myself talking. Perhaps Archie's confidences had disarmed me, or perhaps he was a better interviewer than I gave him credit for.

"My mother more or less raised us, but my dad was the fun one. He liked to listen to the radio with us and read to us from the newspaper," I said. "He collected people and their stories. He was what my mother called 'a real card.' Of course he drank too, but he was one of the happy ones. He sang a lot. He could tell a story to make you fall down laughing. There was a lot of goodwill in him, a lot of the dreamer, and not much judgment. My mother always said I took after him—shiftless but lively. She went to church and prayed for him. There were eight of us kids. We didn't have much money. After my dad died, things kind of went to hell. I ended up leaving home right after high school. I'd run away a couple of times before that."

"So you've come up from nothing too," said Archie. "It's optimism, isn't it? It's looking on the bright side of things. I've always been an optimist. I got out of the house by getting two paper routes, by playing baseball, working my way through high school and college. I always believed that I could change my life, and I did. I made sure that my kids would have a different life." He paused and stared at the lake. "I don't drink much. My father wasn't like yours."

He didn't say what had happened to him, why he had to get out of the house, but I didn't need to ask. I wondered how bad it had been, and what his memories were.

These are some of my memories: I see my older sister Maureen braiding my frizzy hair and buttoning my dress; I see myself feeding one of the babies a bottle, holding it close and smelling its soft sweet breath. I see my father balancing me on his knee, telling me nonsense, singing me songs, a glass always on the table next to us. I also see myself screaming at my older brother Kevin to stop teasing me, or for Maureen or Eileen to leave me the hell alone. I see myself in church fidgeting, see myself not coming home for dinner, staying out half the night. I see my mother's closed face, and her open hand swinging. I was never an optimist, but I knew that I was going to have a different life than that of my family.

I grew up fighting to get a word in. No one sat around waiting to hear me speak, no one took care of my needs without my asking. Words may have been a great source of pleasure, but they were also a necessary means of protection, the only means, besides your fists and fingernails, of getting what you needed.

Maybe Archie hovered too much, maybe Emma had never had to ask for what she needed. Maybe she was just waiting to speak until the time was right.

"So you'll help me with Zsoska?" asked Archie again.

"All right," I agreed. "I'll see what I can find out. No promises though. Can I borrow your dictionary?"

Archie pumped my hand a few times and then left me to return to the dining hall, where Zsoska was half-heartedly polishing glasses.

To my surprise she gave me a friendly smile. "Yes. You wanting?"

"I'm wondering," I said in English, "if you are free tomorrow? I would like to see more of the countryside, and I don't have a car."

"Yes?"

I repeated this in Romanian, with a few gestures.

This time she understood me, but she stuck to English. "Where you wanting going?"

"Oh, anywhere, just to see the mountains and farms."

"Yes. I having car. We going."

"I'll pay you."

"Just you, yes, no others? No Snapps?"

"Just me."

When I went back out to the square nobody was around, so I decided to take a walk before dark. I followed the path leading to the lake and strolled around its shore. Firs hid cuckoo nests; the birds sang their two notes in rounds. A kind of squirrel I'd never seen before lived in these woods: it had long pointed ears like a rabbit. The sun had dropped behind the mountains in the distance and the air was cooler now; the flowery scent of backyard orchards was gone, like a woman who'd passed by.

After I'd rounded the lake, instead of going back to my room, I made my way along a road, paved with small flat stones, that wound up behind the hotels, and in a few moments I had left behind the world of mass tourism and was back in an earlier era. Large villas were set back from the road, surrounded by trees and orchards. There were benches set about in overgrown, but not unkempt, lawns of bluebells, daisies and yellow buttercups. Had they once belonged to Magyar families who spent their summers here, in the coolness of Arcata's woods and lakes? Painted in soft browns and forest greens, the villas were gabled and spired, embellished with scrolls and other carvings around the window and door lintels. Many had fanciful turrets, shingled and conical, and romantic little dormer windows under eaves decorated with filigreed fretwork.

There were evergreens here, but also many birches, white calligraphed with black, their new leaves only a breath, not yet a canopy, of green. Wild abundance was in wait; in July and August these gardens and orchards would explode with flowers and fruit and the heavy, intoxicating scents of summer. But for now, in the twilight of a spring evening, all was tentative, a little ethereal.

Up near the top of the hill were two wooden gates, facing each other across the stone road. They had plump, hollow roofs of scalloped shingles, wide at the bottom, rising pagoda-like to needle spires. Perched on the carved wooden gateposts these roofs were like oversized hats, fanciful and strange. The two gates were carved and painted with stylized blue pots of red tulips and green leaves, which curled in vines all around the posts.

One gateway was much larger and more elaborate; it formed part of a picket fence, broken at intervals by wooden posts turned on a lathe, and all painted that same soft shade of brown. The door of the gateway stood open and I walked through, up a path of tiny river pebbles to an enormous house. It was a creamy chocolate color with window lintels of bright blue. The lower part of the structure seemed to be constructed of logs, while the second story was paneled in an openwork pattern of tulips in pots. The house had two turrets, one a tall peaked tower that looked like a witch's hat, and the other a spire with a weathervane. The doorway was painted dark brown and the door composed of four long panes of glass; the whole was surmounted by a carved lintel and further embellished by a profusion of carved, painted and gold-leafed flowers. There were words, also in gold, running up and down the doorway and the windows close to the door. I saw the names György and Erzsébet Lazsló, 1864-1934.

I looked in the big front window and saw empty rooms. This magical house was uninhabited. Oh, if only I could live here! I sat on the stone front porch and surveyed my new territory. Tall firs surrounded the house, but there had been beds of flowers once, and could be again. Across the road I saw the other, smaller gate, with a blur of wild-flowers visible through its opening. Where did it lead? Was there a house somewhere farther back in the trees? Was it even more fairy tale-like than this one?

I was back suddenly in Kalamazoo, on South Street, where the rich had built their beautiful gingerbread Victorians at the turn of the century. I supposed that nowadays some of the houses were offices or antique shops, but in my childhood they had belonged, or so I imagined, to fabulously wealthy families called Arbuthnot and Churchill. Sometimes on a Saturday, babysitting my younger brothers and sisters, I would drag them from where we lived behind St. Augustine's for a walk down South Street, and together we'd admire the ornaments, the decorations, and especially, the size and orderliness of these houses. The house where we Reillys lived was not small, but there were ten of us before my father died, and I never had a room of my own. I shared an attic dormer room, stuffed with crucifixes and holy cards of female saints, with my two older sisters, Maureen and Eileen. Maureen wanted to be a nun, until she had to get married at seventeen; Eileen held out for a church wedding after high-school graduation. Both of them had little or no interest in school, in books, in art. Nor had I, then; I only knew that there was something else, and that something didn't live in our home, only in houses like those on South Street.

There was one house that had been my special favorite when I was about ten. I called it the fairy-tale house. It had a turret room upstairs and downstairs a big picture window draped with lace, through which a piano was visible. A woman as blond and refined as Grace Kelly lived there, and a stout, prosperous man who always seemed to have on a suit and tie, even on weekends. They had a maid who wore an apron and cap, a large black poodle, and two children, a girl about my age, with a feathery cap of blond hair, and a boy a little younger. I imagined that the girl lived in the tower room, that she was lonely for a friend, and that one day, when I was just walking by, she'd invite me in. I'd say I was an orphan, and the family would adopt me. The girl would become my sister, they'd give me piano lessons, I'd say to the maid, Hilda, bring me my breakfast in bed. I'd have French toast and fresh orange juice every morning.

The girl noticed me, all right. One day as I was walking by with the two youngest in my family, she opened up the door to the fairy-tale house, ran out to the porch and screamed, "Go away! I see you all the time, looking at our house. I'm sick of seeing you out here on the sidewalk. Go away!"

I stared at her only a few seconds before hurrying my little brother and sister away. I saw us all as the blond girl must have seen us, poor Irish, badly dressed in hand-me-downs and St. Vincent de Paul specials, our wild curly hair in our eyes, forbidden longing on our faces.

I didn't walk down South Street again for a long time.

But I could live here! Here in this beautiful house in

Arcata. It couldn't cost that much in Romanian lei. This could be my South Street, my fairy-tale house.

The stone porch was getting cold and darkness was falling. I got up and walked down the pebbled path and through the gate. But where did the second gate lead? A high, trimmed hedge rather than a fence separated the yard from the street, but there was no path once you opened the gate, only a meadow of wildflowers—buttercups, daisies and Queen Anne's Lace. There was something still and peaceful here, here where there was no house, but only overgrown grass and flowers. Had it been a park once? There were two wooden benches with curved, slatted backs. I sat down on one of them, and let the mood of the place enter my spirit. I felt in the presence of something lost and long ago. In the presence of loss, but also of enchantment.

I had first run away from Kalamazoo the summer I was seventeen, following Dede Paulsen, who had not exactly said she loved me back, much less that she wanted me to come with her to her new home in Los Angeles. I had a little money that took me on the Greyhound down to Wichita. From there I hitchhiked across Kansas and Colorado, down through New Mexico and Arizona. I was picked up by the state patrol outside of Tucson and held in jail three days there for possessing no identification and for refusing to give my name. Finally I broke down, and my mother, who had never been farther from home than Grand Rapids, flew down to free me and bring me back.

Neither of us had ever flown before. She had had to borrow money from relatives to manage it.

I had been gone over a month when she saw me. She burst out crying and hugged me; then she gave me a good wallop on the butt, though I was taller than she was. After I'd left home one of my sisters had spilled the beans about my infatuation with Miss Paulsen. My mother couldn't decide which was worse: being in love with a woman or running away.

"If anything like this ever happens again," she threatened, "I won't be coming to collect you. You'll be on your own with your sinful ways. I won't be following you down the highway to hell."

Needless to say, it did happen again, and again, and the last time I left home, just after my high-school graduation, was the last time I saw my mother.

Women and the road thus became irrevocably merged in my mind. I never told my mother this, or any of my girlfriends back at school—because I wanted them to think me a hopeless romantic who'd do anything for love—but somewhere down about Santa Fe I had forgotten about Dede Paulsen. I had fallen in love with travel itself, with movement and change, and I didn't care if I ever reached my destination.

It was completely dark by the time I came back down the cobbled road to the hotel. I stood outside looking up at the building. Most of the windows were dark; only a few glimmered with lamplight. In one of the lit windows, two women stood embracing. The shadow of the smaller one seemed to dwarf the taller, who leaned back to be kissed on the neck.

In another window a small figure held a violin up to her chin. The strains of a simple Bach melody floated out into the Arcadian night.

I remembered once complaining to my bassoonist friend Nicola that, however much I loved classical music, I could never understand it.

"What don't you understand?"

"When I listen to classical music, I often have feelings, but I don't know what the feelings are. It's not like listening to a ballad or the blues."

"Yes. And?"

"I mean, I can't describe the feelings, I can't really say if they're happy or sad or whatever."

"Yes. And?"

"I *mean*, Nicola, that no *words* come to me to describe the feelings."

"Words," she said. "Why on earth would you want words when you can have music?"

But I never heard music without words when I was growing up, and it was the words that gave the music its meaning.

My father had a beautiful tenor and he often sang around the house. He loved jigs and reels, but more he loved sad ballads like "Kathleen Mavourneen."

The refrain that Jack had yesterday forbidden me to sing came back to me now.

Oh hast thou forgotten how soon we must sever?
Oh hast thou forgotten this day we must part?
It may be for years and it may be forever,
Oh why art thou silent, thou voice of my heart?
It may be for years and it may be forever,
Then why art thou silent, Kathleen Mavourneen?

❧ CHAPTER ELEVEN ❧

I SAW JACK AT breakfast the next morning. Bundled in a Nepalese sweater over a sarong, tights and hiking boots, she was alone at a table eating bread and butter. Her skin was paler than usual, with soft violet shadows under her gray eyes, and she had an unusually languid air about her.

"Are you all right?"

"I'm bleeding."

"What?"

She looked at me in surprise. "I mean, I'm having my period. And—I didn't get much sleep last night."

"Jack, she's far too young for you. She's hardly twenty. What would Gladys say?"

"Actually, Gladys did say something. She said she was glad we'd turned up, because she'd been worried about Bree getting bored with just Cathy to talk to."

"If you were just talking, it would be fine."

"I don't believe in being ageist," she said. "It's nice, it

makes me feel young too."

"Well, you don't look young. You look awful."

"You had your chance, Widow Reilly. Is it my fault you prefer to suffer over the charming Eva? Or are you still suffering?"

"Eva would adore me if I were a car mechanic. Anyway, you were the one who had dinner with her last night, you tell me."

"I know you'll hate us," Jack said, "but we found a sweet little outdoor restaurant by a stream, where they served us freshly grilled trout and a lovely bottle of white wine. I think the wine helped put me in the mood. When I came upstairs there was Bree in my room, just waiting . . ."

"Did Eva say anything about me?"

"She says she's never met anyone like you before."

"She really said that?"

"Yes. She said she thinks you're a bad influence on me."

Zsoska met me outside the Arcata Spa Hotel at nine-thirty, only half an hour later than she'd agreed. She was wearing a hot pink training suit of rustling-thin fabric, running shoes, and a great deal of small jewelry, a dozen little gold rings, bracelets and lockets. Also aviator-style sunglasses. Her long, layered, gold-striped black hair bounced as she hopped out of the car to attract my attention with a wave.

She invited me into her Dacia, which was red and newly washed and as sporty as an Eastern European model could be. Gold chains hung from the rear-view mirror. She had stretched a thin tee-shirt with the Playboy bunny logo over the back of the driver's seat.

Zsoska said she wanted to practice her English with me rather than speak Romanian or use the Hungarian phrase

146

book. This meant that I was going to have to find a way to reorganize Zsoska's passionate but fragmented thoughts into more coherent linguistic units. In my travels I've met with all sorts of English speakers, from the brilliantly fluent, with accents straight from the BBC World Service, to those for whom English is a kind of game played with a ball, the object being only to keep things moving. Zsoska was a challenge, requiring intuition and patience, particularly in the matter of pronouns, with which she had a very loose way. I'd read in the Berlitz phrase book that *ő* in Hungarian could mean either he, she or it; in German, which, in her fashion, Zsoska also spoke, *sie* or *Sie* can mean she, they or you.

This gender-bending method of assigning pronouns was part of the reason that Zsoska's sentences were frequently impenetrable. Although they were packed with feeling and assisted by eyebrows, frowns and the occasional charming smile, they tended to lack the logic so comforting to a listener.

"First needing petrol. Petrol very much money for me."

She wore the stern expression that made Archie quail. I suspected that it was pride.

"Oh, don't worry, I'll get the petrol," I said.

She smiled happily. "We having nice day. Going far."

Driving down through the villas and garden houses, we passed many people who stared at her (women) and many who waved (men).

"I suppose you've been living here a long time."

"How that?"

I repeated it.

"I growing up in next village," she said. "Two years, I working here hotel restaurant. Bad, very bad. No money in Romania. No one money."

Her beautiful face wore its fierce expression again. "I

wanting leaving. Deutschland. Deutsch man my friend. Not Deutsch, living Deutschland. *Sass.*"

"*Sass?* You mean Saxon?"

"Yes," she answered. "She growing up Sighişoara, going Deutschland, but no liking Deutsch girls, liking Magyar. Me. They coming back seeing me soon. I wanting leave here, go back Deutschland with her. Living good there."

"He?" I asked. "Him?"

"Yes, he, he, he. I knowing English! He-man. Rolf."

We filled up the tank at a single-pump station just outside Arcata and set off. The sun glistened off the dew on the fields, and the foothills began to turn into mountains. Zsoska put a cassette of German pop music in her car stereo. I had no idea where we were going, or exactly how I should steer the conversation to find out what Archie wanted to know.

"Harghita mountains," she said, waving out the window. "My family Székely, living here long time."

Well, Archie was right about that then. And the Székelys *were* a romantic lot, who had in medieval times protected the border against the Mongols from Asia. I'd heard that the Székelys had never been serfs, that they'd always lived in these mountains and valleys, a law unto themselves. It was easy to imagine Zsoska, with her Tartar cheekbones and hawk-like nose, in an embroidered sheepskin vest, in boots, on horseback, looting and marauding ... easier to imagine her on the range than in the restaurant.

Zsoska had been singing along to a peppy Bavarian pop tune, and it seemed to conjure up happy thoughts. She said, "They having Mercedes."

"Who?"

"My *friend,* Rolf, from Deutschland."

"Oh, right, Rolf."

"You? Car?"

"Me? No."

She looked puzzled. "I car, you *no* car. Why? You American, yes?"

I tried to explain that I didn't live in America, didn't live anywhere, traveled frequently, and had very few possessions at all. She listened to me disbelievingly. "I car, Romania," she said several times, pointing at her gold-locketed chest. "You, *no* car, America, no understanding."

"What if we speak in Romanian?" I said.

"No. Practice English!" She looked affronted. "I wanting tell you my life."

Well, this was good news, that she was going to volunteer information. Perhaps I would find a way to prepare her for Emma.

I said, "So you're hoping to move to Germany soon? Deutschland?"

"I wanting marry Rolf, but with her I having problem, many problem. They jealous." Zsoska turned angrily to me. "Why, why? I having *no* life. I going *not* out at night. I staying home. No jealous, no jealous *me*. She coming visit, bringing friend, that friend liking me. I do *nothing*. You *jealous*."

"No, I'm not jealous. You mean, '*he* is jealous.'"

"How that?"

"Never mind. I understanding, I mean, I understand."

Then a long story followed, punctuated by the sounds of accordians, slapping heels and the occasional yodel from the car stereo. As far as I could make out, this Saxon Rolf was one of the many thousands of German-speaking Romanians who had left the country as soon as Romanians were issued passports after 1989. There was a German law that anyone—no matter if their family had left Germany five centuries ago—who was ethnically German could return to Germany. Zsoska's boyfriend was one of these.

I began to space out on the lengthy story, in which half a dozen people, without names and with a variety of pronouns to describe them, seemed to be distrusting Zsoska. For no good reason. After a while, instead of listening, I only watched the landscape. We had passed through forested mountains into a wide valley, with farms stretching green in every direction. There were no tractors or other farm machinery, though this was probably due more to the poor economy than to a desire to keep to the old ways. From time to time we passed a horsedrawn cart, heavy and creaking, piled with people going to or from the fields. This region must be one of the last places in Europe where you could still get a sense of how life had rolled on for centuries.

"I already having one baby, I no wanting more now," Zsoska was saying, and I suddenly paid attention.

"You have a child?"

"No."

"But did you have a baby?"

"I married only age seven, no, seventeen," she said sullenly. "Bad man, man drinking. We living Tîrgu Mureş, he working, me working. I wanting divorce, he hitting me. I coming back to parents, divorce."

"But did you have a baby?"

"Why asking you?" she demanded, suddenly furious. Without warning she did an abrupt U-turn in the middle of all that green lushness, under a bright blue sky wheeling with birds. "We going no more. We going back my village. Yes." She was calming down, perhaps fearful that I wouldn't think this was enough of an excursion. "There nothing here, boring country, farms, horses, nothing.

You going my house, Lupea, seeing dog." She gave me her radiant smile, and turned up the stereo so that the day was pierced by the nasal voice of a woman singing "Baby, baby, *Ich liebe dich!*"

"Rolf giving me cassettes," she said. "We are liking music!"

Zsoska's village was about five kilometers from Arcata. There was a stream overhung with willows and birches, and fields stretching out on either side of the road. Many of the houses were robin's-egg blue, trimmed with kelly green. These were simpler homes than those in Arcata, but many had the traditional gate surmounted by a long birdhouse. Most had vegetable gardens, edged with tulips and pansies. Off the main square was a Catholic church, but not an Orthodox one; this was a Székely village and many people probably didn't even speak much Romanian. There was no restaurant, but a small shop where Zsoska took me inside. The shelves were practically bare, with only plastic bottles of Pepsi, some chocolate, a great deal of plum brandy, or *ţuică,* and a few glass jars of unidentifiable fruits and vegetables.

"What wanting you?" Zsoska asked. "You see we having nothing."

"How about some Pepsi?" I bought two bottles of it and some chocolate. Zsoska approved of my spending money and said something to the middle-aged shopkeeper that made him look at me with respect.

"America, very good," he said in English. "Clint Eastwood very good. Bang! Bang!"

The main street was the only paved road in the village. Zsoska parked down a dirt street in front of a small blue house, and we went inside. The furniture was sparse and rather low to the ground. There was a kind of divan covered in red shag material and a coffee table with a television set on it. In the kitchen were a table and four chairs, a stove and no refrigerator, and some empty-looking cupboards.

We sat at the kitchen table and poured ourselves some warm Pepsi. A little puppy ran inside and Zsoska swept it up, hugging it tightly.

"This Zizi," she said. "Only one who is understanding me."

"Where are your parents?" I asked.

"My mother..." She searched for the right word. "Building, milk?"

"A dairy?"

"My father, no working. Pension—600 lei month." That was just over a dollar, barely a pound.

I was trying to imagine Emma here. Who would have taken care of her? Zsoska and her mother had to work; her father was probably sitting around with his friends drinking *ţuică* most of the day. The house had four rooms: a kitchen, a small living room, and two bedrooms. There was indoor plumbing, but not much of it.

I tried again. "Zsoska, did you give up your baby for adoption?"

"How that?"

"The baby you had, with your husband, what happened to her?"

"If I keeping baby, husband making me stay. I telling nobody. Baby sick, no food, going hospital. In hospital, Tîrgu Mureş, they saying no problem with baby, we finding parents, rich people from America, from France, from Deutschland. You signing paper." Zsoska mimed signing. "I getting money and buying car, helping parents. Leaving husband. Now I am having *Sass* friend from Deutschland,

152

but they jealous. I am twenty-two. I no wanting more baby, no wanting make Rolf jealous. Now no more baby."

She gestured to her flat stomach and held Zizi closer.

I understood suddenly that Zsoska had just had an abortion, because Rolf thought that she might have been fooling around with one of his friends and she didn't think she could persuade him otherwise.

"Zsoska," I said carefully. "What would you say if your baby, the baby you had in Tîrgu Mureş . . . if you saw her again? How would you feel?"

She stared at me, uncomprehending. "That baby going away. I never seeing that baby. That not baby I am talking about now."

"I know, I know," I said. "But she was a real baby. The nurses at the hospital must have kept the baby for a while and then . . . and then someone adopted her, a couple from America took her back to America."

"How you knowing? How you knowing baby is she-baby?"

"Well . . . because I met the father and sister and. . . . "

Zsoska's black eyes were wide with alarm. She pounded the table. "Snapps!" she said. "Now I knowing why they always trying talking me!"

"Yes, and that little girl, Emma, is . . . "

"Emoke," she said. "Her name Emoke."

Zsoska jumped up, and the little dog fell away from her with a thump, forgotten. "No milk for that baby, cold cold winter. No food anywhere, fighting in the streets, revolution. Baby so sick, I think that baby die. Mother, father never seeing Emoke."

Zsoska paced the kitchen. Suddenly she stopped and looked anguished. "Rolf finding out I having child, no, no, *no*. I telling her no married before!"

"There's no reason he needs to find out about Emma—Emoke. After all, he lives in Germany."

"He coming soon visit. No, no!"

She stopped and glared at me. "What wrong that child? She no speaking."

"Well...you see...the Snapps were hoping to find out if there was anything in your family, anything that..."

"My family, we speaking!" She hadn't sat back down, she was so agitated, and now she grabbed her purse and keys. "Come."

In the red Dacia her child had bought for her, Zsoska drove me back to the hotel. She did not say another word, in any of her languages.

Outside the treatment center we found an alarming scene in progress. Gladys, in a red flannel bathrobe and felt slippers, her white hair damp and disheveled, and without her glasses, was standing in the entryway behind Dr. Gabor, who held out both arms as if to protect her. Two men looking young and unhappy were there in full police regalia: brushed blue uniforms, black boots, guns and tricorn hats. They were gesturing at Gladys and trying to get her to come with them into the open back door of their police car.

Off to the side, in her leather jacket, Bree was videotaping the whole thing.

Zsoska pulled up beside the police car and I jumped out.

"What's going on?"

"Mrs. Really, Mrs. Really," said Dr. Gabor. "You are a witness, these men are trying to *abduct* Mrs. Bentwhistle. I say to them, Have you an arrest warrant? I say to them, This is not Ceauşescu times any longer, my friends. You can not just come and take off innocent people to your tor-

154

ture chambers. Securitate! No more!" He began to shout at the thoroughly cowed-looking policemen again. The crowd of bath attendants, doctors and nurses assembling behind him got into the spirit and all began shouting in Hungarian, probably something along the lines of Ceauşescu was a murderer and all Romanians were murderers. The black dogs that always collected around Gladys howled in unison.

I turned to Gladys. Someone had brought her glasses and she attached them firmly to her straight nose.

"Gladys, are you all right?"

"Sure thing, hon. They'll never take me alive!"

"What happened?"

"I'd just come out of that shower-massage room—you know, twenty minutes of that wakes you right up!—and was going for my next appointment at the mud baths, when these two bozos come up behind me and take me by the elbows. Well, I learned how to deal with muggers in my self-defense class, so I gave one a jab in the stomach and the other a kick in the knee cap, and hightailed it for Gabor's office. They caught up with us right here. Bree was walking by with her video camera, so I told her, Get this on tape. We're suing!"

Someone had alerted Nadia and she came rushing up from her office, out of breath. Her bun had come undone and strands of dark hair fell across her round face.

When the two policemen saw Nadia they burst into explanations, and these I could partly understand: All they had wanted was to ask the American lady a few more questions; they had wanted to take her down to their office to get a statement; whether or not Gladys was a murderer, she had been a witness, and their superiors in Bucharest were demanding that some action be taken.

"Yes, yes," Nadia said. "Gladys, they are not arresting

155

you. Not to worry. They have questions only."

"We know the kind of questions the Securitate ask!" Dr. Gabor shouted. "They turn you into informers, they torture you if you don't answer."

"Doctor!" Nadia said. "These not Securitate, you know these men. These men live here in Arcata. They only do their job. There is murder, in democratic countries also murder, you cannot just ignore."

"Where did the Securitate go then?" Dr. Gabor countered. "After the so-called revolution that keeps the same men in power, you think the Securitate just disappear? No! They are still living all around the country. They are used to torture and intimidation. They are *Romanian*." For the benefit of the police he repeated the same thing in Romanian.

The two policemen, angry now, burst into justifications and counter-accusations. They had dealt with Dr. Gabor in the past. He was trying to protect his clinic as usual. But they were well aware that he and Dr. Pustulescu had had a quarrel, and that Dr. Pustulescu had demoted him the day before the murder. He shouldn't think he himself was not under suspicion.

"I have been under suspicion my whole life in this godforsaken country," Dr. Gabor said scornfully. "Are you telling me something new?"

"Well, I'm not going anywhere without a lawyer," said Gladys. "The idea I'd kill some aging Lothario is a load of bull. They already questioned me and I told them I was innocent. I know my rights. I stand with the Hungarians on this one. Hell no, don't you know. The Ro-manians have got to go!" she chanted, and a few enthusiastic bath attendants took it up. The black dogs, who now numbered six, barked wildly. Bree moved in for a close-up of her grandmother. It was like watching a made-for-nightly-news demonstration.

Nadia stood helpless, hands up in the patty-cake way, saying, "Please, no Yugoslavia. No Yugoslavia."

Finally, the Romanian cops got back in their car, without Gladys, and drove off. A cheer went up from the clinic staff, and Dr. Gabor said to me, "We begin now to make a stand against the tyranny of the Romanians."

Nadia said to him in English, "You just make more trouble for Gladys. They only want her to sign paper. You watch, they come back and arrest her next. And it is *your* fault!"

But Dr. Gabor, flushed with the success of the impromptu revolt, had turned away. "Now, now, Mrs. Bentwhistle," he was saying, "you see, nothing to worry about. We Magyars will protect you."

Gladys gave him a friendly wallop on the arm, and they all trooped back into the clinic.

I began to follow and then remembered Zsoska. One minute she'd been standing next to me; now she was gone.

"Nadia," I said to the distraught tourist agent beside me, "I've got to talk to you."

"*Allons-y,*" she said. "Let's go to my office. There we can speak *in peace.*"

❧ CHAPTER TWELVE ❧

IT IS ONE OF the remarkable aspects of language that we can appear to take on different personalities simply by making different sounds than the ones to which we are accustomed. For those who are truly bilingual this seems so obvious as to hardly bear mentioning: they flit easily between tongues—an English set of vowels and mannerisms flows into Urdu patterns and intonations with scarcely a ripple—though they will talk casually about "my Pakistani self" and "my English persona." But for those of us who came late to another language, it is always something of an odd experience to see and feel it happen, the moment when you notice another personality overtaking your familiar one, the moment when you become "Italian" or "Japanese." It's the moment when you stop worrying about grammar and accent, and allow the other language to possess you, to pass through you, to transform you.

When I speak Spanish, the language that I know best besides English, I find my facial muscles set in a different pattern, and new, yet familiar gestures taking over my hands. I find myself shrugging and tossing my head back, pulling down the corners of my mouth and lifting my eyebrows. I touch people all the time and don't mind that they stand so close to me and blow cigarette smoke into my face. I speak more rapidly and fluidly and I use expressions that have no counterpart in English, expressions that for all my experience as a translator, I simply can't turn into exact equivalents. To speak another language is to lead a parallel life; the better you speak any language, the more fully you live in another culture.

Whatever Nadia's inadequacies in English, in French she was quite at home.

"Oh France!" she said when I asked her about it on the way to her office. "If one could live in France one would be perfectly happy. I did live there once, you know. I studied in Paris for six months. It was the happiest time in my life. The cinema, the cafés, the shops, the French themselves, a brilliant, artistic people." She kissed her fingertips. "I was spoiled forever by those few months.

"France and Romania have always had a special relationship," Nadia went on, opening the door to her bleak, bare office. "We are a Latin people, you know, an island of Latins in a sea of Slavs—language orphans. That is what makes Romania more Western than the other Eastern European countries. The Hungarians, the Polish, the Czechs, the Slovaks, the Serbs: they are heavy, Teutonic, theirs is the barbarian tradition. But we Romanians are Francophiles, we love literature, especially poetry, philosophy, the delicate arts of love and conversation.

"You know Rimbaud?

O saisons, o châteaux
Quelle âme est sans défauts?"

160

Nadia sat down heavily at her desk and gestured to me to take a seat opposite.

"Yes, I have read all the great French authors and poets," she said. "Voltaire, George Sand, Rimbaud, Baudelaire, de Beauvoir. There were once many cultural exchanges between the two countries, and a great deal of Romanian literature has been translated into French. We have a kindred spirit, our two countries. Unfortunately, it is only in spirit. Romania's history has been very different, tragically different."

She pinned up her hair absent-mindedly, "I believe that we were placed on the earth for love and art, to enjoy the beauty that God has given us and make more beauty if we can. And yet, except in places like France, that does not happen. We do not allow ourselves to be happy and creative. We argue, we hate, we punish, we kill. Even here, even here in this beautiful town of Arcata—death and murder!"

"So you definitely think it was murder then. Not an accident? Not just a heart attack?"

"But of course," she said.

"Surely you can't believe that Gladys did it though."

"I think the murderer is Dr. Gabor himself."

"I know that Dr. Gabor is an intensely nationalistic Magyar, but he strikes me as a very honorable man. He admires Václav Havel and . . ."

"I offer no accusations against the honor of Dr. Gabor. He makes my life miserable but I do not accuse him of being a cruel and spiteful man. Still, he is the one who had the most reason to see Dr. Pustulescu die."

"Because he and Pustulescu quarreled?"

"Exactly."

"But that's too obvious. Gabor gets the sack and the next day Pustulescu is electrocuted? That's the stuff of bad mystery novels."

"Real people are not as clever as good mystery writers," Nadia shrugged.

"What did you mean by saying that Gabor makes your life miserable?"

"Did I come to Arcata to be made a fool of?" she said passionately. "No! I came because I love people, because my job is tourism and making people happy. I like solving problems, not making problems."

"But . . ."

"Gabor fights me for the souls of the tourists. I do everything to make the foreigners happy here. I arrange their hotel stays and treatments. I pick them up at the airport or train station and return them. I drive them anywhere they want to go and tell them the history of Romania—in French, in English, in German. Romania has a difficult reputation at the moment, with bad associations for some tourists. It's very important that people enjoy themselves in Romania and see that it is not as they had heard, but that it is a friendly, beautiful, peace-loving country. Yes," she pounded the table, "I do everything to make them happy, and then Gabor fills their heads with lies. How badly the Hungarians are treated. How awful the Romanians are. *I* Nadia Pop, *I* am Romanian. Does he care? No! Does he care that everyone coming to Arcata learns to sympathize with the Hungarians and despise the Romanians? No, that makes him happy."

"I'm sure he doesn't mean to attack you personally."

"Pah. From the moment I came he has said to me, Why can't the government send a Magyar tourist agent? Why did they send *you?*"

"How well did you know Dr. Pustulescu?" I asked, trying to get back on the subject. "Did you work closely with him?"

162

For the first time Nadia looked evasive. "I do my job, and that job is to make people happy. They come here to Arcata to relax, to take the waters and the treatment, many come for the special effects of Ionvital. They have heard about Dr. Pustulescu and his work and they almost worship him. But I, personally, did not know him well."

"How long have you been working here?"

"Only about three years, since after the revolution. Before that I was in Bucharest, but I wasn't happy. Tourism under Ceauşescu at the end of the eighties was pathetic. He needed tourists for the hard currency, but he would not put the money into tourist accommodations. All this," she gestured to the hotel complex above and behind us, "was built in the seventies before Ceauşescu's mania for industrialization completely ruined the country. At that time the hotels were full. People from all over Eastern Europe and the Soviet Union would come to Romania for conferences and relaxation, as well as for medical treatment.

"You know that up until the end of the Second World War Romania was a prosperous country? My parents told me about the food they had, food to spare! But the Soviets stole so much of what we had, our food, our oil, our minerals. Then Gheorghiu-Dej and Ceauşescu made it worse and worse. All the agriculture was converted to industrial crops for export. There began to be more and more food shortages in the eighties. We couldn't feed ourselves, we! Once the breadbasket of Europe.

"By the middle of the eighties Ceauşescu was insane with power and greed. He was tearing down Bucharest, he was tearing down the villages. All his money had to go into his palace in Bucharest. He was sending all our food abroad to pay the foreign debt. While he ate caviar and lit chandeliers in his palace, the country ate bread and potatoes and sat in the dark.

163

"I grew up in Bucharest," she said. "Once it was a beautiful city. They called it the Paris of the Balkans. I remember cafés on hot summer nights. Wine. Laughter. Poetry. I went to the university, I studied French, I wanted to be a teacher. But no, there was little work, I was sent to this school and that school, always in the provinces. I wanted to emigrate, I wanted to go back to Paris, but I couldn't leave my parents. That was my life. Finally I stopped teaching, I lived in Bucharest. After my parents died, I went to work for Carpaţi, the national tourist agency. They sent me here to Arcata, where I am surrounded by beauty, but also by Hungarian fanatics."

"You must be one of the few Romanians here then?"

"More are coming. But yes, my sister and my brother-in-law and their children, the police, a few at the hotel. We are isolated. Never mind," she said. "I have great hopes. Ceauşescu is gone, the tourists will come back."

Outside the window I saw Archie with his tape recorder following Jack and Bree. Seeing him made me remember the real purpose of my talk with Nadia.

"Listen Nadia, we have another problem."

"Don't tell me," she said. "My brother-in-law is working as fast as he can on Eva's car. Tell Eva that I will take her anywhere she wants to go. If she wants to go back to Budapest I'll take her to Budapest. I would like to see Budapest. I would like to see her secretarial office. I will offer to drive her to Budapest. Yes, I will. I don't hold a grudge."

"Let's wait on that," I said nervously. "I think Eva would probably like to take her car back with her. But that's not the problem I meant."

Briefly I explained the Snapp family's presence in Arcata, and Zsoska's relation to Emma.

"So I told Zsoska," I was saying, "and now I'm worried

that it's going to cause trouble."

The effect of this story on Nadia was quite compelling. Her face grew pink with fury.

"So she gave up her baby! Of course! What choice did she have? She couldn't have decided not to have the baby in the first place. It was the law. It was genocide," she said. "Oh, men like Gabor talk about Ceauşescu as a murderer, but what do they know? It was the *women* who had to bear the brunt of his cruelty and madness. Thousands and thousands of women died from abortions—does the world know that? The foreign journalists and television stations came to Romania and photographed the orphanages and everyone said, How could people put their children into orphanages? What choice did we have? There was no birth control, there was no abortion, there was no food. Ceauşescu was worried about the population for his new industrialized country, he said all married women must have five children. They had to undergo monthly exams; they were watched, they were controlled. Many women gave themselves abortions, sometimes badly. If you were bleeding and went to the hospital, before they would treat you you had to sign a paper that said you had given yourself an abortion. Afterwards, if you survived, they would put you in jail. Many women did not sign; they died of septicemia. I have heard that 25,000 women died of septicemia this way. Half a million others were permanently damaged.

"I had a friend, a girl I cared for very much. She was pregnant, she had no money. She tried to abort and was bleeding. We called the ambulance and waited twelve hours for it to arrive. I remember how she bled and bled and we couldn't stop it, and how she got weaker and weaker. When they took her to the hospital they said, Tell us who performed the abortion. She refused. Her kidneys collapsed and she died two days later.

"But if you have the baby, you can't take care of it. You must work, there is no food. You put the baby in an orphanage, the baby gets AIDS, the baby dies. And you too, you die inside."

Nadia bowed her head a minute. I wondered if she were talking about herself. "And then people like the Snapps come from other countries, shopping for babies. They bought our children and walked away with them; they took them away to homes in Scandinavia, Germany, England, America. What could we do? We are not a Third World country. We are not a backward people—economically backward perhaps, but not spiritually backward. But Ceauşescu destroyed us and the women most of all. We could not even protect our own children."

Nadia stared at me. "What does Monsieur Snapp want now with Zsoska? Can't he just leave her alone?"

"It's that Emma doesn't speak. He wants to find out about her family. But you know Zsoska—she's . . ."

"Yes! I know Zsoska, she's always a problem with the guests. Once she hit a man. Another woman, a French woman—can you imagine?—Zsoska spat on. They would like to fire her at the restaurant, but they are afraid of her.

"Yes," she said. "This is a problem." She gazed out the window for a minute or two, and then turned back with a smile, as if she'd found something in the blue sky that was invisible to me. "But don't worry, we will fix it, we will make everybody happy."

I went out to the square, just in time to hear Archie finishing up his interview with Jack.

"Cass, your friend Jack has just been telling me some fascinating things about this part of the world. I had no idea that its history went back so far. What I always learned in school is that civilization started in the Fertile Crescent. Not so! Apparently this whole area was called Old Europe. There are neolithic sites all over Transylvania. Now let's run over those dates again, Jack. What B.C. are we talking?"

"Marija Gimbutas estimates at least 30,000 years of cultures that worshipped the Great Mother. Then, around the year 3,000 B.C. came the warrior invaders from the North, the Kurgans. Their hallmarks were rigid hierarchy, weaponry and enslavement, the ownership of women's sexuality and fertility. It didn't happen all at once though. There were millenia of conflict and adaptation. At first the Great Goddess was still worshipped; then she became the consort of a male god, and finally she was reduced to only being the mother of God. The Minoans on Crete kept the old ways alive longest, but by 1500 B.C. patriarchy was well-established. The only places the Goddess survived were Africa, Central America and in the old Celtic religions."

"Fascinating, fascinating," said Archie, scribbling a few notes. "So do you think this is a new trend, this rediscovery of the Goddess cultures?"

"As far as I'm concerned," said Jack loftily, "patriarchy is a mere blip on the radar of human consciousness. I mean, what, we're talking a few thousand years, compared with tens of thousands. And the rule of the fathers has obviously been a total failure."

"So you'd like to go back to those matriarchal societies, where women have power over men?" Archie looked a little nervous.

"But they weren't matriarchal," said Jack. "Gynocentric, perhaps. Matrilineal. But they weren't about power *over*. That's a male invention. They were partnership societies, not dominator societies."

"Hmmm," said Archie. "Well, I just hope when the war crimes tribunals start, you ladies will all remember that I was a house husband."

"Yes," said Jack. "I think we can put in a good word for you."

"Listen, Archie," I interrupted. "I've got to talk to you about Zsoska."

I pulled him over to the railing above the lake. I could see Bree, from the corner of my eye, putting her arm through Jack's and drawing her down to one of the benches. Jack was dressed in the same sarong as this morning, but with a silk Pakistani jacket over it, while Bree was wearing several torn tee-shirts and a flowered skirt. A couple of Gypsy women, also dressed in bright colors, looked at them approvingly and touched the fabric of their clothes and Bree's nose ring. Jack began to have a conversation with them, apparently in the Gypsy tongue.

"I spent the morning with Zsoska," I began. "I didn't find out much about her family though. They're poor, but Zsoska has a car. Her father's on a pension and her mother works in a dairy. And she's got a boyfriend, one of the Saxons who left to live in Germany. She told me a little about her circumstances when she gave up Emma. She calls her Emma Kay, which is actually Emoke in Hungarian..."

Archie stopped me. "So you told her then? That we were the people who adopted her?"

"She figured it out from my questions. She's not stupid."

"How'd she take it?"

"I don't know... I guess she's thinking it over."

"I hope she's not too upset," Archie said. He looked at

me, but I dropped my eyes. We both knew Zsoska's hot temperment.

"I'm curious," I said. "Why didn't you meet Zsoska when you adopted Emma?"

"It wasn't illegal or anything, if that's what you're thinking," Archie said. He was staring out at the lake, which winked and sparkled in the spring sunshine. "But sometimes I've wondered about the whole thing, the morality of it. It was so easy to get caught up in the craziness of the situation. One minute we were at home remodeling the kitchen and the next minute we were at this Bucharest hotel, with our contact Eugen driving us around from one orphanage to the next."

"Were the orphanages as bad as they sounded in the newspapers?"

"Cass—you couldn't believe them unless you'd seen them. The smell of urine would hit you as soon as you stepped out of the car, before you even got to the door. You'd go inside and see babies in wire mesh cages, just lying there motionless in their own urine and feces. There weren't enough nurses, not enough supplies, and here were Western couples being brought here to look, as if it was a supermarket."

Archie kept facing the lake, and his habitually cheerful voice sounded flattened and distant. "I can't really describe what I saw, it really hurts too much—the disabled kids, the kids who stood in their cribs and rocked back and forth just to get some kind of stimulus. It was a nightmare. People like Eugen took advantage of us and the others, and he wasn't even one of the bad guys. He didn't try to cheat us, he just kept our hopes up, driving us around to these orphanages where the healthy babies had all been adopted and then to hospitals. We found three kids at different times that seemed suitable. One of them, little Iulia, we just fell in love with. But she was HIV-positive. Another little boy—we heard he was available and we drove to his village to speak with his parents. They said yes, but changed their minds as we were going to sign the papers.

"Meanwhile, all around us, other people seemed to be having better luck. Going out for the day and coming back with a healthy little Dan or Adriana. Most of them were going farther afield than Bucharest and most of them, I think, were buying the babies directly from the parents, without bothering with the orphanages and hospitals. They didn't call it a black market, but that's what it was."

Archie turned back to me, his gold-brown eyes earnest and pleading. "You can't blame people. I know how they felt. You get desperate after a while. So when Eugen suggested that we try another city further north we went along with it. Lynn had already overstayed her leave of absence, we just couldn't see any end to it. That's how we wound up in Tîrgu Mureş.

"I remember that we didn't want to get our hopes up when Eugen said he'd heard about a nine-month-old girl in the pediatric ward of a local hospital. Her mother had brought her in with pneumonia and malnutrition and then had abandoned her, they said. Eugen said the nurses were concerned about her because she was well now and they didn't want to send her to an orphanage.

"We didn't take to Emma right away—we'd done that too many times before and had our hearts broken. Anyway Emma was thin and cried a lot, her hair was scraggly and she had blotchy skin. Not an attractive baby. The hospital in Tîrgu Mureş wasn't the worst we'd seen, but it was understaffed and depressing. Emma had been in the hospital for two months; she probably wasn't held much, she didn't smile. But she was healthy. And she was available, they said. It was like the last sweater on the table in the bargain basement. It's not quite the right size, but you think you can make it fit.

"The nurse said the parents were getting divorced and that the mother was living with her parents in a village about an hour away. Lynn put her foot down about doing direct negotiations. We'd been on too many wild goose chases. So Eugen agreed to arrange everything. He came back from the village saying that the mother would give up all claim to the baby and allow Emma to be adopted for about $2,000. Considering how much time and money we'd already spent that seemed very little. We agreed and the papers went through. We took Emma back to Bucharest, and then to the States."

"Why'd you really come back here, Archie?"

"I never felt right about how it happened," he said. "I felt hardened at the end, kind of heartless about it all. Lynn took it all in stride, but I . . . I guess I felt mad at the system, the orphanages, the hospitals, even Emma's mother. Especially Emma's mother. I wanted to blame somebody.

"But after a while I started to feel like we'd made a big mistake in not getting to know Emma's mother and family. I guess I want to make up for that."

I didn't really know how to say it other than bluntly, "I hope you know what you're getting into trying to get to know Zsoska. She's kind of a . . . volatile person."

"I keep hoping that she'll be more friendly, and then we can talk a little, get to meet the rest of the family, see if there's anything that would explain why Emma has a problem. I know that the Kit-Kat isn't too pleased to be here, especially since Bree's been giving her the cold shoulder, but I'm starting to like the place. Didn't have much of a chance to look around and think about all the history before, we were so busy. Besides, we can't just leave Gladys in the lurch."

"Okay, okay, I'm not saying you should leave," I said. "But just be careful." I was thinking of the earlier scene outside the treatment center. "Try not to get the police involved."

"Cassandra, you're a wonderful person," he said. "And I find your life, what little I know of it, just fascinating. Would now be a good time for an interview? I'm so curious about your work as a translator and your life on the road. Is there anyplace in the world you haven't been?"

"Not many," I said. "But there are a lot of places I haven't been back to."

❧ CHAPTER THIRTEEN ❧

DURING ALL THIS time I had not stopped dreaming of
Eva. Not in the urban core of my desire, more in the
suburbs. I had thought of her quite intensely, for instance,
in the mud-packing salon, at the moment when the fiery-
hot thick black mud had been smeared on my belly and
loins. Seeing Jack and Bree together was a reminder of
what I lacked at the moment. There certainly couldn't be
any harm in going to look for Eva.

Besides, if I wanted to find out more about Dr.
Pustulescu, it would be useful to have someone with me
who spoke Hungarian. Almost everyone spoke Romanian, but I wasn't confident enough in my own ability to
understand every nuance of it.

I finally located Eva in the physical therapy section of
the treatment center, in the "medical exercise room."
Wearing only a one-piece bathing suit, she was on the mat
doing handsprings, much to the admiration of a couple of
creaky codgers on exercycles. Her blond hair was tightly

pulled back from her heart-shaped face, and her forehead was beaded with moisture. The scent of sweat off her body mingled with the stale, old-socks smell of the room.

"Eva," I said. "I need you."

She sprang, literally, to my side.

"I mean I need your help with the women who work in the treatment center. I want to question a few of them, and I think Hungarian would be best. Can you translate?"

"Of course, Cassandra," she said. "You know, I'm beginning to like it here. If it weren't for worrying about my car and the business, I would be quite happy. Except for Nadia and her brother, everyone is Hungarian."

She swung up to the vault and sat there.

"I'm curious, Eva. How much of your dislike for the Romanian people as a whole is based on Nadia Comaneçi and her three gold medals in Montreal?"

"What do you think it's like to kill yourself from the time you're six years old and then lose to some Romanian? I wouldn't have minded losing to the Russians—that, we expected. Olga Korbut, she was marvelous, but Nadia Comaneçi! Every time she walked by with her head in the air, holding one of her dolls, I wanted to kill her. The judges were in love with her. Seven perfect tens! Three gold medals! The Hungarian team was sunk before we started," she said, swinging her body on strong arms. "Imagine, and I had spent my whole life preparing for that moment. I went to a gymnasts' school where I practiced six hours a day and squeezed in my other studies when I could. I was six when I started; everyone always said that was almost too old. Some of the girls in my class had started at four years old, can you imagine? Our coach drove us like horses. Once I had a bad fall and dislocated my ankle; he said, You're not to cry and make a scene. It happens to everyone. We'll tape it and you'll go ahead with the program. I was eight."

"You must have liked some of it though."

"Oh, there were benefits. I studied English and traveled. My father, who had lost his job after the uprising in 1956, was given a pension. My aunt, who took care of me after my mother died, was given a modern flat. I know you think our flat is small, but in those days, the sixties, when there was no housing, two people in a flat like that was luxury. I'd grown up in one room, with four people. I was glad to make life easier for my relatives."

Eva jumped off the vault, ran across the room and dashed back again to leap over it. I massaged my newly diagnosed arthritic knee.

"After Montreal, I was finished. Age fifteen. I didn't win a medal, my scores were respectable but not spectacular. There was no reason to go on, I would be too old for the next Olympics. And so I left it and began to be ordinary again. Of course that was impossible too. A fifteen-year-old girl who has traveled widely, who speaks English, who was in the Olympics, who has a flat—that was not normal in Hungary. I'm afraid I grew stuck-up and didn't study. I married very young, at nineteen, to another athlete, a soccer player.

"It was a terrible six years," she said, panting after another leap. "He was often with other women, often cruel to me. I was unhappy. I realized I didn't love him. I made a plan to escape, but the only place I could go was back to my aunt's. This time the flat did not seem so big. I started thinking, what can I do? I knew English, but otherwise I was very stupid. I began again, to educate myself, to use my English to read everything. I found a way to go to London when it was possible to travel and to take a secretarial course for a year, along with some business classes. It was there I became interested in feminism and it was there

175

I got the idea to start a secretarial business."

Eva slowly turned a somersault on the mat. "If I had not been to London I would not have understood the feminist movement in the West. There had been no women's liberation movement in Eastern Europe in the sixties and seventies. They would have said, What do women need to be liberated from? We are all socialist citizens, we live in an egalitarian society. The early communist theoreticians never described what an egalitarian society would really look like. Some of the utopians of the Bolshevik era imagined communal living and crèches for the children, to liberate women for the larger world of work. But that world of work came, during Stalinist times, to be heavy industry, construction and agriculture.

"Yes, women built dams and drove tractors; they also had to stand in queues for food and do the cleaning and washing and childraising. It's no wonder that when women thought they had a choice, they said, I'm not a feminist. Feminists are ugly, man-hating lesbians. They said, I don't want to work. I want to stay home and be a housewife."

"Believe me, they still say that in the West. Without having built any dams," I said.

"The situation since the fall of communism is not better for women, not at all. The Czech women and Polish women worked for freedom as much as the men, but where are they in the government? Now the Roman Catholic church reasserts itself everywhere to make women's lives worse. Abortion is almost illegal now in Poland again. We go backwards even as we go forwards."

"Yeah, pretty soon it will be as bad as Ireland," I said.

Eva addressed me from a pretzel position on the mat. "I don't understand you, Cassandra, I admit. You come from a country where you could have anything, do anything, where there is nothing to stop you, nothing material in your way. You come from America, from the birthplace of modern feminism. And yet you spend your life wandering aimlessly, involved in cultures that are not your own, doing nothing for the cause of women."

"I believe I provide a model of rugged independence for oppressed womanhood everywhere. Besides, you act as if I don't work . . . I just don't work all the time."

"But don't you feel you belong in your country? Don't you have patriotic feelings? Don't you want to help your country?"

"As Virginia Woolf said, 'As a woman I have no country. As a woman my country is the whole world.' Besides, once I left home my class status went up significantly. Being an American in the rest of the world is like being an Upjohn in Kalamazoo."

The two old men had staggered out and we were alone in the room. Eva approached me, sweating, her blond hair in disarray. "You intrigue me, Cassandra. Your lifestyle is extremely anti-social, almost parasitical. I would not like to be like you, and yet . . . "

I took her chin in my hand and kissed her. "And yet?"

"I am sometimes interested in women," she confessed. "I mean, in the way that you and Jack are. In London such opportunities were available to me, but I did not have the courage to take advantage of them. I suppose I was afraid . . . "

I kissed her again. "Believe me, it's easier than you think. Like falling off a vault."

"Not here," she whispered. "Later? Later tonight? Now I'll get dressed and help you ask your questions."

Modestly she turned away. Immodestly, I watched.

*　*　*

Eva and I went first to the scene of the crime, where Ester, the galvanic bath attendant with the morose expression, was cleaning out the four porcelain basins in preparation for a new patient. She reminded me that I had missed my scheduled appointment that morning. Already the excursion with Zsoska seemed long ago, but Ester had given me a new idea.

I asked Eva to inquire if there was a full record of everyone who had had the galvanic treatments, and if so, could we see it. Indifferently Ester pointed to a clipboard hanging on the wall. Eva and I went over and took it down.

"It would have been last week, Friday," I said. "Gladys has said that she and Pustulescu were down here early, at eight o'clock, before the day's appointments started."

"These names are hard to read," she said. "But the first appointment is at eight-thirty."

"So that would have given someone time to come in and tamper with the voltage meter and then enough time afterwards to adjust it back before the first patient."

"But wouldn't there have been a huge commotion after Pustulescu died?" Eva asked reasonably. "How would there have been the opportunity? Maybe it was just time for him to go and a little electrical current sent him off."

I wasn't quite convinced. There were too many people who didn't like Pustulescu. Probably everyone in this clinic, starting with Dr. Gabor.

"Ask Ester if she remembers who were the first people to arrive after the incident."

After a moment, Eva translated: "She says when she heard Gladys scream, she came running, and many others also. Then in half an hour the police came, and they looked at the voltage meter. They couldn't see anything wrong with it but they took it away anyway, and Ester had to find another meter. Then the first patient came and sat there and everything was fine." Eva nodded, and added, "Ester says she knows nothing, all she does is clean the basins between the patients and turn on the meter."

"And who was the first patient that day?"

Eva looked closely at the schedule. "I think—yes— Ackermann."

Well, Frau Sophie obviously hadn't suffered any ill-effects from the treatment. It would be worthwhile talking to her again.

Next we tackled Ilona, Mistress of the Waters. She put Eva and me into adjoining dressing rooms.

"How are *you?*" she asked me, as I took off my clothes. "Your arthritis better here?"

"Much. Listen, Ilona, did you hear about the police coming yesterday to question Gladys?"

She nodded. "Romanian animals. They not care about the baths. They Ceauşescu men. Securitate. I grow up in Arcata. We never need police here."

"You don't think that Gladys killed Dr. Pustulescu?"

"Why Gladys kill Dr. Pustulescu?"

"Somebody killed him."

"No, no, it was accident." Her face assumed a sorrow-ful expression. "Sorry to say, these baths getting old, no tourists, no money to make better. People no have money come here. Understand?"

"But, Ilona, the voltage meter wasn't malfunctioning, according to the police. Is there a possibility the doctor wasn't electrocuted at all? I know that he got an Ionvital shot every day. Who would have given him that shot? Maybe something was in it."

"Accident, accident only," she said serenely. "Life is many accident, yes?"

"Don't you think it was a coincidence that it was Dr. Pustulescu who—1) wasn't a patient and 2) just happened to be showing Gladys how the galvanic bath worked and 3) had just quarreled with Dr. Gabor—who happened to be the one to have the 'accident'?"

But this was all too much for Ilona. She gave me a tender pat on the shoulder and said, "I go now other lady."

When she returned, I decided to ask her something else. "If you grew up here in Arcata, Ilona, you must know the story of that beautiful house up behind the hotel. The brown and blue one with the gate and the little gate across from it that doesn't lead anywhere."

"Yes! I know! It is the house of long-ago family. Their name was Lazsló. He was doctor from Tîrgu Mureş. You see their names on house. György and Erzsébet. I love that house."

"Is it empty now?"

"Yes. Too big for most people. Someday maybe museum, I hope."

"What about the gate across the street?"

"The Lazslós have five children, but one die. A young girl. Her mother puts grave there, and garden."

"It has a feeling about it."

"Yes! I know. Now you and friend get in nice warm water."

"Ask her more about Dr. Pustulescu's amorous activities," I directed Eva when the two of us were floating in the silky mineral baths, and Ilona sat on a bench beaming at us with towels in her hands.

After a few minutes of rapid Hungarian, they were in gales of laughter.

"What is it? What is Ilona saying?"

"Unbelievable," said Eva. "The old man had a wife—a young wife—and a mistress in Bucharest. He even had a

180

mistress here in Arcata. But still he wasn't satisfied. He was always trying to make love to the women in the clinic. Every time he came to the treatment center in Arcata he would follow the women around, trying to make love to them."

"Ask her what women found attractive about him?"

Ilona snorted. "His money!" she said in English. "Doctor very rich man from Ionvital. He can give food, drink, perfume, clothes to women. Women have nothing, how they say no?"

"Ask her about the wife and mistress in Bucharest. Did they ever come here? Could they have possibly killed him, or arranged to have him killed?"

Eva asked her and then told me, "She says they only saw the young wife once. She came and was very critical of everything. But that was over a year ago. She hasn't been back since."

"And what about this mistress in Arcata? How do they know he had a mistress here, who was she?"

Ilona shrugged. "We don't know, we only guess. Someone in a high position."

I thought of Margit, with her nervous laugh and habit of rushing away whenever she saw me. Someone with a guilty conscience if I ever saw one. Had she been having an affair with Pustulescu? Had her husband found out about it and decided to kill Pustulescu? Had the husband plotted the murder or had Margit?

It could have been a crime of passion, but it was more likely to have been one of money. Dr. Pustulescu's wife probably had the most to gain from his death. She would have been left a rich widow. How could I find out that information? Perhaps Nadia could help.

But first it seemed worthwhile to interview Margit.

* * *

"Margit seems kind of unstable to me," I said to Eva, after we'd dressed and were back outside in the corridor. "At first I thought she was having an affair with Dr. Gabor, but then I decided not."

"Is he married?"

"He's a widower."

"Oh, like you?" Eva had heard the rumor, but obviously she didn't believe it. She laughed. "You probably haven't ever even been with a man."

"Please don't cast aspersions on my deceased husband. André may not have been a man in the fullest sense of the word, but he served his purpose."

We went upstairs to Dr. Gabor's office, where we found Margit filing. "Can I... help you?"

Eva took over in Hungarian, much to Margit's surprise. She jumped up from behind the doctor's desk and grabbed her stethoscope. I thought she was going to make one of her fast escapes, so I reached out a hand to stop her. Her arm was wiry but emaciated, and the skin had a dry electric feel.

I burst out, "We need to know about Dr. Pustulescu."

Eva repeated it in Hungarian, and listened to Margit's shrugging answer.

"She says she doesn't know anything. She never had anything to do with him."

"That's impossible. Margit works with Dr. Gabor and together they work with all the foreign patients getting Ionvital treatment. Of anyone at the clinic she must know more about what was going on around here than she's saying. We'll shock her. Tell her we know that she was having an affair with the old guy." Eva looked dubious but spoke anyway.

Margit looked at me with furious and hurt eyes. "Lying!" she said in English, followed by a whole torrent of

Hungarian, none of it flattering to judge by Eva's pained expression.

At this juncture Dr. Gabor appeared, and Margit took the opportunity to rush past him into the corridor.

"That girl," he said. "What's the hurry? I am always asking her. Hallo, Mrs. Really, you have a friend?"

I introduced him to Eva. "A friend from Budapest. We've just heard some troubling things about Dr. Pustulescu," I began.

"But you are Hungarian," Gabor said to Eva. "That is wonderful. You come from Budapest! Budapest, the most magical city in the world! Tell me, how you find this country?"

Eva stammered, "I like it very much."

"No, it is a terrible country," Dr. Gabor laughed. "How much suffering we go through, you can not imagine. But we do not give up. We are working for freedom, someday to be not united back with Hungary, but to be on equal terms. Free borders, Magyar literature taught in the schools, a reconnection with Central Europe, which is our true home. . . . " He launched into Hungarian and Eva responded eagerly. I thought I heard the words Milan Kundera.

I had a suspicion that Margit knew more than she pretended about a number of things. It was time to see where she went when she vanished from Gabor's office.

Aside from my strenuous treatments the day before I had not really investigated the full extent of the clinic's resources. I started right outside Gabor's office, asking everyone in white I met if they had seen Margit. No, no. No Margit. The bath attendants bustled past me with arms full of towels and with baskets of plastic sandals. Some accompanied elderly patients, some slid by me with blank looks, uncomprehending. Then a nurse pointed down a corridor where I hadn't been yet, and I pushed through double doors into a steamy realm of whirlpools and saunas.

"Margit?" I kept asking, and someone pointed me on again. The atmosphere here was as close and muggy as a hothouse. The corridor had a greenish hue, and patients staggered past, all face and ghostly body, like lilies or orchids, white with invisible stems. The water here didn't drip but hissed, like serpents roiling at the bottom of a ravine.

I heard the sound of retching and then bitter crying from behind a ladies' restroom door, and without thinking I went in.

Someone was in one of the stalls, throwing up into the toilet. I had heard that sound in our family bathroom back when Maureen was giving up on the idea of being a nun.

When she came out, Margit's face was pallid and her lipstick was smeared and garish. The superficial impression of vivacity she usually gave was gone and she looked older, and more tired.

"You're pregnant," I said in English, and saw by her expression that she understood me. "Aren't you? Is it Pustulescu's child?"

"Why do you care?" she said bitterly, and her English was clear and unhesitating, as good as Gabor's or better. "You're an American. You don't have to live here. The old man is dead and no one misses him. Why do you keep asking questions?"

"Because of Gladys," I said, but at the moment I didn't quite convince even myself. "Can I do anything to help?"

Margit steadied herself against the sink, facing the mirror. "Help?"

"Why would you sleep with him, Margit?"

"He would have made me lose my job. That was the first reason. Afterwards he said he would tell Gabor. I knew Gabor would despise me if he found out. I was trapped."

"How long did it go on?" I asked.

"Five years, six years. My husband never knew. He would say, Why can't we have children, Margit? But when I became pregnant it might have been the doctor's. I had four abortions in two years; the doctor always arranged for them in Bucharest.

"After that I was more careful; I was able to get birth control after the revolution. I kept thinking, He must die soon. Now he is dead, and I am glad he is dead, but I am pregnant again, and must abort again. I don't want anyone to know. They knew in the clinic about Pustulescu, that I was his mistress. They hate me, everyone except Nadia. Nadia is a kind woman. The others hate me. I hate myself." Margit stared into the mirror. Perspiration had come out on her forehead.

"Did you hate Pustulescu enough to kill him?"

"I hated him more than that. But I didn't kill him. He had a heart attack, that's all."

"Who gave him his Ionvital shot every day? Did Gabor? Did you?"

"What do you mean?"

"I mean that maybe it wasn't a heart attack, either spontaneous or the result of a shock from a problem with the voltage meter. Maybe Pustulescu's death had nothing to do with electricity. It would have been easy enough to substitute something for the Ionvital, something poisonous."

"No one gave the doctor his shot besides himself. He was like his hero Ceauşescu. He trusted no one."

But Margit's eyes didn't meet mine. Suddenly she

bolted again for the toilet stall, though she had nothing left to vomit, except bile.

Back in Gabor's office I found that he and Eva had been joined by the tenacious editor of *The Washtenaw Weekly Gleaner.*

"Hi Cass! I heard you talking about Dr. Gabor being a real Magyar patriot and I decided to get the background for my piece straight from the horse's mouth. No more dull history. Real stories from real people." Archie turned on his tape recorder. "I'll start right in, Doctor. For most American readers, all the countries behind the old Iron Curtain seem pretty much the same. Can you tell me some differences?"

Gabor laughed. "What a big question, Mr. Snapp! I must refer you to Mrs. Kálvin about Hungary, which as you know has already in the last ten years shown many good changes in freedom and economy. In Poland of course you have the strong trade unions, you have since long time Solidarność and Lech Walesa. In the old Deutsche Demokratische Republik, East Germany, there was a coalition of Greens and other liberalizing tendencies —now they are together with the West and everyone is suffering. And then the Czechs! The Czech Republic (not the Slovaks, they are like Romanians, very corrupt and backward) is a country I admire very much. They had a very strong dissident movement for years before their revolution. Not like Romania, where most intellectuals and writers collaborated with the government. In Czechoslovakia they went to jail or took hard manual labor, like Havel in the brewery. There the intellectuals were part of the masses. Here in Romania there was almost no samizdat movement. Typewriters had to be turned in. We did not communicate among ourselves for fear of speaking to an informer."

"So, Dr. Gabor, you're saying that Romania had no opposition movement?"

"Hah! It had no opposition movement then. It has almost no opposition movement now. Because Romanians are used since Turkish times to bow down their necks to rulers. Only in Transylvania did the Magyars organize. But in secret."

"But Ceauşescu's regime didn't just fade away, it was overthrown," said Archie. "It was the bloodiest of all the uprisings."

"Yes, we can be proud we were the only Eastern European country to overthrow such a tyrant. But we are also the only country, except Bulgaria and then later Lithuania, to have voted in another Communist government. The National Salvation Front, coming into existence in the hours after Ceausescu tried to flee the country, is the Romanian Communist Party. It has another name, but the same faces. They pursue many exact same policies, including opposition to Magyar autonomy in Transylvania."

"Romania's leaders always blame Hungary when there is any violence between Romanians and Hungarians," Eva interjected.

"Exactly," said Gabor. "But it is always Romanian nationalists who start the violence. There is a group now called *Vatra Românească,* something like Romanian Hearth, very right-wing, with many members now from Securitate, Ceausescu's old secret police. In 1990, in Tîrgu Mureş, 2,000 Romanian fascists attacked a peaceful demonstration of Hungarians."

Eva said, "I remember that. Many thousands of us gathered in Budapest in solidarity with the Hungarians in Tîrgu Mureş."

"What do you think, Cassandra?" Archie asked me.

"What?"

"About this whole question of nationalism. Isn't it dangerous to revive these sentiments?"

Truth to tell, I had not been paying full attention. I was still preoccupied with Margit. Was it really possible that Gabor knew nothing of what Margit had gone through? Was he trying to protect her? Was he using her to protect himself? Or had the two conspired to kill Pustulescu together? What had Pustulescu and Gabor been quarreling about? If they'd been arguing in Gabor's bugged office the police would have overheard them. Why didn't they arrest Gabor then? Why were they so fixated on Gladys?

"Cassandra is an internationalist," Eva answered for me. "She doesn't believe in patriotism."

"You have brought up a complicated subject, Mr. Snapp!" said Dr. Gabor. "Let us ask ourselves, What is nationalism? Is it the same as ethnic identity? Here in Transylvania we Magyars still have few rights. We ask for cultural rights—to have Hungarian on public signs in streets, to have classes taught in Hungarian at all levels, to have Hungarian radio and television. Not just to *speak* our language, but to have our Magyar identity respected."

"Don't get me wrong," Archie said. "I *support* Hungarian cultural rights. Minority rights must always be respected. What I think you all have to be worried about, over here in this neck of the woods, is anything that smacks of ethnic cleansing."

"The Serbs are beasts," Eva said. "And the Croats are not much better. It's the truth to say that, not nationalism. It's the truth to say that Romanians are corrupt and that Magyar culture is superior."

"Come now, Eva," Archie remonstrated. "Isn't that the

kind of ethnic stereotyping that starts wars in the first place?"

"I believe that some cultures are morally diseased, and that they must be uprooted and destroyed if they're not to infect the rest of us," she said. "You Americans are far too naive with your talk of tolerance. It's not just that some societies are better than others, or some groups of people contribute more to the world, it's that some cultures actually are so horrible that they can damage the rest of us. If you had lived through Hitler or Stalin or Ceauşescu you would know this. You would not be so optimistic and sure that everyone is equal."

"I agree," I said, surprising Eva with my enthusiasm. "I personally have been horribly damaged by Catholicism. And just by male culture in general. So when do we start uprooting?"

Dr. Gabor looked puzzled, and Archie laughed nervously. "Cassandra's such a joker," he said.

There was a knock at the door and Jack came in.

"I was wondering where all of you hang out. If I didn't have my own ways of restoring youth I might be tempted to have some treatments myself. Cassandra's looking younger every day. . . . But I didn't come to tell you that, only," she turned to Archie, "I thought you might like to know, Cathy and Emma seem to have gone off."

He stared at her. "What do you mean, gone off?"

"I saw them getting into Zsoska's car; Cathy said they were going to Zsoska's house. At first I didn't think anything of it. But then I remembered the story and . . . "

Archie was already out the door, and I followed him.

❧ CHAPTER FOURTEEN ❧

Since the Polski Fiat was still in pieces in front of the tourist office, that left only Nadia's vehicle to take us to Lupea, unless we wanted to wait for the bus. But Nadia was at first not to be found. The tourist office was closed, with a padlock and chain on the door, and we had no idea where she lived. Archie and I searched the hotel lobby and half the town before we ran into her coming out of the police station in the lower quarter.

"What were you doing there?" I demanded.

"Autopsy finished. Heart of Dr. Pustulescu stopped."

"But that's good news," I said. "Now they'll believe he had a heart attack and stop bothering Gladys."

"Heart can stop by too much electricity," she said. "Gladys still in trouble. That is why I talk to police," she said, averting her eyes. "Explain they must be careful with American citizen or big trouble with foreign aid. I say we call American Embassy now. Gladys must go to Bucharest before police arrest her. I must take her, but where is she?

Always with those dirty dogs, I can *not* understand. People starving in Romania, she feeds dogs."

"But Nadia, you know that Gladys didn't do it."

"Yes, yes," she said. "Tell that to judge, as you say."

I had wanted to talk to her about Margit, and about the possibility that the doctor's Ionvital shot had contained something to shorten life, not prolong it. But if the autopsy had proved it was the heart, who was I to suspect anything else? There was also something about the way Nadia had seemed to sneak out of the police station that made me hesitate. Instead I said, "What about the wife, the wife of Dr. Pustulescu?"

"What *about* wife?"

"I know that Pustulescu must have been a wealthy man from all his drugs, and that he had a young wife who would inherit."

"Not true! Pustulescu too smart for that. He divorced and married three times. Wives no power."

Archie broke in, "I know Gladys is in a tough situtation, but Nadia, you've got to help us, you've got to drive us to Lupea."

"Lupea? What Lupea?"

"Zsoska has kidnapped my children, Cathy and Emma."

No averted eyes now. Nadia was all indignation. "No! I do not believe! We go, we go right now!"

"I never like that Zsoska anyway," said Nadia in the car.

"Why not?"

"Always bad mood," Nadia said. "Why she worry? She is *beautiful*."

"Even beautiful women have their problems," I said. "I know I do."

192

Nadia stared at me for a minute, then gave a delighted laugh. "You are joking, yes?"

"What I want to know is, why would Cathy let her take Emma," Archie was worrying. "Why would Cathy go herself?"

I privately wondered if Cathy saw Zsoska as an answer to her prayers. Maybe she was thinking that they could just leave Emma in Romania, where they'd found her.

"I don't know what Lynn is going to say," said Archie. "I told her that everything would be just fine. I hate to worry her about this; she's in the middle of a big project."

"What kind of physics does she do?"

"Quantum mechanics," said Archie humbly. "I don't understand much about it. We met in English 101."

The idea of having a physicist for a mother was practically beyond the realm of imagination for me. When I think of Rosemary Reilly, I see an Irish Kali: one hand stirring a pot of chicken stew on the stove, another arm holding a baby for bottle-feeding, while a third long arm snakes out to catch me a smack as I run by. She has seen me out the kitchen window, hanging by my knees from a tree limb, with my none-too-clean underpants showing.

"Catherine Frances, I'll thank you not to set an example of degradation to your younger sisters and the neighborhood. And you twelve years old."

My mother had a lovely rolling vocabulary; she never used a simple word when a more inventive one would do. Sometimes I think it was she who taught me how to be a translator, how to assess the precise meaning of a word, never with a definition, but with a synonym.

"What's degradation?"

"Filth and perversity, young lady."

"Don't you mean perversion?"

"You shouldn't even know a word like that. The idea!"

193

She gives me another smack, as with a miraculous fourth arm she reaches out to catch a softball one of my brothers has lobbed through the open window.

In Lupea I wasn't able to remember the way to Zsoska's, and we spent ten minutes driving up and down dirt streets, looking for the robin's-egg-blue house.

"This is it, I think," I finally said. But it was more sound than sight that made me sure. For from inside the little house came the sound of the violin. It wasn't Mozart, but a folk dance tune, measured and merry. And if I weren't mistaken, there were two violins playing it.

"Cathy," called Archie, jumping out of the front seat. "Emma, Emma!"

The music ceased abruptly and Zsoska came to the door. "Hello, Snapp," she said coolly.

"Zsoska!" said Archie, not bothering with his Hungarian phrase book. "What's the damn idea? You can't just take my daughters off like that."

"Emoke, *my* daughter," said Zsoska. "You sitting table every day. You no telling me, Snapp."

"Well, we were planning to tell you," said Archie. "That was the plan."

"Hi, Dad," said Cathy, popping out from behind Zsoska.

"Kit-Kat! How could you let this happen?"

"You didn't tell Zsoska that it was okay? She said you did."

"Well, I mean," Archie stumbled, "Of course I've wanted us all to get to know each other better. . . . Is Emma all right? That's the important thing."

"Emma," said Cathy, "is in seventh heaven. At least now we know where she gets her musical talent from."

"Zsoska?" whispered Archie, staring in awe at her striped black and yellow mane and fiery eyes.

"Grandpa!" said Cathy.

A ruby flush of alcohol smoothed out his weather-beaten face and gave him a congenial warmth that I suspected didn't always survive into the morning. He had Zsoska's black eyes, hooked nose and high cheekbones, though his mouth sank into a well of toothlessness. Like Zsoska he also had a full, sweeping head of hair, dramatically white. But his imposing head sat on a withered body; one of his legs dangled uselessly.

He was wearing a faded white shirt and an embroidered vest, and in his lap was a beautiful old fiddle. Next to him, clutching her own small violin, was Emma, no longer blank-faced, but smiling, though she was still silent and her eyes gave away nothing.

Grandpa greeted us in Hungarian and offered us a round of *ţuică* from the bottle next to him on the table. Zsoska produced glasses. Archie took a sip and choked, while Nadia belted hers down. I cautiously touched my lips to the glass and put it down again.

"The old guy was totally excited when he saw us come in with Emma and her violin case," Cathy told us. "Zsoska talked a bunch to him and he cried and hugged Zsoska and Emma and even me. Then he went into the other room and got out his violin and they've been playing ever since. It's kind of amazing. I mean, I've heard Emma play a lot, but just classical stuff, over and over. But this is different. Gramps plays part of a tune and Emma plays it after him. Then he plays the whole thing, Emma plays the whole thing, and then they play it together. I can't imagine how Emma holds it in her head like that."

"My father happy," said Zsoska, trying to pour us more brandy. "Emoke stays here."

"No!" said Archie. "Well, just a little. You see, Zsoska, I'm afraid that wouldn't work. I mean, we were just planning to stay here in Arcata a few days, not more than a week. We have to get back to Munich to the children's mother, to Lynn that is, Cathy's mother and Emma's adopted mother. We're very happy to meet your father, in fact, that was one of the things we'd been hoping to do on this trip, and that was to, you know, make contact with Emma's family. There are a few questions we have regarding, you know, family background, things like that, but once we get a fuller picture, we don't really have any reason to trouble you further or take up any more of your time."

Zsoska said something to her father and he shook his white head. He took up his violin again and began a new tune, a loud and lively *csárdás*. After a few seconds, Emma picked up her violin and followed him. It was as if she knew the direction the notes were taking without needing to think about it.

"Emma," cajoled Archie. "Come on, sweetie. Time to go. We'll say thank you to the nice man with the violin, but it's time to get back to our hotel for a nap."

"Emoke staying here, Snapp!" said Zsoska. "My mother coming from work. My mother seeing her."

"Nadia," said Archie. "Can't you help?"

Nadia addressed Zsoska in Romanian, but I knew immediately, when I heard the word "police," that she was taking the wrong tack. In a few moments the two of them were screaming at each other.

Archie, meanwhile, was inching over to Emma's side, while Cathy looked on as if she were watching a scene from Dostoyevsky come to life.

"Can't we compromise?" I finally yelled. The music and the shouting stopped. I continued, "Obviously Zsoska would like her mother to see Emma. What if Emma were to stay here tonight? Would that be so terrible? In the morning, Zsoska can bring her back to the hotel."

"She won't bring her back," said Archie. "You can be sure of that."

I addressed Zsoska: "You know you can't keep Emma here. You gave her up and you have no legal claim anymore. If Archie does let Emma stay here tonight, would you bring Emma back to the hotel tomorrow?"

"Yes," Zsoska said sullenly. "I not lying."

"But Emma will be scared here with these people, without us," said Archie. "Lynn would never forgive me if something happened."

"What can happen, Archie? Have you ever seen Emma so engaged? What could possibly happen?"

"Maybe she won't *want* to come back."

I looked at Emma's shining dark eyes. They were the equivalent of classical music, wordless and full of feeling.

"Snapp," said Zsoska. "I need knowing my daughter."

On the way back to Arcata I sat in the back seat with Cathy, while up in front Archie pulled out his steno pad. I thought he might want to discuss the situation with Zsoska, but he must have judged it safer emotionally to take refuge in journalism.

"I see I've interviewed almost everyone except you, Nadia," he said. "Maybe I could ask you some questions about Romanian history. There are some things I still don't understand . . ."

"I tell you," said Nadia eagerly. "First, here is story: In

197

beginning God give to all countries many things. To Romania he give everything—forest, river, mountains, minerals, good farmland, even oil. Then God say, This country got too much good, I think I give it something bad. So he put Romanian people here. Hah!"

"That's a hard story to tell about your country," said Archie, nonplussed. "The Romanian people I've met have been absolutely wonderful, absolutely . . ."

"Hard, yes!" interrupted Nadia. "Romania very hard, very tragic history. First one thing, then another. All problems start with Turkeys, Turkeys come in middle age, many hundred years we under Turkeys." Nadia made some wave-like movements with the hand not on the wheel. "Up and down, that is us. We revolt, then we are squished—squashed? We are poor, very poor and ignorant. Work in fields, give all to some lord. Lord gives to Turkeys. So. Finally we got some kings. First king from Germany, pretty good. Queen Marie very good, but King Carol very bad, crazy. There are wars. First World War. Second World War. Between wars Iron Guard fascists. After wars, Stalin takeover. What a mess.

"So, we got communists. Gheorghiu-Dej, big Stalinist. Soviets tell us to collectivize farms, make big industry. Then Ceauşescu comes in 1965. First there is some freedoms, but soon bad times. More he get, more he want. Bad to worst. Real craziness starts. Total insanity. No talking to foreigners. No passports. Taxes for not enough children. Women dying abortions. Ceauşescu big man in world politics. He stand up to Soviets, support Czechs in 1968. Americans love him, Nixon visits. Soviets say, Fine, Romania, no more good friends with you! Hah! Ceauşescu says, okay, we do everything ourselves. We pay foreign debt through export, thank you very much. We don't need food here. We don't need electricity. We don't need petrol for cars. We are miracle people, we live on air."

"I've just been talking to Dr. Gabor about the rights of the Hungarian minority," Archie interrupted. "He says all the Romanians suffered under Ceauşescu, but the Hungarians suffered the most."

"That man, he got one idea, one idea only," Nadia said, her voice rising. "And that to make tourists hate Romania. Do we treat him bad here in Arcata? No! We Romanians are the ones to suffer. He is king of Arcata, that man."

Archie continued scribbling. "So you're not in favor of Hungarian nationalism, Nadia?"

"I am in favor peace and quiet! We have been through plenty. Let's just shut up now and be friends."

"Romania has sure been through the wringer, all right," Archie agreed. "But wouldn't you say that things are getting better, Nadia? Ceauşescu's gone, the Soviet Union has disintegrated. You've held democratic elections. Maybe not everybody is happy with Ilescu, but he's not as bad as Ceauşescu. Abortion is legal again. People are free to travel."

"Yes, yes," Nadia said, her habitual optimism reasserting itself. "All this is true. We are dreaming of freedom for years and years. Now we have it and we must be grateful. Romania has many problems still, but when things are bad here, I always say to myself, thank you, God, at least we are not Yugoslavia."

In the back seat I remembered what I had been doing before the commotion with Emma had started.

"So, Cathy," I asked. "Do you know anything about electricity?"

"Like what?" She was slumped in a corner of the car, worrying her split ends and about two-thirds of the way through *The Magic Mountain.*

"Well, like, what is it? How does it work?"

"Didn't you ever take any science classes?"

"Science wasn't invented when I was growing up. We just had miracles. And anyway, I never went to class. I was a juvenile delinquent."

"Huh," she said, clearly not believing me. "So what do you want to know?"

"When we get back to Arcata, I'd like you to come with me."

It was late in the afternoon, and all the patients had left the clinic. A few attendants were mopping the floors, but no one asked us what we were doing down in the corridor that led to the galvanic baths. I didn't know if they were always so lax, or if they recognized us as peculiar foreigners who wouldn't understand the regulations anyway.

"So this is the galvanic bath?" Cathy said. "Wow. You know that guy Galvani, the one with the frog legs? It must be named after him."

"Frog legs?"

"Sure. Back in the eighteenth century. He found out that he could make dead frogs twitch their legs by touching nerve points with metal. It was one of the first electrical experiments. But he got it kind of wrong. He thought the convulsion came from the frog tissue, that there was some electrical life force inside. The electrical charge really came from contact between the two different metals. The guy who came after him, Volta, proved that. Volta figured out that different metals have positive and negative charges, and they produced a current. If he stacked up a bunch of negative and positive metals he could make a battery. Before he did that, Galvani's nephew used to go around demonstrating this animal electricity on the cut-off

200

heads of cows and sheep. He could make their eyes roll and nostrils twitch. Sometimes he got hold of a corpse and gave it an electric jolt and the arms and legs moved. Mark did some experiments like that once."

"Not with corpses, I hope."

"Frog legs," said Cathy. She looked happier than I'd even seen her. "Just like old Galvani."

I quieted my squeamish stomach, and pointed out the voltage meter. "As I understand it," I said, "the meter is set to a very low voltage, and the current runs through these wires into the tubs of water. You get a slight shock, but not much. I tried it, it's more like a tingling."

"It must be really low," Cathy observed, "because if your hair dryer falls in the tub, that's only 110 volts and that's enough to do you in. What's this?" She looked at the meter. "Looks like it doesn't go up very high. Whatever the voltage is in this place it's probably transformed down pretty low."

Cathy went over to the tub contraption, and stuck her finger in the water and then up to her lips. "Distilled, I bet. Okay, you can see here how they've worked it out. With all four limbs in the water you're all set. They've got your pathway going in a circuit, I see," she muttered.

"What do you mean, your pathway?"

"Well, you know when people get electrocuted by a high-voltage wire or by lightning? The current enters at one point, like the head or the hand, and exits through the feet, for instance. It's more dangerous when the current traverses the heart. So how was Dr. Pustulescu doing it?"

"He put both arms in."

"That shouldn't have knocked him off, unless there was a different amount of voltage in each tub. I'm not sure if you could get that to happen through a single source, though." Cathy went back to the voltage meter and fiddled with it. In a couple of minutes she had the back of it off and was peering inside.

"Is there a way you could increase the voltage?" I asked.

"I think so," she said. "The electricity is coming from the usual source, you know, through wires, on an alternating current. You wouldn't be able to increase the voltage past the transformed supply. This isn't the transformer, only the meter. The transformer's somewhere else in the building, I guess. If you put in a new transformer or just removed the old one, a lot more voltage would get through. When Mark and I used to make transformers we would put the coils of wire side by side. The more coils, the more voltage you'd get."

"So there's something besides this meter, a transformer, that someone could have fiddled with? Where would that be?" Cathy shook her head. "We could go look for it," she offered. "But even if somebody fooled around with the transformer, they must have fixed it back by now. They would have had to have fixed it back right away if they weren't going to get caught."

We both stared thoughtfully at Dr. Pustulescu's Nightmare Bathing Machine.

"What I don't get," said Cathy, "is how you'd make sure that the right person was electrocuted."

"That," I said, "continues to be the great problem."

As we left the basement of the clinic, I noticed Cathy's shoulders begin to droop again.

"Thanks for the help," I told her. "You're way ahead of me on the scientific front. Weren't all those hours making dead frogs jump worth it?"

Cathy sighed. "My dad says, if I ever want to be a

writer like him, I'll be glad I had an interesting childhood."

"Do you want to be a writer?"

"I'd rather be a doctor," she said. "But mostly I just
want to be a normal person." She sighed again. "Did you
have an interesting childhood, Cassandra?"

"I don't think so," I said. "It was crowded and eventful
though."

"My dad says he wants to make up for everything he
didn't have when he was growing up. Is your dad like
that?"

"My dad died when I was fourteen."

"That's sad," she said. "I've never known anybody who
died. Anybody close to me, I mean."

I looked at her with her adolescent acne, strong nose and
floppy hair. My name had once been Cathy too, and before my father's heart attack I could have said the same.

"Come on," I said. "I'll buy you a bottle of orange soda
in the lounge. You can tell me the plot of *The Magic Mountain*. I can't remember—does anything really happen in
that book?"

"Not too much," she said. "They talk a lot."

It was porkchops and omelettes again for dinner that
night. Eva was missing. Someone said she was supervising
Nadia's brother-in-law while he repaired the Polski Fiat;
more likely she was making sure that he didn't steal any
car parts. Everyone else, except for Emma—and Zsoska,
who wasn't working—was there.

While Gladys filled everyone in on her brush with Romanian authority in the morning, I went over to Frau
Sophie's table. "May I join you, Frau Ackermann?"

"*Aber ja,*" she said heartily, and ordered me a glass of

vodka. With a conspiratorial wink she opened up her handbag and brought out a jar of pickled herring. *"Bitte,"* she said.

"Frau Ackermann," I said. "You have been coming to Arcata for ten years, isn't that right?"

"Yes," she said. "And I hope to retire here."

She leaned closer and her reddish face beamed like a geranium over her green dotted dress. "I have a plan. I have been thinking of this many years and next year I will do it. The negotiations are now complete."

I couldn't imagine what she was talking about. "Negotiations?"

"With my savings I have bought a house here in Arcata. A villa that I will turn into a small hotel, a *Gasthaus*. The Germans and Austrians will come back to Arcata if there is good food for them here. I will serve delicious food! Bratwurst and Bürenwurst and true Wienerschnitzel and Schweinbraten, with Knödeln and Kraut. There will be Spätzle, little liver dumplings, and lamb and mutton. We will make our own good rye bread and Kaisersemmel, and dozens of kinds of tortes and strudels. I will have pigs and sheep and a cow especially for cream, and a vegetable garden and an orchard. I will do some of the cooking, and I will hire others to help. Perhaps I will buy other villas. Once again, people will come to Arcata for the good air, the healthy walks and swims, the Ionvital treatments with Dr. Gabor. And for the good Austrian food."

At that moment the Arcata Spa Hotel version of Wienerschnitzel appeared in front of both of us, its battered coat pale and soggy rather than golden yellow. It lay like a corpse on a funeral pyre of oil-soaked French fries.

"Grauslich," said Frau Sophie with a shake of her head. "When I open my *Gasthaus* we will have roasted potatoes,

and the Wienerschnitzel will be crisp on the outside, tender on the inside . . ."

"There was just one thing I wanted to ask you, Frau Ackermann," I said. "Did you go ahead with your galvanic bath treatment the morning of Dr. Pustulescu's death?"

"Of course," she said, through a mouthful of schnitzel. "But my treatment was delayed. They had to find another voltage meter."

"So you've never experienced any problem with the galvanic bath?"

Frau Sophie had reached for the salt shaker and was dousing her fries. "Oh no," she said. "I love how it makes me tingle."

❧ CHAPTER FIFTEEN ❧

W HEN WE CAME out of the dining hall, it was clear that
something in the weather had changed and a storm
was building. Archie went off with Gladys to feed her
dogs some table scraps, while I settled down with Jack,
Bree and Cathy in the lounge.

There was still no sign of Eva, but I wasn't worried, yet.
After all, she'd said we would get together "later" and it
was not even eight o'clock.

The lounge had a floor of linoleum and seats of orange
embossed plastic. It had the feel of an American bowling
alley coffee shop, circa 1950. At the counter there was always a handful of men drinking coffee and *ţuică,* and in the
booths were a few young people with Cokes or sometimes
a man and a woman, she with her orange drink, he with
his beer.

There was a sign outside the lounge that recommended
proper attire in several languages. The English version
said, "They require obligatory dress." No one had said

anything about some of us but we definitely did not fit in, especially Bree with her torn tee-shirts, nose ring and chain necklaces, and a tattoo on her shoulder that was occasionally visible. They had heard of such things in the West, perhaps, but not on the streets of Arcata. Jack, of course, was appearing in public in all sorts of interesting combinations. This evening she had on a type of Moroccan djellaba that made her look like a high priestess.

"Tonight is Beltane," Jack said. "Too bad it's going to rain." She looked out the window, where dark clouds had intensified the twilight and where the trees in the park in front of the hotel were swaying like the first dancers in a long festival procession.

"Isn't that some Irish celebration?" I asked.

"Celtic. It's one of the four quarter festivals of the old Goddess-based year: Lammas in early August to mark the first loaves made from the first harvested grain; Hallowmas, which is the time when the crops die and the Goddess goes underground; Candlemas in February to signal the reawakening of the earth and the return of the Goddess; and Beltane, May Eve, to celebrate the flowering of the land."

"I saw a program on public television about that," said Cathy shyly. "It was about Avebury in England."

"That's right," said Jack. "We went to Avebury on this tour I just did. I can't believe I lived in England all those years and never knew about the sacred sites. Avebury was the center of megalithic culture in Britain. They acted out the seasons of the year in rituals at Silbury Hill and the Long Barrow and inside the henge at Avebury itself. The festivals correspond to the Goddess's life story, to the seasons in a woman's life: childhood, youth, maturity, old age."

Jack glanced around at the four of us. "Look at us, we're living illustrations of the festivals. Cathy is Candlemas, the time of initiation, when puberty rites are celebrated; Bree is Beltane, when the Goddess of Love reigns over symbolic weddings; I'm Lammas, symbolizing the lush ripening of nature, the Harvest Goddess, and..." She looked over at me and paused, "...and Gladys is Samhain, Mother-into-Hag, the Winter Goddess, the Lady of the Tombs."

"What about me?" I complained.

"You're on the downside of ripening, I'd say; the grain is starting to go to seed, but the old juices are still flowing. You're more September than October, still a long way from winter."

"I see. Sort of like blackberry season?"

"Yeah. The vines are withering, but the fruit is getting sweeter by the day."

"And what happens on Beltane, Jack?" Bree asked, flushed with the thought of being a Goddess of Love.

"It's the time when the power and sacredness of sexuality are recognized. In Celtic times they lit Beltane fires from hilltop to hilltop, to celebrate the coming of the new moon. The entire community danced with upraised arms in imitation of the horned moon. And then they mated communally in orgiastic rites that went on all night."

"Wow," said Cathy. "They didn't show that on the program."

Jack coughed, and came back to earth. "No, ah, well... and then the next day is May Day, which is celebrated in some form all over the world. The Maypole and so on. In some places in Europe they still do circle dances and drink from sacred wells."

From outside came the sound of excited barking and

then Archie rushed in, followed by a reluctant Gladys. "Hecate and her hounds of hell," said Jack.

"I only wish I had more to feed them," Gladys said. She was wearing her appliquéd Western shirt and coyote bolo tie.

Archie looked dazed. "I counted thirteen, Gladys. Thirteen scrawny mutts out there."

The editor of the *Weekly Gleaner* seemed to have lost his bearings. His felt hat, a reliable indicator, was pulled forward down to his eyebrows instead of pushed back so you could see his mild, excitable expression. His agate eyes were dark with worry and he was less talkative than usual.

For a few moments he simply sat staring at his hands, while Gladys talked about how she'd like to get hold of the whirlpool room for a couple of hours and give some of those dogs a good soaking.

Then he said, "It's so strange not to have Emma here. I keep looking around for her and then realize she's with Zsoska. I hope she's all right. This isn't what I meant to happen. I don't know what Lynn is going to say."

"Oh Dad, Emma's fine," said Cathy. "She's probably better than she's been for years."

"How can you say that, Cathy?" Archie's eyes flashed. "She would have gone from the hospital to an orphanage if we hadn't adopted her. Zsoska never would have come back for her. She's not that kind of person, she's too . . . I don't know."

There was a silence while we all thought about Zsoska.

"Zsoska kind of reminds me of my mother," Gladys said unexpectedly. "Married too young. Short temper. Wild. She ran off for a while with the fellow who owned the local mercantile. But she came back after about a year. She was quieter then. Women didn't have a lot of choice in those days, not like you kids today. There were four of us kids all under six years old. She couldn't take it and left. But she didn't forget us, and when she'd sorted herself out, she came back. In fact, her time away probably made her a better mother."

That wasn't what Archie wanted to hear. He stood up. "Come on, Kit-Kat, it's getting to be bedtime."

"It is not. It's early. I want to stay here!" She looked around for support but, finding none, stood up sulkily and followed her father to the elevators.

"I guess I'll be hitting the sack too." Gladys yawned and waved us good-night.

"Your grandmother is an amazing woman," said Jack. "I hope I'm half as energetic as she is when I'm seventy-five . . . though that's a long time off, of course."

"It's funny, Gram hardly ever talks about her child-hood," Bree said. "She's always so positive that I forget what a hard time she had."

"What happened when her mother came back?" I asked.

"Supposedly things were good for a while, but her father lost his job and then *he* left. It was the Depression and they were in a small town in Arizona. Gram did whatever she could to survive. I guess she wanted to go to college and be a vet, but there wasn't the money. She got married, had my mother, her husband died and she had to support the two of them. That's when she got into the pet business. She makes good money at it. She sent my mom to college and graduate school."

Bree suddenly looked straight at me. Her dark hair tangled against the milk white of her neck. Maybe I'd been overly hasty in turning her down, but it was too late now.

211

She said, "You don't think there's really any danger here, do you Cassandra? I keep telling Gram we should think about leaving, but she says she's having the time of her life. I can't tell with her, I mean, if she's scared or not. She doesn't know about the secret police and everything. And even if she did, she still wouldn't want to back down."

"I think somehow the cops are getting the idea," I said, "that Gladys has great personal resources. But I'd feel better if she weren't involved at all." I remembered Nadia coming out of the police station. I wanted to trust Nadia. I did trust Nadia. But what if she were in league with the police to get Gabor removed from his position, and what if she were using Gladys to do it?

I went upstairs to my room to wait for Eva to turn up, with a forlorn feeling I couldn't quite put a name to. It had been such a long day and so much had happened that I hadn't been able to absorb it all. Before switching the lights on, I walked over to the window and looked out. There had never been a sunset, only a pale stain of red behind the mounting gray clouds. Even now the light wasn't quite gone; reluctant, it clung to the trees and lake, clutching at a leaf, at a wave, even as the wind tried to pull it away from the earth.

I kept thinking about Zsoska giving Emma up for adoption, about how confused and lost Emma must have felt being abandoned and then taken to a new world. I kept thinking about Margit getting pregnant over and over by Pustulescu, having to lie to everyone. The evil spirit that was Pustulescu still seemed malevolently alive. His heart had stopped, but no one had put a stake through it, and that was the only way to really kill a vampire.

I stood there at the window remembering a curious

piece of translation work that had come my way about two years before. Until then I'd never read *Dracula,* much less Le Fanu's story, "Carmilla," and I associated vampires only with drive-in movies in Kalamazoo. The book was a collection of odd little vampire stories from Spain, written by a woman, Rosalia de Vega-Muñoz, and published in Madrid in the fifties. I undertook a sample translation to English for a British publisher, John Molesworth, an elderly and secretive man, more an antiquarian bookseller than a publisher really, though he did put out a book or two a year. Molesworth had discovered the original, *Cuentos de sangre y amor (Tales of Blood and Love)* while on holiday, in a remote hotel on the Galician coast. Try as he might, he could not find out anything about the author, except that she had died in 1976, apparently in a boating accident. She seemed to have no relatives.

Molesworth told me about the book when I visited his shop in Islington one day. As it happened, I was just off to Ireland. My last remaining great-aunt had finally died, and the old people's home notified me that she had left everything—the contents of five boxes—to me. Aunt Maeve and I had never gotten along well, but she had loved my father Michael Reilly and she always said I reminded her of him.

I decided to rent a cottage in the village for a week and to work on the Molesworth manuscript. The village was on the Cork coast, an eerie sort of landscape at that time of year, late November.

I took a xeroxed copy with me (the original book, which was sold to a Japanese collector, was a lovely edition, printed on heavy cream stock with detailed copperplate illustrations). After paying my respects to the nuns and carting away the boxes, I settled down to work in my cottage.

From the first I had trouble getting the mood right. The stories were more perversely ironic than supernatural, yet the language was arcane and self-conscious. It was difficult to translate into English without resorting to a Victorian vocabulary. Words like "phantasmagoria" and "sylvan" abounded, the sun always set in "melancholy splendor" and a hill was never a hill but an "eminence."

Between long walks on days when the sun refused either to shine or to sink, when the sometimes luminous, but often threatening gray-blue sky merged with the cold gray-green expanse of sea, I found myself among Aunt Maeve's old books, pouring over Sheridan Le Fanu and Bram Stoker, looking for a vocabulary that would be as evocative as it was enigmatic. I found it curious, but not at all strange, that the two greatest vampire authors were Irish.

The Galician writer's tales were love stories, or more accurately stories of desire beyond dreaming, beyond fulfillment, beyond mere life: desire between women. The word lesbian was never used; it was encoded in the word "perverse." The acts the women dreamed of were chaste but suffused with longing. One woman was the seductress, more experienced, and perhaps more evil; the other was often a virgin, troubled in mind, yearning for something she did not understand, hesitant and yet willing. The two women met in heightened circumstances: on an ocean liner in the middle of an Atlantic storm, at an opulent hotel on the coast of an unnamed country. In one story, incestuous, they were twins separated at birth. In another they were headmistress and student.

Always they recognized each other, always they seemed to have met before, in another lifetime, in another century. There were haunted glances, white columnar necks with gleaming crucifixes that were slowly removed or ripped aside, heaving bosoms and throbbing temples . . . feverish love consummated by burning kisses, only to be destroyed by jealous fathers and fiancés, only to vanish in the mists.

Men always came into the picture, figures of authority: a doctor, an investigator, a fiancé who couldn't understand the change in his previously docile beloved. There were deaths—servant girls and students began to disappear. The virgin grew pale as death, her eyes glittered strangely. She lost her appetite, wore scarves around her neck, took to walking late at night in graveyards.

In some of the stories, the seductress, the mysterious stranger with the slight foreign accent and riveting glance was hunted down with blazing torches, crucifixes and stakes. Packs of men surrounded her and murdered her, skewering her heart. But in many of the stories, the perverse desires lived on, in the apparently innocent virgin, in the daughter of the house who may have lost her lover but who had gained forbidden knowledge. The spirit of the vampire had entered her. She was ready to begin her own career of seduction.

While I was trying to translate these stories, I often stood at the window of the cottage and looked out on the dark waters of the Atlantic, just as tonight I looked out at where the lake was fast disappearing into the twilight. I had thought then, too, of the persistent human desire that life last longer than it was meant to, that life should return—as a spirit living on in another body, as the winter hag being reborn as a young goddess of spring and fertility, as Demeter and Persephone being reunited.

In the end I never finished the translation. I showed two of the stories to Molesworth when I got back, and he decided that they were less explicit than he'd hoped. Not that he put it quite that way. He said, "The subtle imagination is a wonderful thing. But what the public likes is another matter."

I turned from the window and lay down on my bed, waiting for Eva to knock, longing for Eva to knock, and fell into a dreamlike state, full of despair at the shortness of human life, and yearning for something more lasting, that is to say, eternal.

✤ CHAPTER SIXTEEN ✤

WHEN I WOKE up it was after midnight, and the wind was howling outside. It was not the wind that woke me, however, but the sound of voices in the room next door, Eva's room. Not voices exactly, but sounds: a man and a woman making love. I strained to catch the tone of the man, but I already knew who it was.

You start out discussing the velvet revolution in Czechoslovakia and the next thing you're in bed. It wasn't surprising. Gabor was an attractive man, and he adored Hungary. As for Eva—I should have known. There would always be a Mrs. Nagy or a Señor Martínez or a Dr. Gabor between me and this particular object of desire.

Nevertheless I didn't feel like listening to the sounds of a rapprochement between Magyars from two nations.

I got up and put on my beret, two sweaters and my leather bomber jacket, and slipped out into the corridor with my flashlight. The elevators were no longer running, so I walked down the five flights and into the dimly lit lobby. The bar had closed in the lounge and the reception desk was empty. Through the glass doors the world looked dark and crazed and threatening.

It reminded me that though the name Arcata summoned up visions of enchanted pastoral life, lush green fields and flocks of fluffy sheep tended by singing and dancing shepherds, in reality Arcadia had been a region in ancient Greece where violent human sacrifices took place, and cannibalism as well.

There had been wolves in Arcadia, and there were wolves here too. Or at least half-wild dogs, whose howling echoed that of the wind.

I hesitated a moment, then opened the hotel door and went outside.

Although the wind was blowing hard, to my surprise the air was almost warm. The waters of the lake made a slapping sound, and the light from the waxing moon hooked the waves in fishnets made of silver. The branches of the newly leafed birches rushed back and forth among themselves like women in frothy skirts at a party, while the fir trees and pines creaked and moaned.

I left the lakeside and headed past the blank dark windows of Nadia's tourist office, up the cobbled road to the two chiseled and painted wooden gates across from each other, and went through the one leading to the chocolate fairy-tale villa. I didn't know why this house drew me so. Even in the darkness, abandoned as it was, it didn't seem threatening or forbidding. Not like a ghost house in a horror movie, in spite of the gothic turrets and gables, the weather-vane spires, the overhanging doorway heavily carved with designs that in the moonlight looked archaic and indecipherably mysterious.

The first raindrops hit me as I stood staring at the house, feeling a painfully sweet mixture of home and loss. It felt right to be here, right to be in Arcata, in this spot, on this earth under the trees and the waxing moon, and yet how it hurt me, too, the very shortness of my time on earth.

I was caught in mid-life, between the cramped and chaotic childhood I'd escaped, the travels that had shaped and fed my curiosity and delight, and a future that might lead me finally to take root somewhere, if only because of advancing age and disability. When you defined yourself as a traveler, as a risk-taker, you weren't thinking of rheumatoid arthritis, you weren't thinking of old age.

I stood under the trees to escape from the wind, and wrapped my arms around myself for comfort. But the rain kept coming. The sky flashed above me with mountain lightning and the thunder rolled in a few seconds later. Perhaps under a tree wasn't the safest place to be. Not for the first time in the past few days I wished I'd paid more attention to those lectures on electricity back in school.

I rushed for the covered porch through the pelting rain, feeling as if I were inside a gigantic galvanic bath. I leaned against the door as into an old friend; the house seemed to welcome me, I thought. Perhaps it was lonely, unlived in so long.

What was it like inside? I hadn't thought to wonder before. I pressed my nose against the window. No furniture or carpets, but a fireplace and richly decorated doorways and doors. I tried the door and, to my surprise, it opened with a rusty creak. In a place like Arcata, there was probably no reason to lock your door.

I slipped into the entryway and then the big main room. Ilona had talked about the doctor and his family who lived here while I was in the changing room today.

"He was collector, painting collector, all kinds things collect. My mother remember when she child she walk past, see the paintings through windows. And so many people come, house always full of people visiting. Arcata different that time ago. No hotels, just nice villas and restaurants by the lake. People come to walk and hunt and fish and swim and dance and laugh. When Transylvania belong to Hungary, but even after, before Ceauşescu."

Now I walked through the empty, dusty rooms, imagining a night like this one, a spring night seventy-five or a hundred years ago, with a tempest breaking around the sturdy house and inside a crowd dancing to a Gypsy band, eating and drinking and flirting. They wouldn't have had electricity then, only oil lamps and candles, and the house would have been alight inside and out, protecting, sheltering, embracing.

Upstairs I found bedroom after bedroom, empty of furniture, creaking when I walked on the floorboards. I stood at the curved window of the turret room looking out on the wild night as if I were in a lighthouse and the trees were waves breaking all around me. I had turned off my flashlight and the moon was behind clouds; my only illumination was the intermittent blue-white crackle of lightning. From time to time, through the noise of the wind, came the howling of the dogs, or perhaps they were wolves.

Then, through the trees I spied something white and ghostly. It moved up the street and through the gate. It seemed to be a figure, but because of the darkness and heavy rain I couldn't see a face or hands or feet. Only a pale, translucent, spectral shape, like a spirit floating, not walking, through the trees. I clutched my flashlight, but didn't dare turn it on. It wouldn't reach down far enough, would only serve to highlight me at the window.

The apparition floated up the steps to the house. It was on the porch. I remembered the door was unlocked. My heart was pounding like a dentist's drill in my mouth. I could hardly breathe. I had lived through some adventures in my time, some frightening moments of wondering if I was going to be killed by a mugger in São Paulo, a wretched time of it in Thailand with dengue fever, a terrifying half-hour when our boat overturned on the Amazon and it was found that one passenger had been eaten by piranhas. But all those adventures had happened in the real world. They gave an edge to life, a feeling of having survived, and—afterwards—were very good stories indeed.

This was my first encounter with the spirit world and I didn't like it one bit. I pressed myself against the window and wondered if I could possibly climb out and onto the roof. But if a banshee could float into the house like that, it could surely float out of the window after me. Oh Sweet Mary, have mercy on my soul, I knew now my mother was right: the only thing between me and evil was my little silver crucifix on a chain, and I had stopped wearing that when I was fourteen.

Well, that was a big mistake.

Perhaps this house was haunted after all, and the ghost was the daughter of the family, who still lived on here at night, and didn't take kindly to tourists.

Or—a more frightening thought—perhaps it was the undead body of Dr. Pustulescu, risen from the autopsy table and stalking the dark countryside in search of new victims.

From downstairs I heard a whispering sound, as if the apparition were talking to someone or calling for me. I couldn't help it: I got down on my knees and prayed.

"Dear Lady Mary, Mother of God, I know I've been out of touch for the last thirty years, but it's not that I haven't thought of giving you a call from time to time. I've got your number somewhere in my book. . . ."

Now it was coming upstairs. I jumped up, and pulled

out my Swiss Army knife. *Donnerwetter!* Like hell I was going to lie down and let some banshee stop my heart with fright. It was more likely that this was the Galvanic Killer, and I had been getting too close to the truth for comfort. Never mind, I'd defend myself to the death. I stood away from the window in the shadow and waited to attack. But it knew my name, how did it know my name?

"Cassandra," it hissed loudly. "Cassandra?"

I couldn't do anything but clutch my knife and wait. It was coming down the hall, coming closer; it was standing in the doorway. . . .

"Nadia?" I said. "What the hell are you doing here in your nightgown?"

"I saw you go by," she said in French. "My flat is above the tourist office. I couldn't sleep because of the wind and because . . . I had so many thoughts. I was looking at the lake, I saw you go by. I was only going to go out for a minute . . . to tell you something . . . but I couldn't see where you had gone. Then the thunder and lightning started. I came to the house. . . . "

She was shivering with cold and her nightgown was soaked clear through and sticking to her body. Her long dark hair was no longer in its untidy bun, but hanging in wet strands down her flushed cheeks. She wasn't wearing her glasses, and her slippers were coated with mud.

I was glad I'd put on so many clothes. "Take off that nightgown right away," I said. I stripped off one of my sweaters, the long one, and gave it to her, along with my heavy socks. "There's wood in the fireplace, I saw some. I'll light a fire and we'll get you dried out."

The maelstrom increased outside, but within ten minutes I had a good fire going. Whoever took care of this house must have to keep it warm in winter, for there was kindling and some paper as well as birch logs. Nadia said little as I worked on the fire, but draped her wet night-gown nearby so it could dry out. Although she was rounder than me, I was taller, so the sweater came down to her knees. This was a relief, as the sight of her full stomach and large, pendulous breasts through the clingy wet white nightgown had been mildly disturbing.

Finally I asked her what it was that she had needed to tell me.

"Today you asked me about Dr. Pustelescu," she said. "I didn't tell you all I knew."

"Ah."

"And do you know why I didn't tell you?"

"No."

"Because I knew you would not understand some things."

"Try me."

"It is complicated."

"Yes."

Nadia was silent a moment and then said softly, "I'm not used to speaking freely, to telling the truth. I keep looking over my shoulder to see if anyone is here, and deep in my bones I feel that the walls must have microphones, even though my head knows they do not."

The flames caught and I moved closer to the fire with my hands out to warm them. Nadia crept closer too.

"What must be hard for you to understand," she said, "is that there are so few in this country who are not implicated, who did not collaborate in some way with the Ceauşescu regime. It was a moral poison. In the right universe you should have a clear choice. If you choose one thing, it will affect you like this; if you choose another, something else will happen. But here it wasn't simple. The

Securitate was not often violent in Romania. They did not usually put people in jail, they did not usually torture us, they didn't send us to concentration camps. They simply created an atmosphere—how can I explain it?—that they knew everything and controlled your life and that if you did not cooperate you would be punished. We were all afraid, and the worst fear we had was that everyone around us was in the Securitate and that there was no one to trust. You talked perhaps to your family, perhaps to a very trusted friend, but not to most people, not to neighbors. And many of us cooperated with the Securitate too. They came and said, This is what we want to know. Often it was nothing. Simply about your job, who you worked with, et cetera. You told them, because it was easier than not telling them. So you got into a habit of talking to them, not thinking that you were betraying anyone, not thinking that you were doing anything wrong. Until one day they asked you a different question, and it was not so easy then to stop answering, to say, I told you other things, but not this. And often, they knew the answer already to something you were holding back, so you thought, Why not tell them, if they know already."

"But this was all before the revolution, yes?" I asked.

"Old habits continue," said Nadia. "And old memories. I came to Arcata to get away from Bucharest, to start over. But there were those here who knew me. Pustulescu knew about me."

"What did he know about you?"

"About my work."

"But you were a teacher."

"No. I mean the work I did after I stopped teaching in the provinces and came back to Bucharest."

Nadia looked down at her plump knees poking out from under the sweater. Had she been a prostitute? I wondered. A baby broker? A spy?

"I was one of those . . . who helped women abort," she said. "Because it was illegal for doctors, and because many women did it themselves and hurt themselves, I helped them. For a fee. It wasn't long before the Securitate knew. They threatened to jail me at first. Then they said I could continue—everyone knew that abortions were still going on—but that I would have to tell them the names of the women. In this way they were able to go to these women and let them know that they knew, and so extend their influence. This was my choice, my false choice. I could stop helping women and perhaps go to jail myself. Or I could continue to help them and to betray them at the same time."

"But I don't understand. Dr. Pustulescu wasn't a gynecologist. How would you have come in contact with him?"

"He had a wife, didn't he? He had girlfriends, he had mistresses. He had Margit right here. I have given four abortions to Margit. I told her I would not do this one. She must ask someone else, she must go to Tîrgu Mureş, a proper hospital, not my bedroom." Nadia covered her face with her hands. "That time is over for me now. I work for Carpaţi, I am a tourist agent, I try to make people happy."

I was still trying to take all this in, and the possible implications.

"Why were you afraid of Pustulescu knowing what you'd done? After all, the Securitate knew and didn't put you in jail. And it was before the revolution—abortion is legal now. People should admire you for what you did."

"Carpaţi said when they sent me to Arcata that Dr. Pustulescu hardly ever came to this hotel, that he was old and sick and ready to die. But very soon after I arrived he came to me, very healthy and strong, and said, *Bon,* Nadia, we have a secret, don't we? He didn't care about the abortions. He knew that I had been an informer for the Securitate, that was the hold he had on me. He said he would tell Gabor and everyone in Arcata if I didn't help him."

"What did he want from you?"

"Only information, he said. Just like the Securitate. *He* was part of the Securitate too, you know. Information on tourists, information on the clinic, on Gabor. He had been used to controlling the treatment center before the revolution and he still thought he should know everything that went on and that he should get most of the money from the tourists. He didn't need money, he had plenty of money. He just didn't like Gabor to have money."

"And then he quarreled with Gabor about something and then he was killed, and you think Gabor killed him."

"Yes. . . . " Nadia was more hesitant than this morning.

"Was it money they fought about? Was it control? Could it have been anything else?"

"One was Romanian, the other Hungarian." Nadia shrugged. "They could have fought about anything."

"Tell me the truth, Nadia. I won't care if you killed him. But . . . did you?"

"I know it appears I had a reason. I *did* have a reason. But I didn't kill him."

"Do you still report to anyone?" I thought of Nadia coming out of the police station this morning with her eyes averted.

Again she hesitated. She clearly wanted to say, I'm only a tourist agent, I only want to make people happy. But she said, "It's not easy. They still ask, but I don't answer anymore."

I put another log on the fire. Her nightgown was still

soaking wet and the night outside as stormy as ever. Nadia had moved closer to the fire and closer to me during her story. I felt the warmth of her full body at my side, and it was both nourishing and erotic. For such a small woman she had a lot of flesh on her.

We sat for a long while looking into the fire and feeding it with more logs that I found on the back porch. When we touched each other it was in French, the best language for love. The storm went on most of the night, but after a while the fierce bursts of lightning and thunder stopped and there was only the steady, strong drumbeat of rain on the roof and against the windows.

❧ CHAPTER SEVENTEEN ❧

WHEN I AWOKE the next morning, Nadia was gone and sun poured through the windows of the villa. My sweater and socks lay in a neat heap and the nightgown was gone. If it hadn't been for that evidence I would have been tempted to believe that the night had been just a dream, and Nadia a visitor from the spirit world.

I walked out into a world transformed. A brilliant morning sky stretched above me, blue as a bright birthday ribbon tying up a splendid and dazzling universe. Water droplets everywhere sparkled like tiny globes of light, and wildflowers—rose, canary yellow, ivory and sapphire— were more abundant than only yesterday. Yesterday was April. Today was May. The air was soft in the sun and crisp under the firs. You could drink air like this. You could swim it.

"*O saisons! O châteaux!*" I shouted. Then I remembered the rest. "*Quelle âme est sans défauts?*" What soul is guilt- less? Had Nadia been trying to tell me something? Oh well, I'd worry about that later.

The porch gave a friendly creak as I stepped off onto the pebbled walkway. I looked at my watch. If I hurried, I'd be in time for my saline bath, followed by a nice hot packing of mud. At the moment, nothing sounded better.

While soaking in the tub I took the opportunity to question Ilona about Nadia. Did people in Arcata like her even though she was Romanian? Did she come often to the treatment center? Was she friends with anyone in particular? I was afraid that after last night I might not be as objective about her as I should.

"Nadia very nice woman," said Ilona. "No husband, no children, just like you. But not widow, never married. Sad." Ilona shook her head. "A woman not married, not happy. Alone. No . . . sexual relations . . . sad."

"She seems happy enough to me," I said. From a few hints last night I had a suspicion that Nadia might have had some previous practice. "So you don't mind her being Romanian?"

"Hungarian, Romanian—if you woman you suffer under all government. Important thing, Nadia try to help Arcata. She help everybody. Is good."

On the way to the basement I ran into Gladys, who was also due for an hour of hot mud. She'd just had her shot of Ionvital from Dr. Gabor, and was manifesting the energy and euphoria I'd heard about. In her red flannel bathrobe she looked like a firecracker about to ignite.

"Cassandra, I can't tell you how great I'm feeling. Twenty years younger," she said exuberantly. "Thirty or more. Heck, I didn't feel this great when I was in my twenties! And to think that before I left the States I was thinking of selling my business and moving to a retirement home! No way, José! The only thing that makes me sad is that Evelyn couldn't be here with me."

"So is it Margit or Dr. Gabor who gives you the shots?"

"Dr. Gabor, of course. Between you and me, I'm a little worried about Margit." Gladys tapped her forehead. "She's covering something up. You think she did it?"

"If she did, he probably deserved it. He'd sexually abused her for years. But having a motive doesn't automatically mean you're guilty. It takes someone who's willing to cross a moral line, or who doesn't see that the line is there. Who's capable of that? I don't know."

"Well, I'll tell you this: I'm not going to be driven out of Arcata by those Romanian bully-boys. Nadia's been trying to convince me to go to Bucharest and take refuge in the American Embassy, but I'll be damned if they're going to hound me out of here before I've finished my treatments!"

Optimism in Archie's case often seemed more like denial, but Gladys's positive outlook was the real thing. She didn't think she was in any danger of being arrested or jailed, but if she were she'd put up a fight. She probably didn't need my help at all.

But I had gotten curious about the incident at the galvanic baths. Whether or not it was murder, there was some mystery surrounding Pustulescu's death, and I wanted to know what it was.

I was getting with the program on the mud packing. Lie still and turn obediently and, most important, don't shriek when the hot black mud hits your pubic zone. My medical diagnosis was rheumatoid arthritis of the knee, but I guessed the mud-packing ladies were so used to fertility problems that they just glopped it on in the area of my dormant reproductive organs anyway.

Mummified in my little mud-and-cotton cocoon and listening to the soothing swoosh and drip of water, as the thick silty heat squeezed between my thighs, I thought of Egypt. Yes, I'd been there, but it was long ago. Perhaps the second half of my life would be about retracing my steps. Egypt was one of the first countries I'd dreamed of going to, one of the first places, with its pharaohs and pyramids, that had caught my imagination as a child. I remembered a *National Geographic* I'd seen in fifth grade about Queen Nefertiti, and how it had not been enough just to read about her, but necessary to vow to go to where she'd lived.

My mother had said, "You're not going anywhere if you don't start minding your mother and paying more attention in church. You'll be going to hell before you go to Egypt."

But my father, who was, after all, brother to the aunt who gave us the *National Geographic* subscription, had been encouraging.

"Someday we'll take the whole family to Egypt. Why not?" he'd said.

He'd been drinking, of course, but even a drunkard can dream.

It set *me* dreaming, dreaming in cold Michigan, of heat, alluvial mud, palm trees and ruins submerged in the Nile. Of King Tut's gold and precious metals, of slit-eyed stone cats and women with thin gauze dresses. Of asking the Sphinx some hard questions. About God, families and why things had to be the way they were.

Yes, this trip I'd go to China, but after that definitely Egypt. Egypt for months and months, and after that all of

Africa, never to return to England, always to be on the move, she-who–does-not-stop, that was me, Cassandra, that was what made me different from my family working for the Upjohn Company and having children and buying pickup trucks and going to Mass and drinking and having heart attacks. I wasn't only a dreamer but a traveler, heat and love were my elements and I would never stop never go back never be cold again. . . .

Far away in the land of the twin crowns, under the hot African sun, it took me a few moments to become fully aware of a loud commotion somewhere at the other end of the room. A series of screams traveled down the row of cubicles like vocal dominos.

"What's going on?" I asked in all the languages I was capable of. In vain. The woman on the table next to me in the cubicle was frantically wiggling out of her cocoon of sheets; she'd managed to get one arm out and was unwrapping herself.

"*Rendőrség!*" she said. Archie's Hungarian phrase book could have helped me, but unfortunately I had no arms to reach for it. The muslin trapped me like a shroud around a mummy.

There must be a fire, I thought. The mineral smell of the mud would mask any scent of smoke. Or an earthquake. Hadn't Ilona hinted at the fact that this place was falling down? I looked up at the ceiling and saw cracks. Big buildings like these shouldn't be constructed on soft saprogenic mud. In a few minutes perhaps we'd be part of the element that we originally crawled out from.

These thoughts took milliseconds, as I writhed frantically inside my muddy winding sheet. A feeling of panic was palpable in the corridor. The screaming got louder, and the attendants ran back and forth shouting either warnings or instructions. A minute or two later the first

233

black-bedaubed figures began to appear, in flight. Their white hands, faces, and feet made them look like pale root vegetables recently pulled from dark wet earth.

Finally, I squeezed my hand up to the top of the muslin sheets and looked for the start of the folding. The woman next to me was already unwrapped; she was just starting to help me unpeel my cocoon, when we heard men's voices shouting above the female shrieks, and with that my companion was off, leaving me to unfold the last of my chrysalis myself. Feet pounded past; it was a stampede of turnips. I sat on the side of my narrow table, the blood rushing to my head and muddling my escape plan. Should I run too? Yes, if it were a fire; no, if an earthquake. Then I should get under a doorway.

"Oh no you don't." To my astonishment these words were shouted in English, and in a very peppery way too. A blackened Gladys appeared in the open space by the showers, with a bucket of mud in one hand and a wooden mop handle in the other. She seemed to be fending off someone or something. Or else she had just gone crazy, like everyone else around me.

I peered around the corner of my cubicle and saw that her antagonists were the two young Romanian policemen of the day before. One of them looked cowed and horrified, but the other was steadily advancing on Gladys with a pair of handcuffs.

I got up unsteadily and went to her aid.

"Gladys, what's going on?"

"They're trying to arrest me!" She feinted with the bucket of mud, and the two boys drew back. One of them looked as if he would never get his eyes back to their proper shape. I consoled myself by thinking that I wasn't *exactly* naked. All the important bits were covered, so to speak.

I mustered up as much Romanian as I could, and where I didn't know the Romanian, threw in a kind of Franco-Italian.

"You can't come down here and arrest this American woman. You don't have any proof. First of all, you don't know that Pustulescu didn't have a heart attack, and secondly, I think that Gladys was set up. But the main thing is timing, boys. This is a sacred place, this is women's space."

"It's no use, Cassie," said Gladys. "They don't want to talk about it. Better grab some mud."

It was a scene from of one of the First People's creation myths. Out of the chaos of darkness and water, out of the pulsating mysteries of the fecund earth, out of the loins of the Great Mother herself, two almost indeterminately-sexed figures had emerged—me and Gladys. We had met-amorphosed from chaos, from a fertile soil that contained within it every sort of potency and possibility. Primal beings, we stood alone, confused and yet alert. Then, as if realizing a vital impulse to dive into the goo whence we'd come and to create other beings like ourselves, we looked around until we saw one of the hot-mud-bucket carts behind some curtains. Quickly I filled a bucket of my own with steaming globs of black silt and, rushing back to Gladys's side, tossed it directly at the stiffly pressed blue uniform of one of the policemen.

"Okay, now we're talking," said Gladys, letting fly her own bucket of mud and coating the other cop in oozy black earth. "Now we're going to town."

The mud-drenched Romanians, furious now instead of just aggressively doing their duty, came towards us with renewed determination. The younger one held out the handcuffs, but the bigger and older one took out his gun and pointed it first at Gladys and then at me. He didn't speak, judging that actions spoke louder than words.

"Holy Moly," said Gladys, slopping him with another bucket. "You've got to disarm him, Cassie."

"Me! What if it's loaded?"

"Oh heck, the big chump isn't going to shoot us. Probably. Jump him."

I made a flying leap and the two of us came down hard in a fertile puddle of hot mud, the big chump somewhat harder than me because I was sitting on him. The gun went flying. "Now what, Gladys? He's squirming uncomfortably."

Gladys gave me and my hostage another good slopping. The other policeman, the younger one, who was not quite so bespattered, seemed to be thinking twice about this whole adventure. He didn't take his gun out from his holster. "Ladies, ladies," he said plaintively. "It's my job."

"Sit tight, honey," Gladys instructed me. "Don't let the big guy get away. I'll deal with this other babe in the woods. He's going to be putty in my hands."

But already the big guy under me was rolling towards his gun. We grappled. In some respects, I had the advantage. Naked, I was like an oiled seal, squeezing through his grasp.

Sweet Jesus, this was probably my mother's worst fantasy about the kind of thing I'd been up to since leaving Kalamazoo.

"Gladys, I'm losing him. Do something or he'll get the gun again."

"Sorry Cassie, I've got my hands full with the young'un." She combined a karate kick to his knee with a bucket of mud over his head. The bucket stayed there a moment, giving the boy the look of a robot.

I couldn't help laughing and the big guy chose that moment to heave me off him so that I went sliding stomach-first through a big black puddle.

He was reaching for the gun. . . .

And then, from an unexpected direction, a huge slurp of mud came flying. It hit my hostage squarely in the face and momentarily blinded him.

I turned to look: a battalion of women, coming in twos and threes, was massing behind us with buckets. None had showered or gotten dressed: they were all wonderfully barbaric with streaks on their faces as well as their thighs and shoulders, with their torsos caked with black as if they wore breastplates. Their bedaubed faces were set in expressions of resolution. For most of them this was probably the first time they had stood up to authority of any sort, much less Romanian police authority, much less stood up en masse, in solidarity.

As if to an unheard clarion call to arms, they began to plunge their hands into the hot mud and to fling handfuls at the cops. One of the women grabbed the gun and buried it in a bucket of silt; another helped me to my feet, while the others barraged my hostage with a steady rain of mud.

And as they fought and threw and tossed, the women began to talk, and then to shout and then to laugh and then to scream. I could only imagine what they were saying, since most of it was in Hungarian, and all of it was at a very high volume.

Perhaps it was something like: "You stinking Ceauşescu agents, you worked for a man who took the wealth of this country and spent it on a goddamned palace, a man who turned off the electricity and heat all over the country and let the people starve while he dined on caviar and strawberries in winter. You stood by while he destroyed our traditional villages and moved us into apartment blocks so that people like you could spy on us. You made us inform on each other."

237

Maybe they were saying something like this: "You tried to control our bodies for twenty years, denied us birth control and watched us to see if we got pregnant. You wouldn't let us have abortions, and let us die when we did it ourselves. You made us put our children in orphanages because we couldn't feed them, you gave them AIDS because you refused to sterilize the needles or to import rubber gloves. You did all this to us and now you deserve everything, every grain of mud we're heaping on you. May you rot in hell!"

Or maybe they were just shouting, "Nyah-nyah-nyah!"

The men had descended into our netherworld, into the realm of women, into the domain of the primal womb; they were two pathetic mortals surrounded by powerful creator hags who were rapidly reducing them to slimy slugs of ooze. They were emissaries of the sky gods being driven back by the earth goddesses. They were marauding Kurgans with weapons of death who had been met by the handmaidens of the Old Religion, by votaries of the Great Goddess who weren't going to put up with any shit. By Inanna, by Artemis, by Durga and Afrekete, we should have done this a long time ago.

"Say Gladys," I said. "Do you really think you should be holding his head under the mud like that? After all, we don't want to kill him."

"Sorry, Cassie. You're right. I'm getting a little carried away here." When she released her victim, he bolted sideways, scrabbled to his feet and began to run, slipping and wobbling, away from us, all the while emitting a low wheeze that sounded like a squashed rubber duck.

"Get moving, toad-face!" Gladys shouted. "And don't forget your pal."

The two policemen, almost unrecognizable in their coats of black, staggered and slipped past us into the hallway, while the women shouted their triumph and crowded around me and Gladys, touching our faces and shaking our hands.

What a moment! What a victory! Jack was right. If history had recorded more events like this in the books, it would have been a lot more fun to study in school.

"Now how the heck," said Gladys. "are we going to get this fool stuff out of our hair?"

It took us a long while to clean the mud off the walls and the floor, and then off ourselves. I felt, even more than the first time I'd had the mud-bath experience, like a wet spaghetti noodle. At this rate, I was going to need a rest cure after I left Arcata.

When Gladys and I finally got ourselves clothed and out of the basement, we encountered Dr. Gabor and his new friend Eva Kálvin strolling the corridor.

"Oh Cassandra," Eva said nervously. "Zoltán, that is, Dr. Gabor, suggested I teach some medical gymnastics while I'm here."

"Were you practicing last night?"

She had the grace to blush. "I knocked on your door after dinner, but you didn't seem to be in. I didn't find you this morning either."

"That's because I was celebrating Beltane out in the woods."

"Doc," Gladys broke in. "We've had another incident, have you heard? We headed them off at the pass though. I don't think they'll be bothering us any time soon."

"I agree," said Gabor. "I think we will not see the police again. I saw them running out of the treatment center. They looked very bad, very muddy."

"We had 'em on the run, Doc. You should have seen

Cassie. She was my right hand through the whole battle, she stuck with me, and I mean *stuck* through the whole bust–up. We were firing rounds at them like we were defending the Alamo. Pow! They never knew what hit 'em."

I left Gladys giving Gabor and Eva a blow-by-blow account of the recent attempted arrest and Alamo defense, and went out into the square in front of the hotel. I intended to find Nadia; I found, instead, a small crowd of familiar faces gathered around a big Volvo station wagon with German plates that had apparently just pulled up.

A tall woman in jeans and a sweatshirt, with taffy-colored short hair and glasses, was standing quietly listening to Archie as he waved his arms about and pointed at the hotel and then in the direction of Lupea. Cathy Snapp was shrugging in a kind of counterpoint rhythm to her father's gesticulations, while Jack and Bree looked on.

What next? I thought, and went to investigate.

❧ CHAPTER EIGHTEEN ❧

LYNN SNAPP HAD LEFT Munich the moment Archie had called her yesterday afternoon and had driven all night to get here. She didn't look like the sort of woman to be fazed by much of anything.

"This is Cassandra Reilly," Archie introduced us. "Cassandra's a world traveler and translator and she's been a lot of help."

"It may look problematic at the moment," I said. "But at least you don't have to worry about Emma missing any violin lessons."

"I brought all the food from the house with me," Lynn said. "And a bag of fresh rolls and bread. Is anybody hungry?"

Is anybody hungry? Frau Sophie would go crazy if she could see the bags with salami and bread sticking out, the boxes full of fresh fruits and vegetables. We stood around the car like ravenous beasts and for at least ten minutes no one said anything but "Oh my god, a banana" and "To-matoes, I'm dreaming."

If Archie was an exploding sun, radiating good will and curiosity in every direction, Lynn was an imploding sort of celestial object; she absorbed energy like a black hole and never grew any larger or brighter. Information went in her direction and somehow vanished without obviously being heard. She gave only infrequent signs of reacting to what anyone said. In a peculiar way, she reminded me of Emma.

"Mom," Cathy said with her mouth full. "I am so *glad* you came."

"There's really nothing to worry about, honey," said Archie.

"This has been a totally weird experience," said Cathy.

"I think that Emma has probably been having a ball," said Archie.

"Mom, I can't believe you actually came here in the first place to get a kid."

"Honey, this time we've seen so much more of the countryside than you and I did three years ago. I don't think you and I realized how ethnically diverse it was. You're going to love hearing about the Székelys. I didn't realize that this part of Romania had so much history. The Székelys were warrior tribes that were encouraged to settle here in the Eastern Carpathians as border guards in the twelfth century. Well, can you imagine, it turns out that Emma is a Székely, not a Romanian. Now isn't that going to be something to be proud of when she gets to school and wants to tell people about her ethnic background? You know, I'd like to do a piece for the *Gleaner* on the Székelys and their customs and traditions, I think our readers..."

"Cathy," said her mother. "I'm a little worried about Willa Cather. She seems to have lost the top of her head.

Was it a brainstorm, or did you have a fight with someone?"

"Uh, no... it's just the way you wear it these days.
Mom, I've been thinking—how would you feel if I went
someplace else besides Harvard? Like Stanford or even...
Berkeley?"

"I think right now we'll all concentrate on going to
Lupea."

A decision was made to leave immediately and somehow
Jack and Bree were invited along. The three of us sat in the
back seat, while up in front Archie and Cathy competed
for Lynn's attention (how could poor Emma have gotten a
word in edgewise, even if she'd been able to speak?) and
occasionally brought us into it.

"What's this about Berkeley?" Archie said at some
point. "Isn't that where Bree goes? Have you been talking
to her?"

"No," said Bree firmly.

"Where did you go, Cassandra?" he asked. "Western
Michigan? Ann Arbor?"

"Neither."

"A little farther afield, eh?"

"You could say that."

"Even if I went to Berkeley," interrupted Cathy, stung
by Bree's indifference, "I wouldn't do anything stupid like
Film Studies. I'm thinking of pre-med. I'd like to help
people with incurable diseases."

"That's my girl," said Archie.

"Are you still reading *The Magic Mountain*?" asked her
mother.

"I'll find the cure for AIDS," said Cathy, somewhat
wildly. "Then you'll be sorry."

"Well, you might as well go somewhere else," said Bree. "You wouldn't fit in at Berkeley."

"Why not?" Cathy turned all the way around and fixed Bree with a look compounded of equal parts hopeless attraction and fierce antagonism. "Because I'm not bisexual? How do you know I'm not?"

Bree laughed contemptuously. "In your dreams."

"Did you go East to school?" Archie asked me, in some desperation to change the subject.

"No."

"West then?"

"People know they're gay when they're my age," said Cathy. "Don't they, Mom?"

"I don't know, dear. That's wasn't true for me."

"Don't say you went to a southern college, Cassandra," Archie said.

"Archie, what does it matter?"

"Background, background," he said. "I'm working on your profile for the *Gleaner*." Suddenly he thought of a solution to this uncomfortable conversation. "Okay, Jack. Cassandra. Let's talk about travel. I want to hear about the best trip you ever took."

"Best as in best, or best as in worst?" asked Jack.

"The best trips are always the worst trips," I explained. "Terrible journeys become delightful in recollection, chiefly by becoming even more terrible than when experienced."

"I think I see," said Archie. "How about the best of the worst then?"

Jack and I pondered this. Was an earthquake worse than dysentery? Was being lost worse than being on a bus ride from hell, crammed in between goats and sick children? There were so many ways that travel could go wrong. Some problems—transport that arrived late or not at all, unwelcome male attention (that irritant of our youth had diminished as we'd grown older, though never entirely), food that did not agree—had happened to each of us so often that they seemed more inconveniences than disasters. The bottom line was that the things you were afraid of in travel were the things you were afraid of in life. To get through fear was to survive, and to tell a story about survival was to testify both to your own inner strength and to the general beneficence of the universe.

Jack began. "I was on a bus in Bolivia. I'd been traveling with my friend Edith from Germany, but she got dysentery and ended up in a hospital in La Paz. They didn't think I had it, but in fact I did, and was getting progressively sicker. I'd left La Paz and was on my way to the Yungas valleys. The bus was a local and very slow. Because it didn't have a loo and I was needing to relieve myself pretty often, I'd get off at every stop and look for someplace halfway hidden. We were passing through a stark, high landscape, gaining in altitude; it was bitterly cold and night was falling. I couldn't see my way very well away from the bus and fell into a kind of gully. While I was squatting, something stung me, I couldn't see what, but I panicked, thinking it was a scorpion.

"I staggered up from the gully, weak from dysentery, with a stinger in my behind, and saw the bus roaring off without me. I tried to run for it, but because of the twilight I couldn't see a thing, and tripped and sprained my ankle. All my stuff, except for my passport and money, was on the bus.

"I hardly ever cry, but as I lay there on the ground, I thought, This is the absolute end, this is the worst moment of my life, nothing could be worse than this. Then I heard footsteps. . . . "

Jack paused so that we could imagine rescue and went

on. "When I looked up, two men in uniform were standing over me with submachine guns pointed at my head."

"Don't forget their German Shepherd," I murmured.

"*And* they had a huge German Shepherd that looked ready to tear me limb from limb."

"And you didn't speak enough Spanish to explain."

"Cassandra, I'm telling this! So I'm lying there, thinking, Go ahead, put me out of my misery. But no, they say something, and then when I don't move, they haul me up and drag me to their guard house and they . . . "

Archie interrupted anxiously, "Is this something Cathy shouldn't hear?"

"Dad, you keep treating me like a baby. I'm not a baby!"

"And they dressed my ankle, pulled out the stinger and showed me it was just a nettle, gave me some hot soup, and put me into a warm bed with blankets. And the next day they drove me to the hospital in La Paz, where I spent the next two weeks!"

Bree said, "You've lived such an incredible life, Jack!"

"I've got a South American story too," I said. "Jack and I had been traveling in Ecuador ["Not fair!" Jack poked me in the side], and had decided we wanted to go to the Galápagos Islands. Actually it had been my big dream for years to get there. We'd made our boat reservations from Quito and then the day before we were supposed to leave we traveled to the port city of Guayaquil.

"The next morning we had a big argument about something . . . "

"You were being completely obnoxious . . . "

"And I took my stuff and said I'd meet up with her at the boat at six that evening. I went to a bank to change some money and a few blocks later someone robbed me at knifepoint and took my bag with all my money and identification.

"This turned out to be one of the times when having two passports was a very mixed blessing. When I went to the police station to report the loss, I told them I was American. Meanwhile, someone had found my bag and brought it in. It had my boat ticket to the Galápagos and my Irish passport. Apparently the thief had decided to keep the American one. The police found this all very suspicious. They said I wasn't going anywhere until they found out who I *really* was.

"I don't know if you've ever had one of those dreams where you're late for the airport and you haven't packed and you have too many clothes to fit in the suitcase and your taxi hasn't come and all the time the clock is ticking very round and large on the wall, and you keep only having five minutes before departure but you know you'll never make it. Well, that was what my day in the police station was like. They locked me up in a cell and wouldn't let me make any phone calls. I kept telling them that I had a boat to catch and that my friend would be worried about me, but they ignored me until finally they got a confirmation from the American Embassy in Quito that I really was an American citizen. They let me go just before six o'clock.

"I raced to the dock. I *knew* that Jack would have been terribly worried about me, and that she would have been searching the entire city, and that she would never let the boat leave without me . . ."

"I just thought that you were mad at me and had decided not to come," Jack said. "Hell, I'm going to be hearing this story for the rest of my life! Aren't I?"

"Yes, you are! I still haven't been to the Galápagos, and

now there are too many tourists."

"Well," said Archie. "If that's the life of the world traveler, maybe it's better to stay home. I'm glad I don't have stories like that to tell."

"But our first trip to Romania was a little like that, Archie," said Lynn. "Don't you remember the day when we were in a taxi with our lawyer Eugen and suddenly we were surrounded by a gang of men in blue shirts and blackened faces who were supposed to be miners? They surrounded the taxi and smashed one of the windows and were rocking it back and forth. We were terrified; we made it to the American Embassy but the doors were locked. Finally we got back to our hotel with the other people looking for children, and we had to barricade ourselves in for two days."

Cathy looked at her father accusingly. "You never wrote about that, Dad."

"Well, it's not an experience I like to remember," he said. "Besides, I'm sure it wasn't directed at us *personally*."

In the robin's-egg-blue house, it was as if time had stood still. Emma and her grandfather were still practically in the same positions, fiddling away. We could see them through the window.

An irate and tired-looking Zsoska came out of the house. Her frosted hair was piled loosely on her head and she was wearing a rayon negligee with a sweater over it. She made sawing motions with her arm.

"Driving me crazy. No sleeping, only music."

"She's like that at home, too," said Archie. "We have to take the violin away from her at night."

"Hello," said Lynn, holding out her hand. "You must be Zsoska. I'm Lynn, Emma's adoptive mother."

"Emoke staying," said Zsoska, not taking Lynn's hand, but regarding her suspiciously and crossing her arms over her chest.

Lynn just smiled and went over to Emma.

"Hello, Emma," she said.

Emma appeared glad to see her. At least she stopped playing for a moment and smiled at Lynn and allowed herself to be embraced. I wondered if Archie had ever noticed that his wife didn't actually talk very much. Next to the laconic Lynn, Emma's speechlessness didn't seem so unusual.

Cathy's voice broke urgently through the quiet reunion. "Mom, maybe we should just leave Emma here, I mean, this is her real family and everything. She's got a mom and grandparents and everything."

"Don't be ridiculous, Cathy," said Archie, trying to interpose himself between her and Zsoska, so the latter wouldn't understand. "How can you even say such a thing? Emma's your sister. She lives with us. We went to a lot of trouble to get her."

"You spent a lot of money, that's what you did! You bought her! I saw that show on *60 Minutes.*"

"Emoke staying," said Zsoska, arms still folded, her face looking more hawk-like than before.

"Archie," said Lynn easily. "Why don't you bring in the food from the car?"

Eating put Zsoska in a better mood. While Jack and Bree went out to explore the village, Zsoska invited us to sit down. She was prepared to bargain. "I going United States. With Emoke."

"But Zsoska," said Archie. "You wouldn't want to leave your parents. Not your old parents."

249

"Mother, father coming too. You building us house, Snapp."

"Well, Archie," said Lynn. "There's always that prefab yurt you've been threatening to put together for the last five years."

Archie didn't smile. "It's not that you aren't welcome to visit anytime, Zsoska, but think about it. You live in a fascinating culture, the Székely culture. Your roots are here, your folklore, your traditions. It wouldn't be fair to your parents."

Zsoska said something in Hungarian to her father. Bright-eyed, he slapped his knee and nodded. *"Igen, igen"*—the Hungarian word for yes.

"My father wanting come to America."

Cathy said, "Mom, you're not going to let these people live in our backyard in a yurt, are you? It's too totally weird. Everybody in the neighborhood already thinks we're completely insane. You should just leave Emma here if she's happy."

"I suppose we could see about getting them all visas, Archie," said Lynn. "I don't imagine that Zsoska has much of a future here."

"What's she going to do in Ann Arbor?" Cathy demanded. "Work at Denny's? She's a terrible waitress, Mom."

"Lynn, think about it," pleaded Archie. "The complications. Who would be Emma's mother? You don't know Zsoska, she's out of control. She'd be running our lives with her temper tantrums and whims. And her parents? We haven't even met her mother. What if she's like Zsoska? No, Lynn, it's one thing to meet the relatives, it's another to give up Emma. We're going to have to. . . ." he touched his pants pocket lightly to indicate his wallet. "You know."

The gesture wasn't lost on Zsoska.

"Money not enough now, Snapp. United States of America. Or Emoke staying."

"Mom, why don't you ask Emma if she even *wants* to go. Maybe she's happy, maybe she *wants* to stay here."

"All right," said Lynn, turning to Emma, where she sat watching everything with her usual lack of expression.

"Lynn, Emma doesn't know what's going on," said Archie. "You can't ask a four-year-old what she wants. Especially when it's a question that will have a major effect on her whole life."

Lynn ignored him and stretched out her arms to Emma. "Emma. Do you want to come back home with Daddy and Mommy and Cathy, or do you want to stay here?"

"Emoke," said Zsoska, and presumably repeated the same question in Hungarian. She also stood with her arms out, but more as if she were imitating Lynn than expressing her natural desires.

While Lynn looked like Athena, balanced and fair, Zsoska was more like Lilith, cast out of heaven for not being subservient enough, defiant, rebellious, a she-demon dangerous to men and small children.

"Emma doesn't understand what's going on," moaned Archie. "This is inhuman."

"She's nodding," said Cathy. "She wants to stay."

Emma *was* nodding. She stood in the middle of the room between the two women with their arms outstretched and she nodded her head up and down, just like her grandfather a few moments before.

And then she opened her mouth and said, *"Igen."*

I left the house after this, partly to tell Jack and Bree the amazing news that Emma had spoken for the first time, and partly to escape the argument that ensued. As with any Delphic oracle, interpretation was everything. Had Emma meant yes, she wanted to go back to America, or yes (*igen*), she wanted to stay in Lupea?

I found Bree down the road videotaping some picturesque chickens in a yard hung with the bright red and pink washing of a Gypsy family, and Jack examining in great detail one of the carved gates in front of a nearby house.

"I was just reading somewhere," she said, "that there's a centuries-old tradition in this part of Europe of women illustrating embroidery and other folk art with images of the Goddess. Isn't that incredible, that in spite of domination and repression, women have been able to keep their own traditions alive? To find a non-verbal way to tell their own stories? It was women's work, so nobody noticed."

She traced a stylized pattern on the tall wooden gate. "I think I see some Goddess imagery here too."

"You're seeing Goddess imagery in so many places that I'm starting to see it too. And I'm not a spiritual person."

"You can't fight the Zeitgeist," said Jack. "The Goddess is returning." She flashed me her wicked white smile. "I'm thinking about going over to the States for a while," she said.

"You *hate* North America."

"This is the second Californian I've been involved with in four months," she said. "It might be a sign. You know the women's spirituality movement is very big in California."

"What about Eva? Aren't you supposed to be running a business in Budapest?"

"Eva just needed a tax write-off, a financial break, my Australian passport number. It's time to move on."

"Then why not come to China with me? It'll be like old times. It'll be more of an adventure than California, that's for sure. You don't want to lose your edge."

For a moment Jack's gray eyes lit up. I knew she had never been south of Shanghai. Then she shook her curly head. "The ley lines are calling me," she said.

"I give you two months with Bree. Max."

"Not every relationship between an older and a younger woman fits the evil headmistress model, Cassandra. Which you should know very well."

I thought about Dede, who used to joke that I had seduced her. Was that the reason I'd been so edgy around Bree? Because I saw myself at her age, myself with her wild, frightening desire? I'd been less self-assured and more repressed than Bree, unable to name what I felt, but still driven to act. There had been no political movement, no obvious role models to emulate or rebel against. The words for how we felt and what we wanted weren't in print or spoken aloud, though if you knew where to look, you could see the signs everywhere.

"Just don't let her put you in a lesbian vampire film," I said.

"I'm surprised that the subject of vampires hasn't come up more often," she said. "After all, we are in Transylvania."

"Frankly," I said, as we watched a big car come roaring up the dirt road towards us, "I'm starting to think that vampires are the least interesting thing about Transylvania."

What was a Mercedes doing in this part of the world? What was a new Mercedes with German license plates doing stopping in front of Zsoska's house?

A husky blond man in his thirties, dressed in a form-fitting training suit and Adidas sneakers, got out of the car, carrying a big shopping bag and a boom box playing an amplified polka. There were gold chains around his neck and more on his heavy wrists, along with a huge gold watch that shone in the sun.

Could it be Zsoska's jealous Saxon lover, Rolf?

"Excuse me," I said to Jack. "I think the third act is just beginning."

❧ CHAPTER NINETEEN ❧

SOME YEARS AGO, when I was visiting Taiwan, a Chinese friend pointed out a poster of the film *Rebel Without a Cause*. The title had been translated as "To Give Birth To Children Without Teaching Them Whose Fault It Is."

In the extended Reilly family, where the Cult of the Baby was diligently practiced, birth control was forbidden and motherhood was sacred, but motherhood had less to do with raising children than with procreation for the glory of it. Every Reilly woman who became a mother was a goddess of fecundity, but every Reilly child who survived was on his or her own. My mother might think she had too many children, but she never seemed to feel she'd had too many babies. She loved babies so much that she wanted everyone to have them, even Maureen, especially Maureen, who would rather have had an abortion if she'd only known where to go.

Does giving birth make a mother? What about women who are forced to be mothers? Maureen, who had sobbed hysterically on her wedding night and whined bitterly throughout her pregnancy, said, "Once I held that little innocent in my arms, I couldn't imagine not being his mother." But not every reluctant mother feels that way.

Is a mother merely a gateway through which a new soul passes into the physical universe? Is she a snack bar open twenty-four hours a day but only for nine months? Is a mother a house you can live in through your childhood and longer, a house big enough to hold you both, a house where the rooms connect and the doors are open? Or is a mother a hotel? Sometimes with a vacancy, and sometimes full up.

The man was so tall and deep-gutted that he made the front room of the little house seem to shrink to playhouse size. I had missed the first moment of greeting, but Zsoska and Rolf were still at it when I came in. Rolf had lifted Zsoska off the ground and was kissing her vigorously, while the others looked on: Grandpa and Emma indifferently, the elder Snapps in some bafflement, and Cathy with an expression of intense repulsion and curiosity. The atmosphere had changed from that of a Greek tragedy to a television domestic farce. The Bavarian pop music had followed Rolf inside and now sat blaring polkas on the table. A glow of German prosperity transformed the room. Part of it had to do with Rolf, who must have just splashed himself with cologne before he got out of the car, and whose gleaming gold jewelry, solid girth and engineered tan suggested access to all the fabulous riches of the West; and part of it had to do with the riches themselves.

He released Zsoska, lifted the shopping bag up to the table and started pulling out gifts: cassettes, Lindt chocolate bars, a sweater for Zsoska, perfume and a bottle of schnapps, which made Grandpa's eyes light up.

Zsoska got out some small glasses and Rolf poured himself a drink. He had a boxy head under a thatch of thinning, wheat-pale hair and surprisingly small ears. His eyes were blue, not intelligent but not exactly dull either, more like animals in a state of hibernation, surrounded by all that prosperous flesh. If you didn't mind jealousy, he looked like a safe enough bet. Zsoska removed her old sweater and slipped the new one on over her negligee; she unpinned her dramatic hair, sprayed herself with perfume, got out glasses and poured everyone schnapps; keeping up a deliberate whirl of activity and laughter, she took Emma by the shoulders and edged her gently in the direction of Archie and Lynn. She hoped, obviously, that Rolf wouldn't even notice Emma. But there came a moment when Rolf clearly asked Zsoska who all these people were, and then came what I could only guess was something about us being hotel guests from Arcata.

"English? American?" asked Rolf. "I am *German,*" he said with great pride and, raising his glass to us, downed the schnapps in one gulp. Underneath the tanning-salon brown, a ruddy flush was spreading over his cheeks. After Zsoska poured him another shot he held the glass up to her in the manner of a toast, and made a short speech in Hungarian.

The effect on Zsoska was electric. She rushed to him, her yellow and black mane flying, her gold necklaces jingling, and wrapped her arms around his hefty trunk. Then she surprised us all by bursting into loud, gulping sobs.

Archie asked me frantically, "What's going on? Is that the boyfriend?"

"Just a wild guess," I said, "but I suspect Rolf might have asked Zsoska to come with him back to Germany and perhaps even to marry him."

"But what about . . . ?" Archie whispered.

Zsoska wrenched herself out of Rolf's arms. Her mascara was running down her high Tartar cheekbones. She lifted up her glass and smiled brilliantly.

"Going Deutschland," she said. "Going Deutschland tomorrow to live. No more bad times for me. Rolf is missing me!"

Rolf pointed at his chest. "I live Stuttgart since one year. Work Mercedes factory."

"Congratulations, Zsoska," said Lynn. "I hope you'll be very happy." She raised her glass in a toast, and we all joined her.

"Cathy, put that down," said Archie. "You're too young."

Zsoska's eye suddenly fell on Emma. The little girl stood, holding her violin, between Archie and Lynn. Did Emma know Zsoska was her mother? Did Emma understand she was being abandoned again?

Zsoska almost opened her arms, then she folded them tightly across her chest and turned back to Rolf. No, she wasn't going to risk telling him and lose this chance to leave Romania.

Lynn had figured it all out on her own.

"Well, Zsoska," she said cheerfully. "We've enjoyed meeting you and appreciate your hospitality, but it's time for us to get back to the hotel."

"But Lynn," whispered Archie. "We still haven't decided . . ."

"Yes, yes," said Zsoska, herding us towards the door. "You must go, I understanding. Thank you very much. I seeing you another time. You visiting me in Deutschland please."

"Say good-bye to your friend, Emma," said Lynn. "You'll be seeing him again, don't worry."

I didn't really think that Emma had understood, but she went over to the old man and gave him a kiss. Tears came to his eyes and he turned to Zsoska to speak.

She cut him off sharply in Hungarian and practically slammed us out the door.

"Do you think she didn't want Rolf to know about Emma or something?" Archie asked.

Lynn and I looked at each other. "You know, you might be right, dear," said Lynn mildly.

"I guess the question's settled then," Cathy said, sighing heavily. "Emma's coming back home with us." She paused, and took her little sister by the hand that wasn't holding the violin. "I would have missed you, Emma."

On the drive back to Arcata, I sat in front with Lynn and Emma. In the crowded back seat Archie regaled his captive audience with information about the diminishing Saxon population of Transylvania.

"They're all going to Germany now. It's the promised land. They never lost their German citizenship, after all these centuries—even though the Turkish and Greek immigrants we saw all around us in Munich can never become citizens, not even if they live in Germany their whole lives."

Bree sat on Jack's lap and Cathy was noticeably miserable.

I would have liked to tell her something encouraging, but in fact unrequited love never gets any easier.

"What do you think's going to happen?" I asked Lynn.

"Oh, we'll figure something out," she said serenely. It must be reassuring to look at the universe from the perspective of quantum mechanics, to know that even apparent unpredictability and randomness are subject to certain laws and eventually form a pattern.

Lynn reached over and smoothed Emma's forehead. The little girl was tapping out a polka rhythm on her violin case, memorizing it. "You know, I was a lot like Emma as a child. No one ever heard a peep out of me until I was three. I couldn't read until I was seven. I tell Archie not to worry, but he can't help it, you know. Being a writer, words are important to him. But Emma will speak when she has something to say, won't you, Emma?"

"*Igen,*" said Emma.

It occurred to me that Lynn, being a physicist, might know something about the properties of electricity.

"Galvanic baths?" she said. "Well, well. Yes . . . go on."

I told her everything I knew.

"And you say that as far as you know no one tampered with the voltage meter?"

"Nobody noticed any tampering. After it happened, the place was full of people, and the police apparently came immediately."

"Was the doctor holding on to any metal object?" she asked. "A copper pipe that could have led into the ground, for instance?"

"Gladys said he put both hands in the water."

"Hmmm, then it's a puzzle. You say he was very old. Maybe his heart just gave out. Because otherwise I don't see how. . . ." Lynn continued to think. "Unless of course . . . it *was* just distilled water in the basins? Did anybody check?"

"I checked, Mom," Cathy squeezed forward from the back and hung over the seat between us. "I tasted it."

I remembered how several people had referred to the tubs as being drained and washed out between patients.

"What if it weren't distilled water? What difference would it make?"

"Different substances conduct electricity differently," Cathy said, and Lynn nodded.

"That's right," she said. "For instance, even a mild saline solution would conduct the current better than plain H_2O. It wouldn't change the voltage, of course, but it would affect the conductivity, and that might possibly give the solution enough charge to make his heart stop. It's an interesting proposition. If someone made a mistake and filled the tubs with a saline solution. . . . "

I thought of the brochure Gladys had showed me on the train: "Arcata, well-situated on a salt massif. . . " I thought of myself floating in the saline baths. They got the water from the lake, Ilona had said.

"How salty would the water need to be?" I asked.

"An interesting question," Lynn said. "The more the better, I suppose. Water can absorb lots of salt."

I thought of the hundred dusty linen tablecloths in the restaurant, each with its salt and pepper shaker. They might not have much food in Arcata, but they did have lots of salt.

I found Nadia in the square outside the hotel. She and her brother were washing Eva's Polski Fiat with water carried in buckets from the tourist office. Nadia looked completely different from last night. Her dark hair was back in its untidy bun, and her oversize glasses were settled firmly on her pudgy nose. She had on the flowered pink and green dress and the orange polyester suit jacket, and the sharp-toed high heels that made her legs wobble.

Daylight was always a shock, but this could be very awkward.

"Bonjour, ça va?" she said. "Eva's car is finally fixed. Nicolae has fixed it. Show her, Nicolae."

Nicolae crammed his big body in behind the wheel and started it up. After a few unimpressive clunks, the Polski Fiat hummed to life.

"You see, Cassandra?" Nadia beamed. "Eva will be happy now, I think. Now you can go back to Budapest."

She was so cheerful that I wondered if perhaps I'd dreamed the whole thing. I rubbed my neck, where I had seen a slight bruise this morning.

Nadia noticed and winked at me. "The weather has changed very much, hasn't it? Last night it was wild, rough and wild. Today it is calm, like nothing happened."

"Oh, a lot has happened," I said. I told her about Rolf taking Zsoska away to Stuttgart.

"It's better," Nadia declared. "She only causes problems here at the restaurant. If possible I would like to eliminate all problems."

"You eliminate some problems, other problems crop up," I said. "It's the way of the world. Dr. Pustulescu was eliminated, but that caused problems for Gladys."

"Listen, Cassandra," said Nadia. "When you go to Budapest tomorrow, please take Gladys with you."

"But Gladys is happy here. Besides, we know that Gladys didn't murder him."

"Oh, now you say murder? Not just a heart attack?"

"Murder, Nadia," I said firmly. "And I believe I know who Dr. Pustulescu's murderer is. But I don't know what I should do about it. I don't want to tell the police and get this person in serious trouble. I can't help liking this person, and thinking they had a very good reason to kill the doctor."

Nadia stared at me. "All murderers have a reason," she said without flinching. "It is still murder."

"Then you think I shouldn't protect this person? Shouldn't give them a chance to escape?"

"You must do what you think best," she said. "Maybe this person doesn't want to escape." She looked over at Jack and Bree, sitting on a bench by the lake, arms entwined.

"I often think of Paris when spring comes," she said, before turning away to her office to refill the bucket of water. "In the end it is love, not death, that is the important thing in life, *n'est-ce pas, chérie?*"

CHAPTER TWENTY

DR. GABOR WAS sitting in his office reading his Hungarian political review. Because of the microphones in his walls—and I had no reason to suspect they weren't there—I asked him to come outside with me and take a short walk.

We started in the direction of the lake. The May sunshine was warm and the air was as deliciously fresh as ever. It was almost impossible to think that anything had ever disturbed the peace of this idyllic spot.

"So, Mrs. Really. How is your health?"

"I'm feeling very sprightly these days," I had to admit.

"You see? Our Arcata is the best place in the world to live."

"And to die?"

"No one ever dies here," he said jovially. "We live forever."

"Except for Dr. Pustulescu."

"He already lived long enough. Was he going to make

trouble for us for next twenty years?"

"So you're saying he *was* murdered?"

"Murder, always murder on your mind," said Gabor, undisturbed. He really was a very attractive man, except for those demonic eyebrows. "You must be private investigator, I think. You know the clever crime stories of the Czech writer Josef Škvorecký, with his Lieutenant Boruvka? No? But you must read him. He is in exile in Toronto, Canada since many years. He is translated into Hungarian like all important writers."

Not for the first time I noticed that Gabor never mentioned any women authors from Eastern and Central Europe. What about Christa Wolf from the former East Germany? What about the Croatian novelist, Slavenka Drakulić? What about the Hungarian lesbian Erzsébet Galgóczi? She wrote mysteries too.

"Dr. Gabor," I said. "I'm not a private investigator, but I do have an interest in making sure that Gladys isn't punished for a crime she didn't commit, and I admit I have gotten interested in what happened to Pustulescu. I can hardly blame you for wanting to kill Pustulescu. He sounds like a monster."

"Yes, he was a monster," said Gabor, "in thousand ways you cannot begin to understand," and then he went on softly, "But you know, Mrs. Really, I do not kill him. I am a doctor and I take the vow of Hippocrates. Even to do good, I cannot kill. When one lives in a country that is morally corrupt, one cannot do as they do, think as they think, live as they live. The only sanity is to remember that there are countries not like this, other places where the purpose of life is not to lie and cheat and steal, but to create health and happiness for all."

"But you had a motive to kill him," I said. "The two of you had a quarrel and he made you leave your office and took all your patients."

"That is true," said Gabor. "We did quarrel. I had found something out, and I was angry."

"What was it?"

"I am afraid I cannot tell you."

"I know all about Margit."

He was quiet a moment. "I have not said anything to Margit about what happened. I will not say anything to her. It is too painful for both of us."

"You're protecting Margit, aren't you? You quarreled about Margit and what he'd done to her, and then Margit killed him."

"Margit is even less capable of killing someone than I am," said Gabor. "Yes, I quarreled with Dr. Pustulescu about how he had treated her. But I did not kill him for that reason. You must not think so harshly of us, Mrs. Really. We are survivors of a wicked regime, and we try to keep our humanity. If there is a murderer, you must look for someone with no conscience."

"I suppose you think that Nadia did it, that Nadia sneaked in and put a saline solution in the galvanic bath. Just because Nadia is Romanian you think she's capable of murder, don't you?" It was my worst fear that he would say yes, because if Gabor and Margit were out of the running, Nadia seemed like the obvious choice.

"Nadia Pop, oh no," he said. "No, as I said, you must look for someone with no conscience. Nadia has a very big conscience—for a Romanian. But I am interested," he said. "What is it you say about saline solution in the bath?"

We had rounded the small lake and were crossing the road that led up to the fairy-tale house. I could hear the yapping of half a dozen excited dogs.

"Lynn Snapp, Archie's wife, said that was a possibility. That a saline solution might have been substituted for the

267

distilled water in the tubs, and that such a solution might have conducted the electricity more strongly than otherwise."

"If that is the case," said Gabor, "then I apologize. For then it is indeed possible that I have contributed to a crime. But you must excuse me, Mrs. Really, I have now a patient. We will continue to discuss this later, yes? I may have something to tell you."

I let him go, more confused than ever, and continued up the cobbled road, where I could see Gladys and Frau Sophie. The stray dogs that Gladys had managed to collect over the past week were jumping all around them. Like Dr. Pustulescu's evil deeds, their number seemed to increase every time you turned around.

Gladys was bursting with energy, throwing sticks for them and feeding them cold French fries. Frau Sophie, pink-cheeked and effervescent, laughed and kept saying, "*Jesusmaria,* so many dogs." Her rayon dress was as smooth, her pocket handkerchief as crisp as the first time I'd seen her. She'd be going back to Graz soon, radiant and Ionvitalized. Maybe I'd made a mistake not even trying the stuff.

"There you have it," said Frau Sophie to me with a proprietary wave.

"What's that?"

"The villa. My *Gasthaus.* I have just purchased it."

With horror I saw she was pointing to the chocolate fairy-tale house, *my* house. In an instant it was mine no longer and I saw it filled with big boisterous Austrians gobbling wurst and schnitzel, washing everything down with steins of beer served by hefty waitresses in dirndls.

"I think Soph's got the right idea buying that old house," said Gladys. "She's going to bring this town to life again. Between Gabor and Soph, Arcata will be one jumping place. I know I'm planning to come back next year, and I'm going to tell all my pals in Tucson about it. Heck, maybe I'll even start a home for stray dogs here."

She tossed the dogs the last of the French fries and then dashed after them up the hill.

I was still reeling from Frau Sophie's announcement. I wouldn't even be able to stay at the *Gasthaus*. In the first place I wouldn't be able to afford it, and in the second place I wouldn't be able to eat all that rich, heavy, over-salted . . .

"Oh my God," I said. I suddenly saw, in my mind's eye, Frau Sophie's hand poised over her food with the salt shaker. "You!"

Frau Sophie looked at me, puzzled.

"Did you really mean to kill Pustulescu, Frau Ackermann, or just scare him?"

Frau Sophie didn't miss a beat. "It was time for him to go," she said. "I only helped him along a little. Without some help a man like that might have lived forever." Her rosy face looked to me for understanding. "We're all better off with him dead, you know. Many years I've come to Arcata, many years I've taken the treatment. If I go on living to ninety or a hundred, I'll be coming here twenty or thirty more years. Dr. Gabor understands that. He has plans for the clinic, plans for Arcata. I want to help him."

"Did Gabor put you up to it?"

"Oh no," she said proudly. "It was all my idea. I hadn't met Dr. Pustulescu before. But a few days ago, when I arrived in Arcata for my treatment, he was here.

"I had come to do business as well as take the treatment. I had come to meet with the local authorities about my *Gasthaus* plan and to sit down with Dr. Gabor and figure out how to advertise Arcata to Austrians and Germans so they would come again. And what do I find? Dr.

Pustulescu sitting in Dr. Gabor's office, saying Dr. Gabor does not work here anymore. Of course you can imagine how I felt. My long friendship with Dr. Gabor, all my plans: up in smoke!

"I knew I had to do something, but I couldn't think what. I was sitting and waiting for my shot, when Gladys came out of the office after her visit with Dr. Pustulescu and I went in. The doctor was laughing. He told me that Gladys was afraid of the galvanic bath, and he was going to meet with her the next morning to show her she had nothing to be afraid of.

"In that instant I thought, Aha, I will just see if I can surprise this evil man!"

"But how did you know that adding salt would increase the conductivity of the water enough to electrocute him?"

"Because once Dr. Gabor had said something to me about an assistant who had given herself a shock by putting saline water in the tubs instead of distilled water," said Frau Sophie. "It was an easy thing for me to do, to go to the *alimentari* and get a bag of salt. They do not have a great deal in the stores, but they always have salt. Then, that morning I came in early and poured the bag into all four basins. I stood behind the door watching. I was sure the doctor would put his hands in first to show Gladys. I would have stopped Gladys."

"And afterwards?"

"I was surprised, of course. I thought he would perhaps have a heart attack and be very sick and go in the hospital and Dr. Gabor would come back. But I found I wasn't sorry he was dead. It was the best thing."

"And no one saw you?"

Frau Sophie shook her head. "It was easy in the confusion to come in as I would have for my treatment. I saw them check the voltage meter, but they never thought to check the water. I insisted I must have my treatment, and while Ester was looking for another meter, I quietly let the water out, and told her the police had done it."

"But how could you let Gladys be suspected of his murder?" I looked at Gladys frolicking with her flock of dogs. "She might have been imprisoned for life."

"First of all, Gladys is American. Secondly, she had no motive. Thirdly: why would she electrocute the head of the clinic in a way that would make her immediately suspect? Believe me, Gladys will never be charged. And neither will I."

Frau Sophie took my silence for agreement. "Now, if you'll excuse me, it will soon be time for dinner. I like to have a small aperitif beforehand." She beamed at me with her accustomed look of goodwill and began to walk back to the hotel.

I stood staring at her portly back. There you had it: Frau Sophie had the simplicity, single focus and self-absorption of the true criminal. She was a murderer, but not so much a murderer without a conscience as one of the goddesses of the underworld, helping a tiresome human being slip his mortal bonds. I could only hope that having once achieved success in removing someone who stood in her way, she would not make a habit of it.

No, Frau Sophie had seen her chance and taken it, and now she'd confessed to me with no expectation that I would report it to the police.

And she was right. It wouldn't help Dr. Gabor or Nadia if Frau Sophie went to jail. She was one of the clinic's most loyal patients. Her plans for the *Gasthaus* would be a boon for the local economy. It was hard to dislike Frau Sophie, and easy to hate Dr. Pustulescu. Old Man Coyote had brought nothing but trouble into the world. That didn't make it right that Frau Sophie had killed him, but it made it easy to keep silent. I wondered what Nadia would say if she knew, or if she would go on suspecting Dr. Gabor forever. He'd played a role, certainly. Dr. Gabor must have realized when I mentioned the saline solution that unwittingly he'd passed on the means for murder to Frau Sophie.

"Gladys," I said, as she came with her dogs in my direction. "Jack told me that Bree wants to come back to Budapest with us. It might not be a bad idea for you to leave Arcata too. When you come back next year, I'm sure the whole thing will have blown over."

"You know, Cassie," she said, "I was kind of thinking the same thing. After all, without you gals and the Snapps, I might be kind of lonely here. So I thought I'd find out more about this cheap fare to China you're getting. Maybe I'll run into you somewhere in the Gobi Desert."

"Gladys," I said, slinging an arm around her shoulders. "Can I be like you when I grow up?"

After Gladys and her pack of hounds headed down the cobbled road back to the hotel, I lingered a little. Tomorrow we'd be leaving this place. And I was strangely sorry.

I wondered if Emma would become a world-famous child prodigy on the violin, if Grandma and Grandpa would be coming to live in the yurt, if Emma would go on to develop a vocabulary beyond *igen*. It was beyond me why anyone, given the chance, would choose to speak Hungarian rather than English. But if you had to choose one word to begin with—or to end with—it might as well be *yes*.

I would miss them all. Nadia and Gabor and Ilona, Mistress of the Waters, and the kind attendants who wrapped me in mud and helped defend the Alamo. I would miss Gladys and the Snapps, and after I left Budapest I would miss Eva and Jack. Jack I'd see again, of course, but who knew when? That's my way. I miss everyone, even my mother, who said she never wanted to see me again if I persisted in my unnatural desires. That was almost thirty years ago, and still I miss her.

The wind had come up now and the small fresh leaves on the birches fluttered with a thin papery sound. The warm late-afternoon sun bathed the turrets and dormers of the villa in a radiant gingery light, and its windows were like gold bars. I had always wanted to live in a house like this, all my life. But houses like this were always filled with other people, if not rich families, then tourists with money. I longed for a place to belong, and yet I knew I wouldn't stop traveling, wouldn't give up the feeling of being a leaf in the wind for stationary walls and ceilings, however comforting shelter could be.

I stood in the middle of the cobblestoned road and looked through the elaborate carved gate to the chocolate fairytale house, the house that had briefly taken me in and protected me. It would stay in my memory, a reminder of having been loved once, of having been warm, safe and at peace.

And then I turned to the other gate, the gate that had no house behind it, and that's the gate I went through, into the flowering wilderness.

FROM KALAMAZOO TO TIMBUKTU

CASSANDRA REILLY:
PORTRAIT OF AN EXPATRIATE

by Archie Snapp

She's a woman who makes her words count—and those words come in many languages. Spanish translator Cassandra Reilly, 46, who has seen more of the world than most people, says travel is a way of life for her. "I couldn't stop now even if I tried," she admits.

I met Cassandra on our recent trip to the Transylvanian part of Romania. Most of our readers know that while Dr. Lynn was busy with her research in Munich, Eldest Daughter Cathy and I took our little adopted daughter Emma (or as we now call her, Emoke) back to her homeland for a visit. As I mentioned in last week's story about Emoke's grandparents, who have come to stay with us for an extended visit, we had a marvelous time and met numerous warm and fascinating people in the small town of Arcata and its spa.

Cassandra Reilly was one.

I asked her about her background. "I started out in

Kalamazoo, Michigan," she explained. "My grandparents were born in Ireland, which is how I got an Irish passport."

Reilly uses the Irish passport to venture into territories most Americans wouldn't dream of going to. I often heard her reminiscing over past harrowing adventures with her good friend, Jacqueline Opal, 42, from Australia. The two met in South America in the late seventies, and found themselves traveling companions for almost a year, a period that ended when Reilly missed the boat to the Galápagos Islands.

Jacqueline, or "Jack" as the Australian is nicknamed, has established herself in Budapest where she helps run a secretarial agency. But Cassandra Reilly says it's unlikely she'll settle down anytime in the near future, in spite of advancing age.

"I'm on my way to China," she says, with a faraway look in her hazel eyes. "I don't know how long I'll be there or where I'll go next."

For all her wanderlust, Reilly still has to make a living. She chose translation as the occupation most conducive to her way of life. Well known as the translator of Venezuelan author Gloria de los Angeles's magic realism novels, Reilly has also played a role in bringing the destruction of the rainforest to the notice of the British public.

Adept in many languages, including Romanian, she nevertheless is reticent about her personal life. A large family meant little time for Reilly, though her father, Michael Reilly, whom she is said to resemble, was a bon vivant and a storyteller. Spanish was an early interest, encouraged by a favorite high-school teacher, whose example spurred Reilly into a traveling and translating career.

The fact that Reilly was recently widowed may have

something to do with her sometimes melancholy air of detachment. Her strong Catholic upbringing has stood her in good stead, however, and given her a concern for the welfare of others and a desire to see justice done. A refreshing sense of humor is also part of Reilly's traveling portmanteau.

I asked Reilly if she had been born with the name Cassandra and she smilingly admitted that she'd chosen it. "Jane Austen's sister was named Cassandra," she said. "There's also a line in *Troilus and Cressida* that I liked."

Not being familiar with this Shakespearean play I looked it up when we returned home, and I think I may have found the line:

Pandarus: "And Cassandra laughed."

Bon voyage, Cassandra!

MYSTERIES FROM SEAL PRESS

The Cassandra Reilly Mysteries by Barbara Wilson. Globetrotting sleuth Cassandra Reilly gets herself into intriguing situations no matter where she is—from Barcelona, Spain, to the Carpathian mountains of Transylvania.
GAUDÍ AFTERNOON. $9.95, 0-931188-89-X.
TROUBLE IN TRANSYLVANIA. Also available in cloth: $18.95, 1-878067-34-6.

The Jane Lawless Mysteries by Ellen Hart. The Twin Cities are turned upside down in these compelling whodunits featuring restaurateur and sleuth Jane Lawless and her eccentric sidekick Cordelia Thorn.
HALLOWED MURDER. $8.95, 0-931188-83-0.
VITAL LIES. $9.95, 1-878067-02-8.
STAGE FRIGHT. $9.95, 1-878067-21-4.
A KILLING CURE. $19.95, cloth, 1-878067-36-2.

The Meg Lacey Mysteries by Elisabeth Bowers. From the quiet houses of suburbia to the back alleys of Vancouver, B.C., divorced mother and savvy private eye Meg Lacey finds herself entangled in baffling and dangerous murder cases.
LADIES' NIGHT. $8.95, 0-931188-65-2.
NO FORWARDING ADDRESS. $10.95, 1-878067-46-X; $18.95, cloth, 1-878067-13-3.

The Pam Nilsen Mysteries by Barbara Wilson. Three riveting mysteries, featuring Seattle sleuth Pam Nilsen, take us through the world of teen prostitution and runaways, political intrigue and the controversial pornography debates.
MURDER IN THE COLLECTIVE. $9.95, 1-878067-23-0.
SISTERS OF THE ROAD. $9.95, 1-878067-24-9.
THE DOG COLLAR MURDERS. $9.95, 1-878067-25-7.

STILL EXPLOSION by Mary Logue. $9.95, 1-878067-46-6; $18.95, cloth, 1-878067-29-X. A gripping mystery featuring the sharp-witted journalist Laura Malloy and the timely subject of abortion.

SEAL PRESS has many other feminist titles in stock: fiction, self-help, health and psychology, women's studies, sports and outdoors and international literature. Order from us at 3131 Western Avenue, Suite 410, Seattle, WA 98121. Please include 15% of the total book order for shipping and handling. Write to us for a free catalog.

BARBARA WILSON is the author of two novels, a collection of short stories and four previous mysteries, including three featuring Seattle printer-sleuth Pam Nilsen, and *Gaudí Afternoon,* which first introduced Cassandra Reilly. Like Cassandra, Barbara Wilson is also a translator—of Norwegian —and was awarded a Columbia Translation prize for *Cora Sandel: Selected Short Stories.* Her own work has been translated into German, Italian and Finnish. She travels widely and lives in Oakland, California.